CHASING

THE

SUN

Books by Tracie Peterson

www.traciepeterson.com

House of Secrets • *A Slender Thread*
Where My Heart Belongs

LAND OF THE LONE STAR
Chasing the Sun

BRIDAL VEIL ISLAND*
To Have and To Hold
To Love and Cherish

SONG OF ALASKA
Dawn's Prelude
Morning's Refrain
Twilight's Serenade

STRIKING A MATCH
Embers of Love
Hearts Aglow
Hope Rekindled

ALASKAN QUEST
Summer of the Midnight Sun
Under the Northern Lights
Whispers of Winter
Alaskan Quest (3 in 1)

BRIDES OF GALLATIN COUNTY
A Promise to Believe In
A Love to Last Forever
A Dream to Call My Own

THE BROADMOOR LEGACY*
A Daughter's Inheritance
An Unexpected Love
A Surrendered Heart

BELLS OF LOWELL*
Daughter of the Loom
A Fragile Design
These Tangled Threads

LIGHTS OF LOWELL*
A Tapestry of Hope
A Love Woven True
The Pattern of Her Heart

DESERT ROSES
Shadows of the Canyon
Across the Years
Beneath a Harvest Sky

HEIRS OF MONTANA
Land of My Heart
The Coming Storm
To Dream Anew
The Hope Within

LADIES OF LIBERTY
A Lady of High Regard
A Lady of Hidden Intent
A Lady of Secret Devotion

RIBBONS OF STEEL**
Distant Dreams
A Hope Beyond
A Promise for Tomorrow

RIBBONS WEST**
Westward the Dream
Separate Roads

WESTWARD CHRONICLES
A Shelter of Hope
Hidden in a Whisper
A Veiled Reflection

YUKON QUEST
Treasures of the North
Ashes and Ice
Rivers of Gold

*with Judith Miller   **with Judith Pella

LAND OF THE LONE STAR ★ BOOK ONE

CHASING THE SUN

TRACIE PETERSON

BETHANY HOUSE PUBLISHERS

a division of Baker Publishing Group
Minneapolis, Minnesota

Published by Bethany House Publishers
11400 Hampshire Avenue South
Bloomington, Minnesota 55438
www.bethanyhouse.com

Bethany House Publishers is a division of
Baker Publishing Group, Grand Rapids, Michigan

Printed in the United States of America

Library of Congress Cataloging-in-Publication Data
Peterson, Tracie.
    Chasing the sun / Tracie Peterson.
      p.   cm. — (Land of the lone star ; bk. one)
     ISBN 978-0-7642-0951-2 (hardcover : alk. paper)
     ISBN 978-0-7642-0615-3 (pbk.)
     ISBN 978-0-7642-0952-9 (large-print pbk.)
     1. Texas—History—Civil War, 1861–1865—Fiction. I. Title.
  PS3566.E415C47 2012
  813'.54—dc23   2011040754

This is a work of historical reconstruction; the appearances of certain historical figures are therefore inevitable. All other characters, however, are products of the author's imagination, and any resemblance to actual persons, living or dead, is coincidental.

Scripture quotations are taken from the King James Version of the Bible.

The internet addresses, email addresses, and phone numbers in this book are accurate at the time of publication. They are provided as a resource. Baker Publishing Group does not endorse them or vouch for their content or permanence.

Cover design by Jennifer Parker.
Cover photography © Hugh Beebower/Corbis.

12 13 14 15 16 17 18   7 6 5 4 3 2 1

To Ted and Marietta Terry
for their unfailing support
and witness for God.
Thank you for your friendship.

1

TEXAS
OCTOBER 1863

Hannah Dandridge struggled to keep her voice even. "Father . . . has been taken . . . prisoner?" She lowered her voice and inclined her head forward. "Mr. Lockhart, why would the Yankee army take my father . . . a civilian . . . into custody?"

The bearer of bad tidings dabbed his high forehead with a folded linen cloth, the unusual warmth of the day causing beads of sweat to form at the man's receding hairline. "I do apologize, Miss Hannah. The information my man managed to obtain was reliable, but not as detailed as I would have liked."

"But there would be no reason to take Father prisoner." She folded her hands and leaned back once again. "He's a good man and a fine upstanding citizen."

"Beggin' your pardon, Miss Hannah, but he's a Confederate citizen, and Vicksburg has fallen to the Yankees. The Yankees control the whole of the Mississippi River and the travel upon it. Why, there are renegade bands of soldiers marauding throughout Louisiana and Texas."

It had been six weeks since Hannah's father left their ranch in Texas to go to Mississippi. In that time she'd anxiously awaited word that he had reached her grandparents' house in the war-torn town of Vicksburg.

"But that makes no sense. He's not a soldier and certainly not a threat to anyone. He's only going there to see to my grandmother." More likely, he had gone to bury his mother beside her husband and Hannah's brother Benjamin, both of whom had died the previous June when the Yankees attacked Vicksburg. It had taken two months to get word to the Dandridges regarding the deaths of their loved ones. In that same letter they were told that Grandmother Dandridge was ill—most probably dying. Hannah's father had been beside himself.

Hannah got to her feet and Lockhart did likewise. She walked to the large window, praying he would remain where he stood. She didn't want to be fussed over. Raising the window, she prayed for a gentle breeze to ease the temperature. Any flow of air, however, was absent. She took note of her younger brother and sister playing in the courtyard. They seemed unbothered by the warmth of the day.

Andy was eight and Marty just five. How could she tell them that their father might never return home? She turned back and looked at the man her father called partner. Their joint efforts in real estate and law had proven to be successful, despite the war. But Mr. Lockhart wanted to extend the partnership—to include Hannah. She gave a sigh. Lockhart wasn't a bad fellow, and she supposed an old maid of twenty-four should be honored that any man would look at her with thoughts of marriage.

"Miss Hannah . . ." Lockhart made his move and came to join her. "I hope you aren't worrying about the future. You know that your father considered me an honorable man."

"Yes, Mr. Lockhart, I do realize that. I am certain you are most honorable."

He smiled and rubbed the back of his hand across his mustache. "Your father knew—or rather, knows—how I feel about you. I will see to it that you and your family are provided for. You needn't worry."

"Sir, I was hardly worried about myself." Hannah wiped at a tear. "Father . . ." She knew if she said more she'd break down. "You must excuse me." Hannah felt his gaze upon her even as she turned to walk away.

"We must do whatever we can to help Father," Hannah said, reaching the arched entry of the room. "But for now, say nothing to the children. I don't want them to know what's happened." She paused at the hall and turned toward the open front door, hoping Mr. Lockhart would take the hint to leave.

"Of course not." He crossed the room in quick, precise steps. "Miss Hannah, given this news and trouble with the Comanche, I must insist that you move with the children to Cedar Springs. You can stay at my place. There is more than enough room, and with my servants, no one will consider it inappropriate. I will, in fact, take my residence to the hotel to further dissolve any rumors."

"Sir, that is completely unnecessary. I do not intend to leave the ranch. If your news is wrong, Father will return here or at the very least send word to me here. I will remain."

"You can hardly remain here on your own," he protested. "The Comanche and Kiowa uprisings have left many a man dead."

"But most of those attacks have come to men out on the open range," Hannah countered. She had no desire to leave the ranch for Mr. Lockhart's house.

"Miss Hannah, you have your siblings to consider, as well. It could prove fatal—"

Hannah held up her hand to halt his comments. They would never see eye to eye. He was twice her age and worried overmuch about everything. There would be no reasoning with him or hoping he might see things her way.

"I have a great deal to tend to, Mr. Lockhart. I do hope you'll excuse my bad manners and show yourself out. If you should want further refreshment before your ride back to Cedar Springs, please see Juanita. She's just out the back door in the summer kitchen."

"Miss Hannah, I hope I didn't offend you."

She turned and pasted on a smile. "Of course not. I appreciate that you have brought me the news. I do hope you will do your best to see Father returned to us. Perhaps we should inquire in Dallas. Since he has helped the Confederacy, perhaps they could arrange for my father's release."

He bobbed his head, but his expression suggested he didn't believe it would do any good. "I will see to everything," he said. "I will not rest until we know what has happened. I give you my word."

"Thank you, sir." Hannah curtsied. She could see that he wanted to say something more, so she hurried on. "I simply must get to my tasks." Without waiting, Hannah broke with etiquette and scurried away. Her mother and grandmother would be deeply ashamed of her behavior, but Hannah couldn't help it. Mr. Lockhart would only try to persuade her to leave the ranch.

She made her way out the side door and across the yard to check on the laundry. Lines of clean sheets hung dry in the still air. To her surprise Pepita, Juanita and Berto's youngest child, hurried across the yard with a basket on her head.

"No, Miss Hannah. Mama send me to get them."

"That's all right, Pepita. I'll help you." Hannah reached up to take one of the sheets from the line. She needed to keep busy, and she needed to think.

The Barnett Ranch, as it was called, had been her home for less than a year. Hannah had come to Texas with her father and young siblings five years earlier, much to her dismay. She hadn't wanted to leave her childhood home in Vicksburg—there she could be close to her grandparents and brother. There, she had friends and a life of ease. When her stepmother died giving birth to Marty, everything changed. After that, her father wanted only to leave Vicksburg and his memories. His jovial nature became more serious; he thought only of work and making money. Her beloved papa was only a shadow of his former self, and the man who had come to replace him seemed cold and unfeeling.

Hannah's brother Benjamin and their grandparents had tried to talk John Dandridge out of leaving—especially with two young children, one only an infant. Grandmother had offered to let the family remain with them while their father traveled west to grieve, but he would have none of that. His children were his responsibility. At seventeen, Benjamin stood his ground and told their father he wouldn't leave Vicksburg. A terrible fight ensued . . . a fight that hadn't been resolved before Benjamin lost his life defending Vicksburg.

Hannah frowned at the memory of those days. In Vicksburg she had been nineteen and carefree, engaged to a wonderful young man, now long dead to the war. Unfortunately, the war hadn't initially separated them—her father had managed that on his own. When he went to Hannah's fiancé and demanded the engagement be broken or extended indefinitely so that Hannah could care for her siblings, she was livid. She carefully rehearsed what she would say to her father for hours. When he finally arrived home, she marched to the barn, ready to declare her anger and refusal to be obedient to his wishes. Instead, she found her father bent over his horse's neck, in tears. His pain was raw and heartbreaking. . . . It was the first and only time she'd seen him cry. He hadn't even cried at the loss of his wife. It shook Hannah to the very core of her being.

When he returned to the house, Hannah's father told her how sorry he was that life could not have been better for her. It was as close to an apology for ruining her love life as Hannah would ever get. They departed Vicksburg the following week.

An old friend of her father's had welcomed them to Dallas when they'd first come west. Hannah had tried hard to have a positive spirit about the move. She busied herself with the children and tried to forget her anger and pain. They stayed for quite a while in Dallas, but it proved much too rowdy for her father's taste. For hers, as well. To escape that boisterous town, they moved to Cedar Springs, some six or so miles away. This was where her father teamed up with Mr. Lockhart. The town offered a calm, stable environment for raising small children. Unfortunately for Hannah, it provided very little in the way of friendship.

"Miss Hannah, he come back," Pepita said, pointing to the walk. Herbert Lockhart was making his way toward them with determined strides.

"Oh bother," Hannah said, pushing aside her memories. She wadded up the sheet and stuffed it in the basket. "Have you forgotten something, Mr. Lockhart?" Hannah asked as she straightened to face the man.

"Miss Hannah, I know this is sudden, but my intentions are only the best." He pulled his hat off to reveal a balding head and bent to one knee. "Marry me. That will solve all of your problems. Marry me and I will see that you and your family never want for anything."

Pepita giggled and quickly ducked behind one of the sheets. Hannah wished she could do likewise.

"Mr. Lockhart, you are indeed quite gallant. Please get up, however. I cannot consider your proposal while Father's welfare is so uncertain." She smiled, hoping it might ease the blow.

Lockhart did rise, but he wasn't about to give up. "Miss Hannah, I hold you a great affection. I know that you do not love me, but love will grow in time. I assure you of that. You have my word."

She looked at the would-be suitor. There was nothing wrong with him—nothing that should keep her from loving him or at least accepting courtship in the hope that love would, as he said, grow in time. He was twice her age, but that wasn't unusual in southern marriages. Why, Andy and Marty's mother had been only a few years older than Hannah.

Hannah gave a moment of serious consideration to his offer. Mr. Lockhart was a man of some means, although his appearance didn't necessarily support that truth. His suit was ill fitting and out of date, and his teeth were not at all well cared for. However, those things could be overlooked—if love existed. But she felt nothing for him . . . not even true friendship.

"I am touched that you would honor me in this manner," Hannah finally said, trying to let the man down gently. "But, Mr. Lockhart, I must decline, given the circumstances. I'm certain you understand." Hannah didn't even pause to give him time to respond. "And of course my brother and sister will need my devotion now more than ever. Now, as I said, I have a great deal to accomplish before the end of the day and you have a long ride. Let us say our farewells."

"But, Miss Hannah, you aren't safe here. The Comanche are raiding all around us. Every day they move in closer. Since the forts have been closed and the soldiers have gone to fight the war, the Comanche feel they can reclaim that territory. You haven't enough people here to even put up a good fight."

Ignoring the facts, Hannah turned away. "We knew the dangers when we came here, Mr. Lockhart. My father apparently considered the risk acceptable. After all, he brought his young children here."

"Believe me, I tried to talk him out of that, as well," Mr. Lockhart replied. He stepped forward and put on his wide-brimmed straw hat. With his hands free he reached out to take hold of her arm.

"Miss Hannah, if you won't consider your own safety, think of your brother and sister. The Comanche are known for taking white children captive. Even if they didn't attack and burn you out, they might sneak in here and steal the children."

Hannah had considered this before. It was the reason they were firm with the children about staying close to the house. Still, she wouldn't allow Lockhart to dictate her decisions. She'd endured her father's demands all these years because of her deep abiding love for him. She wasn't about to let his partner, a man for whom she felt nothing, pick up the task in his absence. Hannah stared at Mr. Lockhart's hand for a moment, then returned her gaze to his face.

"Mr. Lockhart, we've already had this conversation. Now I must get back to my chores." She pulled her arm away from his touch. "I will make sure that Berto knows about the Comanche and that the others are apprised, as well. I'm confident we can manage." Hannah could see that Pepita was finishing up with the last of the sheets. "Come along, Pepita. We must get those ironed."

She helped the thirteen-year-old manage the overflowing basket by taking up one side while Pepita took the other. They made their way to the outdoor kitchen area, where irons were heating.

"*Señor* Lockhart find you?" Juanita asked, looking out from the open back door of the house.

"He did," Hannah told her.

"He wants Hannah to marry him," Pepita said, unable to stop her giggles.

Hannah rolled her eyes and maneuvered the basket to an awaiting table. "He also brought bad news." She turned to meet Juanita's questioning expression. "He said that word has come that Father might have been taken hostage by the Union." Pepita's laughter stopped in an awkward, abrupt manner that only served to impact the statement.

"*Es verdad?*" Juanita's dark eyes assessed Hannah for the answer.

"I'm afraid it is true." Hannah didn't speak much Spanish, but she knew enough to recognize Juanita's question. "He said that one of his people was able to get word to him that Father was taken by the soldiers—possibly imprisoned." She left it at that. She couldn't bring herself to add the possibility of his demise.

"What they want with him?" Juanita asked, moving to where she had several pots hanging over an open flame. She lifted the lid off of one and stirred the contents. "Will they keep him long?" It seemed to Hannah that Juanita tried to keep her questions casual, but there was a tangible current of concern lacing her tone all the same.

"I don't know. I don't even know where he is. Mr. Lockhart is trying to find out, but right now we have very little information. Mr. Lockhart wanted us to move to town because of this and the Comanche threat. I told him no."

"And then he ask Hannah to marry him," Pepita declared, only this time her tone was quite serious.

"But I told him no," Hannah said matter-of-factly. "I don't know how he could even imagine I would consider such a thing with Father in danger." She looked to the woman who'd been running the household since long before Hannah and her family had moved onto the ranch. The tiny Mexican woman had become a dear friend, and Hannah greatly appreciated her encouraging spirit.

Juanita and her husband, Berto Montoya, had been hired by the Barnetts. Hannah didn't know the previous owners except through the Montoyas and the other ranch hands. Apparently the man who'd purchased the ranch with his wife and sons had gone off to fight. Unfortunately, they were on the wrong side of the war as far as most Texans were concerned. Their ranch had been taken from them and given to her father as a reward for his help to the Confederate government. Although Hannah was never quite sure what that help had been.

Jason Barnett had settled on the land some twelve years earlier, intent on building a large Texas cattle spread. He had managed a good start with two sons and a wife. Juanita said they were generous, loving people, and Hannah felt sad that they should have fought so hard to carve out their dream only to lose it. She'd said as much to her father, but he'd told her they were traitors. The men had gone to fight for the Yankees and deserved nothing but their disdain.

"What will we do, Miss Hannah?" Juanita asked, replacing the lid atop the cook pot.

Hannah shrugged. "I suppose this is one of those times we do nothing but wait."

"We can pray." Juanita smiled. "God always listen to us pray."

Hannah found the woman's thick accent endearing. Juanita was strong in her faith, too. That was something Hannah hadn't experienced much since leaving her grandmother's home in Vicksburg. Oh, there were plenty of churchgoing folks living in Cedar Springs, but Hannah's father had never wanted her to spend time socializing, which was all he considered church good for.

The sound of Andy and Marty drew Hannah's attention. "Say nothing to the children," she commanded. "I don't want them to know until we are certain what has happened to Father."

"Of course," Juanita said, looking to Pepita. "We say *nada*."

2

"There's your proof," a grizzled, menacing man told Herbert Lockhart. He pointed to several items on the desk. "I took 'em off him just like you said. Now pay me."

Lockhart considered the pieces for a moment. A gold pocket watch and chain, a leather wallet, and a small daguerreotype framed behind glass. He picked up the watch and noted the inscribed initials. Just as quickly he cast it aside. Next he examined the photo of John Dandridge's pretty wife. She was dead, and it was a real pity. The woman was quite attractive. Not as beautiful as Hannah Dandridge, but very pleasing to the eye. Looking through the wallet, he found nothing of interest and very little money. "Where's his cash?"

The man threw him a smile. "Well, I had to pay to get him buried. Couldn't very well just leave his body out there to rot on the road."

"No, I suppose not." Herbert returned the wallet. He opened a desk drawer and pulled out a small bag. He tossed it to the man, noting the chinking sound of coin. "There you are, just as we agreed."

Sneering a smile, the man pocketed the money without bothering to count it. "I'll get right to that other job you wanted me to do. Should have some results by tomorrow."

"See that we do," Lockhart said, closing his desk drawer. "And remember . . . not a word about any of this to anyone."

The man tipped his filthy hat. "I ain't the talkative type." He left the office without another word.

Lockhart frowned at the reminders on his desk. With a swoop of his arm, he dumped them into another drawer and slammed it shut—as if he could shut out the truth, as well. He'd just paid a man for ending the life of John Dandridge. Leaning back in his leather chair, Lockhart wrestled only a moment—a very brief moment—with his guilt. It had to be done. Dandridge was in the way.

"In the way of progress," Lockhart murmured. He smiled to himself and got up from the desk. He wasn't exactly sure when he would tell Hannah Dandridge about her father's death. He would have to plan it carefully to work to his best advantage. No doubt there would come a time when all hope seemed lost and that things couldn't possibly get any worse, and then . . . they would. He would tell Hannah how her father had been killed by Union soldiers, and how he had personally arranged for a proper burial.

Frowning, he realized he hadn't asked Jesse Carter where he'd buried the old man. Well, he'd get the information next time. There wouldn't be any need to rush the declaration to Hannah. Lockhart crossed the room to a locked cabinet and pulled keys from his pocket. He quickly retrieved a stack of papers and took them back to his desk.

Herbert smiled as he glanced over each of the deeds. This was his future. The real estate business was slow due to the war, but there were benefits even in this. The area around them continued to be depleted of people. Folks were moving out—at least temporarily—for safer, more populated areas of the state. Some had even left the state all together, wanting no part of the war, and that was just fine by Lockhart. Added to this, the Comanche had scared off or killed a good number of folks on the open frontier. He had used this to his advantage, paying pennies on the dollar for land that was worth a great deal more. Of course, it wasn't worth much in wartime, and that was what he counted on folks understanding. He also counted on their fears—their ridiculous, unfounded fears. Texas was definitely no place for those fools.

⁓

"C-A-T," Marty said, holding up her slate. "That's cat."

"Very good," Hannah praised, looking to her brother. "And what about you?"

"I can spell *ranch* and *longhorn*. Wanna hear?"

She smiled. "I do. Can you write them out, as well?"

He nodded with great enthusiasm and went to work. "R-A-N . . ." He paused and looked up. "That spells *ran*." Looking back, down he continued. "C-H. Ranch."

"Very good. And *longhorn*?"

Hannah watched as he quickly managed the letters. "L-O-N-G, that spells *long*, and H-O-R-N spells *horn*. Longhorn."

"And what kind of a word is *longhorn*, Andy? Do you remember what I told you?"

He frowned and thought for a moment. "A confounded word."

She shook her head with a smile. "Not confounded, although longhorns are often exactly that. No it's a compound word. You made one larger word by compounding two smaller words together."

"I did it with ranch, too. You got *ran* and *ch*."

"Yes, but *ch* isn't a word. It's a sound made by two letters. See the difference?"

Andy's brow knit together as his frown deepened. "But *ran* is a word."

"It is indeed. However, let me show you another compounding of two words to make a larger one." Hannah took his slate and wrote out *bunkhouse*. "There, do you know what that spells?"

Andy looked at the word and attempted to sound it out. Finally he shrugged and gave up. Hannah pointed to the first four letters. "This word is *bunk*." She drew a line between the two words. "And this one is *house*."

"Bunkhouse," he declared proudly.

"That's right. Each word can stand by itself. The letters *c* and *h* cannot stand by themselves. It has no meaning."

Marty grew bored with this nonsense. "I want to draw pictures now."

Paper was a precious commodity, but Hannah had saved a few pieces of brown paper from her purchases at the mercantile. "I think that would be a good idea. Why don't you draw pictures of the words you know how to spell? You could draw a dog, a cat, a bird, and a cow."

"And a bunny," Marty added. "That's my biggest word."

Hannah laughed. "Indeed it is." She got up and went to retrieve the paper.

This was Marty's first year to participate in regular studies. The year before, Hannah had worked with her sister on letters of the alphabet and numbers, but it was usually related to her cross-stitch work. Marty's short attention span made it difficult for her to sit for very long at a time, so Hannah always tried to limit the child's activities. It seemed if she kept Marty occupied with a variety of things, the child did better.

Andy, on the other hand, would sit and pour over books for as long as Hannah would allow. He constantly looked for words he recognized and passages he could read. Perhaps one day, he would attend a university and do something important with his life. Not that ranching wasn't important, but Hannah saw how very hard the men worked to keep the animals and land. It wasn't a job she wished for her brother. Her family had always been educated, and she wanted to carry that tradition forward with her brother.

Seeing that Marty was engrossed with her next activity, Hannah went back to Andy and pointed to his reader. "Why don't you spend time reading the next story while I check your arithmetic sums."

The boy nodded with a big smile. His hair, so blond it was nearly white, bobbed down over one eye. Hannah noted the length and realized they would soon have to rectify that. She could trim his hair as well as anyone, but the last time it had been cut, Andy had asked to go to the barbershop in Cedar Springs. He wanted a man to cut his hair just like his father did. Maybe she could plan a trip to town for the days to come. She could see if there was any more word on Father.

Hannah frowned and turned away from the children. How could she ever hope to explain to Andy and Marty what had happened to their father? Andy went out of his way to try and please this man who hardly seemed to notice him. Despite that, he was Father's biggest fan. To lose him at this age would be horribly difficult. And then there was little Marty.

Hannah turned back to observe the five-year-old. Marty, too, sported blond hair, although hers wasn't quite as light as Andrew's was. She wore it in braids that framed her round cherub face. Marty was a handful, with a penchant for telling tall tales and misbehaving. Because their father was so often busy, the discipline had fallen on Hannah's shoulders. Of course, so, too, had the nurturing and loving. She couldn't have loved either child more than if they'd been her own.

Marty seemed to sense Hannah watching her and looked up. "I drawed a boy in there, too, 'cause I can spell *boy*. B-O-Y."

"Not *drawed*, Marty. The word is *drew*. You drew a boy." Hannah stepped closer to look at the artwork. "You are doing very nicely with your animals, Miss Marty."

"This one is a cow. She was gonna be a cat first, but I made her too big." She looked at the picture as though assessing a famous work of art. "I think she's a good cow. See . . . here's her others."

"Udders," Hannah corrected casually. She smiled at the strange animal. "Yes, she's a fine cow."

She went back to checking Andy's sums and heaved a sigh when her mind refused to stay focused.

Where are you, Papa? Why aren't you here with us?

What would she do if he never returned? How would she care for her siblings? The last few years of her life had been centered around Andy and Marty. She had been responsible for all of their needs. She'd been the one to find a wet nurse for Marty before leaving Vicksburg, although the young woman had only stayed a few months before becoming so homesick that Hannah insisted on sending her back. One of the Texas women had helped Hannah by nursing Marty for a while, but it was donkey milk that had actually saved the day. When the nursing mother went dry and cow's milk proved too rich for Marty, Hannah tried to feed the baby with canned milk. Marty didn't fare well and grew ill. An old Mexican woman in Dallas heard of the situation and came to Hannah with the solution. At first Hannah thought the woman was joking, but she was desperate to try anything . . . and did.

The woman assured her that donkey milk was most like a mother's breast milk, and within days, Marty began to thrive. Luckily, as Marty grew older she also managed a tolerance for cow's milk. Hannah experimented by diluting the rich milk with water and finally found a solution that worked. It was a good thing, too, because the old woman and her donkeys moved away not long afterward. Hannah had always seen the old woman as a godsend—maybe even an angel in disguise. Either way, she had saved Marty's life and Hannah would never forget it.

"I'm hungry," Andy said, looking up from the book. "Is it time to eat yet?"

Hannah checked the clock. "In about ten minutes we can stop and then you can wash up for lunch."

"Me too?" Marty asked.

Laughing, Hannah nodded. "Of course, silly girl. Then this afternoon you are going to work on your sewing stitches."

Marty clapped her hands together. "I like to sew. I'm gonna make you a dress."

"Maybe one day, but for now you're going to work on your handkerchiefs." Hannah saw Andy fidget and strain to see the clock. "Oh, all right. We'll stop now and see what Juanita has fixed for our lunch."

"I hope she made burritos." Andy quickly closed the reader and jumped up to see for himself if this might be the case. "I can eat two whole ones by myself." He patted his stomach and headed for the door.

"I can eat three," Marty declared.

Hannah waggled her finger at the child. "You know that's not true, Marty. You are exaggerating. You cannot eat three burritos, now, can you?"

Marty hung her head for only a moment. "No, but I want to."

"Well, that isn't the same. There are a great many things that I want to do, but I cannot do them."

Perking up, Marty lifted her head. "Like what?"

Hannah felt stumped. "Well . . . there are a lot of things. Like . . . riding. I wish I had time for a nice horseback ride. Or sailing in a boat. I remember when I was a little girl we sometimes went for rides on the river. It was great fun."

"I want to go on the river, too."

Putting her arm around the child, Hannah guided her to the door. "Perhaps one day we shall all sail the river again."

⁂

That evening, Hannah yawned and turned the lamp up in order to see her stitching a little better. She was trying to get some special things made for Christmas presents. There would be new doll clothes for Marty's baby doll as well as a matching dress for Marty, and shirts for Andy. Andy wanted his own horse, though. If only Father . . . A heaviness clung tight to her heart. If Papa was still missing by Christmas, or worse yet, dead . . . "If he's dead, I don't know what we'll do."

She bit her lower lip and cast a glance at the loft stairs. The children were probably asleep, but she didn't want to take a chance they might overhear her. Hannah tried hard not to fret about the matter, but there were horrible stories about the prison camps for soldiers. If they put Father in such a place, he might not be able to survive the brutal treatment.

Stop borrowing trouble, she told herself. *Even Mr. Lockhart doesn't know for sure what happened.* But something deep inside her told Hannah things were not good. She didn't know if it was some sort of special intuition or perhaps even God trying to ready her for the worst of news, but she had felt this way only a few times before . . . and each time someone had died.

Her mind whirled as the weight of responsibility draped over her like a heavy mantle. There was some money to run their affairs, that much she knew. Father had hidden a small amount of gold under the floorboard in his bedroom. It wasn't all that much, he'd told her, but in case a need arose that couldn't be managed with the household account she'd be set. She'd given it little thought because the household funds had appeared quite sufficient. Although, Hannah had to admit, she'd never figured to head into November dependent on those monies to sustain them. She knew there was a reserve in the bank, as well. Her father had told her how to draw on the account if for any reason he was delayed. Well, now he'd been.

"But surely that's all," she murmured. Surely he was simply delayed.

She tried to imagine him sitting before a Union commander, explaining that his mother lay dying in Vicksburg. Who could not understand the purity of that motive? He had not gone east to fight or raise havoc against the Northern aggressors. He was merely trying to come to the aid of his mother. What decent man would do otherwise?

She suppressed another yawn and closed her eyes for a moment. The evening had cooled off nicely and Hannah relished the slight chill in the air. She hadn't even bothered to light a fire in the hearth, nor would she. There were plenty of blankets should they get cold in the night.

In the silence she tried to pray, but the words stuck in her throat. God had been her lifeline when Hannah had been certain she'd drown in sorrow. And now, alone in the stillness of the evening, Hannah thought of the father she'd adored as a girl . . . and the shell of a man he became in the wake of loss.

Father God, I don't mean to be such a ninny. I honor you and I honor my father. I want to be a godly woman, but I don't understand any of this. Why did my father bother to bring us here instead of leaving us with our grandparents? It seems to me we only caused him more sorrow—more reminders of what was lost. I know that it's to our benefit that we are here instead of in Vicksburg—especially now. But I don't understand the road my life has taken.

She sighed and shook her head. *I want to do whatever it is you have for me to do, but I also want something more—something infinitely more personal. Is that selfish of me, God? Is it wrong to want a love of my own—a home of my own?* Guilt washed over her. She'd gone right into praying for herself and hadn't even thought of her father's situation.

"O God, I don't know what has happened." She glanced at the stairs again and fell silent.

Please deliver Father to us, Lord, she prayed. *Keep him safe, and God, please let Father come back a happier man. Maybe this experience could help him realize what he has and that life is good. Maybe he could find joy in it again. Then we could be happy, too.*

Was that too selfish of a request to pray? Did God listen to self-serving prayers?

3

Pablo came running through the house, panting. The normally sedate, even shy fifteen-year-old was afire with excitement, yelling for his mother and Hannah.

Juanita looked up from where she was helping Hannah learn to weave a basket and addressed him sharply in Spanish. He rattled off an answer that Hannah couldn't begin to keep up with.

Juanita turned to her. "There's trouble."

"Comanche," Pablo said. "JD and Thomas saw them. Papa told me to come tell you. Everybody is supposed to stay in the house and close up the windows."

Hannah felt a shiver go up her spine. "I'll get the children." She pushed aside the basket and jumped to her feet. Nearly tripping over her long brown skirt, Hannah barely righted herself before hurrying off to find Marty and Andy.

She climbed up the ladder and found her sister playing with her doll in the loft. It was a good place for her, Hannah decided.

"Marty, you need to stay up here for the time. There might be trouble."

The little girl came to the ladder and looked down. "Injuns?"

Her comment surprised Hannah. "Don't call them that, but yes, there are problems with the Indians. I need to go find Andy, so you stay here. Promise me you'll stay there."

"I could shoot a gun," Marty declared.

"No. You need to stay put. It's much too dangerous and I need to know that you are safe. Stay right there. Promise me."

Marty's tone betrayed her disappointment. "I promise, Hannah."

Hannah stared up into the innocent expression. The child was full of brave notions but had no idea what they were truly up against. Back in Vicksburg they wouldn't have had to worry about Indian attacks. Of course, if they'd remained in Mississippi, they might all be dead from the siege and battle that had killed so many others.

Hannah pushed those thoughts aside. She needed to find her brother. "Andy?" she called out, but there was no answer.

It didn't take long to ascertain he wasn't in the house, and Hannah realized she hadn't seen him in some time. Why hadn't she kept better track of him?

"Juanita, I'm going to the barn to see if Andy is there," Hannah told her as she headed for the back door. "Marty is in the loft playing."

"Go quickly," Juanita encouraged. Pepita worked with her mother to secure a wooden bar across the shuttered window. "Berto will help you."

Hannah nodded and made her way from the house. The

skies were turning dusky. It would be dark before much longer. Where was her brother?

"Andy?"

Berto appeared, rifle in hand, from around the corner of the barn. "What are you doing here?"

"I can't find Andy," Hannah replied. "Have you seen him?"

The man frowned. "No." He glanced around. "I get my brother and we search for him."

"What of the Comanche? Were they close by?"

Berto nodded. "Close enough. Thomas and JD saw them about five miles away and rode back fast to tell us. There were about six Comanche warriors."

Hannah swallowed hard and touched Berto's arm. "Please find Andy."

He left without another word, and Hannah turned to survey the grounds around her. The area between the house and barn was mostly hard-packed ground with little grass. The women kept a large vegetable garden to the far side of the yard and had even planted a few flowers and herbs along the front of the otherwise unadorned house. Beyond this, there were pens for the horses, a coop for chickens, the outhouse, the bunkhouse, and the small house where the Montoyas lived. In other words, plenty of places for a young boy to hide.

"Andy? Are you out here?" she called. She scanned the horizon beyond the house.

About a half mile away, there was a river lined with brush and trees. A little farther the land was cut with rocky ravines. What if he'd fallen down one of those? Hannah knew Andy loved to frequent the area. He was always asking Hannah to take them there to explore. She thought to go investigate, but Berto and Diego came running full speed from around the back of the house.

Berto took hold of Hannah and motioned wildly. "Get in the house. The Comanche are coming."

"But we haven't found Andy yet. We have to find my brother!" She heard the fear in her voice, and it startled her. This wasn't just a game. The light was fading and the Comanche were closing in. Six warriors could wreak havoc on a tiny homestead. Larger numbers than theirs had faced small bands of Comanche and been wiped out.

"Berto, he must be close by. Maybe he went to the river," Hannah suggested. "I can go see."

"No. You go to the house, Miss Hannah. We will look for him if we can. Go now before it is too late. You and Juanita— get the rifles."

Hannah froze. They never armed the women unless the threat was grave. She waited only a second more before heading back inside, calling for her brother the entire way. "Andy! Andy, please don't hide from us! Come to the house right now—there's danger!"

She paused at the door to the house. How could she seek shelter knowing the eight-year-old was still out there somewhere? Glancing skyward, she prayed as she'd never prayed before. Surely God would protect her brother. He was just a child, after all. Hannah pushed aside thoughts that other children had been lost at the hands of the savages—why should she imagine Andy to be any safer?

"God, please help us."

"You find him?" Juanita asked, coming to her side.

Hannah turned, tears in her eyes. "No. Berto and Diego are looking for him. . . . They said—they—we're supposed to get the rifles."

Juanita nodded, her dark eyes fixed on the horizon. "*Sí*. I get them."

❧

William Barnett rubbed his right leg and grimaced. Sometimes the pain was so great, he wanted nothing more than to give up and die. His father and brother were dead—so why not him? Why had he been left behind—a cripple?

For months now he'd been recovering from the wound given him in battle. He probably should have lost the leg. The ball that hit him in the thigh had gone clear through, splintering a bit of bone on the way. The surgeon had overlooked Will's situation at first, but Will's own men had ministered enough care to ward off gangrene. The wound festered for some time, but little by little the leg healed and the bone reknit. Of course, it left William with a limp and a great deal of pain that the doctor told him would probably follow him throughout life.

Closing his eyes, William tried to forget the sights and sounds that continued to haunt him. War had not been his choosing, but rather his father's and brother's. William wanted only to remain behind and care for the family ranch, but his father determined they would go and support the Union—as a family. Berto and the hands could manage the ranch. After all, it wasn't as if they could send cattle to market. The borders had been closed and the South was quickly depleting of supplies and money.

His father believed the defense of the Union was every man's responsibility. It wasn't a war about slaves or individual ways of life—it was about preserving what had been so fiercely won not even a hundred years earlier. America—their country, their United States—deserved faithful protection.

William frowned. The war had taken his father and brother, and Texas had taken his mother. There was nothing left now, except a piece of land they had all once loved.

He was headed back to that land now. William knew he was nearly there; he should arrive just after dark at his current pace.

It hadn't been easy. After being wounded, William had been transported upriver to a Union hospital. It was there that he had done most of his recovering. It had taken weeks to heal enough to get back up on his feet, and even longer to feel capable of heading home. And then there was the war itself—as a former Union soldier crossing the lines to head south, he'd been at the mercy of both sides. That was why he'd done most of his traveling at night, sticking to the shadows. He'd followed the rivers, staying close to the shorelines and trees to avoid being seen. He'd learned as a boy to live off the land, but that had been prior to his injuries. Trying to hunt or fish with his lame leg hadn't been easy.

He'd wisely cut across Indian Territory for the last part of the journey. It seemed odd that the risk he faced with the Kiowa and Comanche should be less than that from white soldiers, but so far he'd managed quite well. The farther west and south he went the safer he felt. He wasn't sorry to leave the war behind and could only hope it wouldn't follow him to Texas.

Easing up to look over the edge of the rocks, William felt a sense of peace at the empty landscape to the east. He was nearly home. This ravine made an adequate hiding place in which he could stay out of sight and rest until darkness could cloak him. Hopefully, he'd make it back to the ranch in time for supper.

He smiled at the thought of Juanita's cooking. She made the finest spicy pork and rice. Her tortillas and *frijoles* were the best to be had. William had longed for such meals since leaving Texas. He'd missed the ranch and the people who'd acted as family to him over the last twelve years.

Picking up his few things, William struggled to his feet and moved on. The river wasn't wide or deep, but it afforded him water and pointed the way home. That alone was worth everything. William longed so much for the comforts of home. The war and its sufferings had been his existence for so long now. It seemed to have lasted a lifetime, instead of just years. Things would be different now, he promised himself. He would put the war behind him and forget the horrors he'd experienced.

His fervent hope was that the war would soon end. Gettysburg and Vicksburg had caused even the staunchest Southern supporter to reassess the war, but then a win at Chickamauga had encouraged their dreams of winning yet again. And so the cycle of destruction continued. . . . But it had to end soon. It just had to.

Winding through the narrow cracks and crannies, William thought of his life and what he would do now. He could imagine his mother telling him to pray, but prayer seemed almost foreign to him now. If God cared, He certainly had a strange way of showing it. For all of his life, or at least a good portion of it, William had trusted that God was good and that He cared for His children. William's mother had always believed it to be true and her stalwart faith had sustained her younger son. Now, after living through her death and the ravages of war, William knew he could no longer rely on his mother's faith.

A noise up ahead caught William's attention. Familiarity with the land had caused him to let down his guard. Crouching low, William leaned heavily on his left leg and balanced himself against a rock as he brought up his rifle.

"Come on now," William heard a child say. "Don't be afraid." And then he heard the unrelenting distress of a longhorn.

He edged forward and flattened himself on the ground. Creeping closer, William could see a small towheaded boy working to free a young steer from where it was caught in the brush. The animal was more than a little agitated, and William feared the boy could be harmed.

"You shouldn't have come out here," the boy chided the beast.

William smiled at the comment. The little guy was certainly determined. William decided to lend a hand and started to straighten when another sound above them caught his attention. He pressed back against the rock and waited. He saw the legs of the horse before catching sight of the rider: a Comanche warrior. And from the looks of him he wasn't full grown—maybe no more than sixteen.

It was easy to see that the Comanche had spotted the little boy. He moved his horse closer to the edge of the ravine and pulled back on his bow. William quietly maneuvered his rifle to take aim. He didn't want to have to kill the young warrior, but he couldn't allow him to take the life of the child.

Before he could pull back the hammer, however, something spooked the horse. William rose up just enough to see the boy glance overhead. His eyes widened in fear. William thought to rush to the child, but everything seemed to happen at once. The pony reared and bucked wildly, sending the young Comanche off the back and over the ravine. Crashing to the bottom below, the boy lay motionless—his left arm bent under him at an awkward angle.

William stood, but not before the blond-headed boy moved away from the steer and went to the unconscious warrior's side.

Squatting down, the boy shook the shoulder of the silent figure. William kept his rifle on the warrior. He'd seen Indians play dead before. The boy hadn't noticed William.

"Hey, you hurt?" He shook the Comanche again.

Coming up behind the boy, William tried not to startle the child. "Looks like we're in a bit of a predicament."

The boy turned and jumped to his feet. "Who are you?"

William smiled. "William Barnett. Who are you?"

"Andy Dandridge. Are you the Barnett that used to own our ranch?"

Used to? William's brows knit, but he didn't pose the question on his mind. "Look, his people are going to be looking for him. We'd best get out of here."

"But we can't leave him. He's hurt."

William searched the top of the ridge for the Indian's horse, but it was gone. He knelt down and pressed his fingers to the

Comanche's neck. He could feel a steady pulse, but Andy was right—the Indian was hurt.

"Do you know how to handle a gun?" William asked.

"Sure. I've been learnin' to shoot real good."

William leaned the rifle against a rock and reached for his pistol. "This thing has quite a kick," he said, handing the boy a long-barreled Colt. "You stand back—over there. Keep the gun aimed at him. I'll see what I can do."

Andy didn't argue. He took the pistol and backed away, seeming to understand the importance of his job. William gently turned the warrior on his back. There was a large knot forming on the Comanche's forehead.

William checked the boy over, but he didn't so much as moan. The left arm appeared to be broken, but besides minor cuts and the blow to the head, William saw no other evidence of injury. Now the question was what to do with the patient.

"Did you say you're living at the Barnett Ranch?" William asked Andy.

The boy nodded. "We moved there. I can show you the way."

"Thanks, but I know the way." William stood and motioned Andy to his side. "I need to scout the area and see if there are other Comanche out there." He pointed to the unconscious Indian. "He's dressed to raid, so he's probably part of a larger group."

"I gotta get to the house then," Andy said, his expression taking on a panicked look. "I wasn't supposed to come down here this far, but I lost track, and then I heard the steer."

William had nearly forgotten the animal. He looked back to see the steer was still entangled. It could wait. Right now the most important thing was to get this child back to his family. The family that had apparently taken up residence on his ranch.

"Stay here. I'll be back in a minute." He took the rifle and crawled up the ravine. It wasn't exactly the homecoming he'd figured on, but at least he would sleep under his own roof tonight. At least he hoped so.

4

Pepita cried softly against her mother's shoulder, terrified of what the Comanche raiders might do. The last year had only served to heighten everyone's fears. So many ranchers had been burned out or run off. With only a small number of soldiers to keep peace in the West, the Indians were raiding closer and closer to the towns. The stories of stolen children, murders, and mayhem ran rampant. Hannah had to admit she'd not worried overmuch until now. Her father had implied that many of the stories were most likely exaggerated, and since the Barnett Ranch had been untouched, it was easy to believe him. Now, however, facing the possibility of an attack, Hannah wondered at the foolishness of having stayed.

Marty tried hard to pretend she wasn't afraid. She sat in the corner, hugging her doll closer and humming. She had wanted Hannah to hold her, but that was out of the question. Hannah had to be ready to defend the house with her rifle.

Dear God, please don't make me have to kill someone.

Hannah couldn't help but wonder if Marty was worried about her brother. Marty often followed Andy around like a puppy to his master, so his absence was bound to cause her alarm.

Where are you, Andy? Hannah's mind raced with horrible thoughts of him being taken by the Comanche.

JD, a lanky sixteen-year-old who'd been hired just a few months earlier, came bounding into the living room twisting his hat in his hand. "They've up and gone," he announced. "Berto and Diego are following a ways behind to make sure they're not hiding out to attack in the dark."

"Why would they just leave?" Hannah asked.

The young man shrugged. "Don't rightly know, ma'am. They may have seen something that spooked them. Maybe soldiers are headin' this way."

"God has heard our prayers," Juanita said, hugging her child close.

Hannah nodded and headed for the door. "What about Andy, JD? Did you see anything of him?"

"No, ma'am. I ain't seen him."

She tried not to let the comment worry her. Hopefully Andy had taken cover. Maybe he just couldn't get back to the house. She vacillated between being angry that he'd broken the rules and terrified that he might be hurt or worse.

"I'm going to look for him." She leaned the rifle up against the wall in order to open the door.

"But Berto say to stay here, Miss Hannah," Juanita declared, getting to her feet. "You don't know the danger."

"I can't just leave him out there. I mean, what if the Indians have him?"

"Then you no find him here. Wait for Berto."

Despite Juanita's urging, Hannah opened the front door. In the growing darkness she could make out someone approaching. Hannah reached out to take up the heavy rifle. Had the Comanche thrown the men off and circled around to attack from the front of the house?

Andy's excited voice filled her heart with joy. "We found a hurt Comanche."

Hannah quickly discarded her weapon. "Andy! Where have you been? I've been so worried."

Andy came running. "I found Mr. Barnett, too."

The man stepped forward, the Indian slung over his shoulder. "I reckon we found each other," he announced.

Hannah didn't know what to say or do. For a moment she locked eyes with the handsome stranger and froze. It was Juanita who brought a lamp and welcomed the man.

"Mr. William, you come home."

He grinned. "Juanita, it is so good to see a friendly face. I'm afraid I'm pretty much done in—otherwise I'd give you a big hug."

"Your arms are full," she said, handing Pepita the lamp. "You bring him in?"

They both looked to Hannah, who stood in the doorway. She couldn't think rational thoughts. "I suppose . . . I . . . well, we could take him to Father's room."

Juanita reached out for William's rifle. "I take this for you."

No one said a word to Hannah as Pepita led the way, with

Juanita close behind. William and Andy traipsed past her as if she'd not even been there. She didn't know which shocked her more, the fact that they'd just brought a Comanche into her house or that the former owner of the ranch had returned.

Not knowing what else to do, Hannah closed the door and followed the others into her father's room, noticing that the man was limping under the weight of the load he was carrying. The Indian was hardly more than a boy. Hannah could see he was hurt, and her fears were quickly replaced with a desire to help.

"Pepita, fetch some hot water and rags," she instructed. "Andrew, you go watch your sister."

"Ah, I wanna see what happens when he wakes up."

"You'd best do as you're told," Hannah instructed. "You're already in a world of trouble for giving me such a fright."

Andy looked to the floor. "Sorry. I was trying to help a steer get out of the brambles."

"We can talk about it later," Hannah said. "Please go tend to Marty for now." When she looked back to the bed, Juanita and William had managed to strip the boy's leather shirt from his body. He looked even smaller.

"What happened to him?" she asked, coming alongside the bed.

"Horse spooked on the edge of the ravine. The boy fell to the bottom. I figure he's got a broken arm," William answered.

Hannah met his gaze and found herself momentarily lost in his dark blue eyes. She shook herself free of the spell just as Pepita returned with the water. Hannah took the basin and busied herself by washing away some of the grime from the boy's face. The stench from his body assaulted her senses and Hannah couldn't help but wonder when he'd last had a bath. The boy stirred just a bit, startling her.

William reached out for the rag. "I can do that if you want."

Hannah steadied her nerves and shook her head. "I'm fine."

He pulled back and rubbed his right thigh. Hannah wondered if he'd hurt himself but turned her focus to the Comanche boy. She'd never seen an Indian up this close. Their skin really wasn't red at all—at least not this boy, who was more brown, like Juanita and Berto. Maybe Indians could be different skin colors.

"Mr. William, how your father and brother?" Juanita asked. "They coming, too?"

Hannah startled at this. Was it possible that the Barnetts had returned to take control of their ranch? If that were the case, what would she do? A fleeting thought of Herbert Lockhart begging her to come to Cedar Springs flitted through her mind.

"My father and brother are dead," William replied. "They were killed in battle. I took a bullet in the same fight. It's left me lame."

Juanita's eyes filled with tears. "Mr. Jason and Mr. Lyle are dead? Oh, this is terrible news. *Lo siento mucho.*"

"I am sorry, too," William said softly. "Their loss cuts to the heart of me."

Juanita nodded and Hannah couldn't help but throw him a sympathetic glance. She knew her father said they were traitors for fighting with the Northern troops, but given her own situation, she couldn't help but feel bad for the man. She'd already lost a brother and grandfather to the war, and perhaps her father would also be a victim.

Hannah wiped the cloth over the boy's wounded head. "Looks like he fell hard. Has he been knocked out for long?"

"The last couple of hours. We had to wait until we were sure the rest of the raiding party was gone before we could make our way here. Then with my leg the way it is, I had a tough time carrying him and walking."

She nodded but didn't look at him again. How strange it was that a man she'd never met before could make her feel so odd. Perhaps it was just the knowledge that this had been his home and was now hers. Would his appearance only serve to be the start of more problems?

Berto and Diego appeared at the door. "Andy said you have a Comanche in here," Berto said, stepping forward.

"Es verdad," Juanita declared. "And look, Mr. Will is here."

Hannah straightened to see Berto and Diego's faces break into smiles. Berto rushed to William and embraced him. They slapped each other's backs.

"It's good to see you again," William said. "I thought it might never happen."

"You have been missed, *amigo*," Berto said as they pulled away.

William nodded. "All I could think about was getting back here." He frowned and looked at Hannah. "But I guess from the sounds of it, we have a bit of a problem."

Hannah had been waiting for him to acknowledge her residency. "My family has been living here for not quite a year." His scrutiny made her feel uncomfortable, and she looked to Berto. "My father was given title to this ranch . . . after . . .

after. . . ." She looked back to her patient. Juanita was applying a cloth to the swollen lump on the boy's head.

"After we traitorously left to fight for the North?" William asked.

Hannah nodded without looking at him. She wanted to change the subject but knew they would have to address the matter sooner or later. Her stomach growled loudly, giving her a good excuse to speak about something else. "Are you hungry? I'm starving. Juanita, let's have supper right away."

"I could definitely go for some grub," William said, seeming to understand.

"We can talk about what has happened while we eat," Hannah said. She looked at the young Indian. "I suppose someone should sit with him. We can take turns."

"I will stay," Diego said. "Just bring me some food," he added with a grin.

"I come and take care of him when the meal is on the table," Juanita offered. She hurried from the room and Hannah did likewise.

"I apologize for putting you out," William said. Hannah could only nod. He assessed her as if trying to decide on purchasing a horse. He smiled. "Andy told me you wouldn't mind. I hope that's true."

Hannah felt a reply stick in her throat. She nodded again and hurried away to check on the children. The last thing she had expected was to have this man and a Comanche in her home.

"Look," Andy said as Hannah approached. He pointed to the checkerboard. "I'm teachin' Marty to play."

Hannah thought how very young they were and for the first

time felt guilty for having remained at the ranch. Herbert was right. The area had become much too dangerous. Perhaps she would have to reconsider moving into town.

She paused for a moment. "Andy, where were you? We couldn't find you."

"I was just playin'. I was running after a rabbit. Then I heard something down by the river. I found a longhorn stuck, and I wanted to help him. That's what ranchers do."

"I appreciate that you wanted to help him, but, Andy, you know that we have rules about going that far away. Rules for your protection and safety. Look what happened. The Comanche came and I couldn't find you. What if that boy had killed you instead of falling off his horse?"

Andy bowed his head. Hannah had always known him to be very contrite for his wrongdoings and didn't expect that this time would be any different.

"I'm sorry."

Hannah knelt down beside him. "I know you are. But sometimes an apology isn't enough. You broke a very important rule, Andy, and there must be a punishment for that."

He looked at her seriously and nodded. Hannah wanted to hug him close, but she held off. Marty was the one who broke the tension of the moment, however.

"You gonna whop him?"

She might have laughed at her little sister's question had the situation not been so grave. Hannah straightened and looked at Andy. "I haven't decided what the punishment will be. We have guests in the house right now, and the matter will need to wait. We can talk about it more after supper."

Andy looked as though he might burst into tears any moment, and Hannah was afraid that if she didn't leave she might well follow suit. Getting to her feet, she found William Barnett watching her from the hallway. She pretended not to notice him there.

"You and Marty get washed up for supper and then set the table. We'll have Mr. Barnett with us, so be sure to set an extra place."

"Yes'm," Andy and Marty said in unison.

They abandoned their checkers and headed from the room. "Mr. Barnett, you can sit by me at supper," Andy declared.

Hannah heard the man respond favorably to this idea. Marty was babbling to him about sitting by her, as well. He was quite kind to both of them, and when Andy suggested he come wash up with them, William agreed.

She was relieved to not have to face him for the moment. Goodness, but she didn't know what to say to him. If only Father hadn't gone away. For a moment she almost wished that Herbert Lockhart were there to confront the man and explain the situation. Instead, she would have to handle it herself. But how could she explain to him that the Barnetts' ranch had been confiscated as spoils of war and given to someone else?

Making her way to the kitchen, Hannah was relieved to see that Juanita had things well under control. She and Pepita were hurrying around the room, each one seeming to know the steps and plans of the other.

"What can I do to help?" Hannah asked.

Juanita pointed to the plate of tortillas. "Take those to the table. I bring the corn bread and *frijoles*."

Hannah picked up the platter. "Juanita, you and Berto are good friends with Mr. Barnett, aren't you?"

"Sí," Juanita said, stopping in her work. "Why you ask?"

She put the plate down and moved closer to the woman. "What do you think he wants?"

"I don't know what you mean."

The woman's face betrayed her confusion. Hannah glanced at the doorway and lowered her voice. "Why is he here?"

"This is his home. He come home."

Hannah shook her head. "But it isn't his home anymore. The government took it away from him—from his family." Juanita shrugged as if she didn't understand. *And maybe she doesn't,* Hannah thought. *After all, I don't understand any of this.*

It wasn't going to be easy to figure this out in an amicable way. After all, mention of the man being a traitor against the Confederacy was bound to enter the conversation. Hannah couldn't very well explain their presence at the ranch without that being at the center of the issue.

She sighed. "Never mind. I suppose God will just have to help me work this out."

Juanita smiled. "God, He always have a plan."

Hannah went back to retrieve the platter. "I hope so."

～

William hated to admit it, but he liked the changes in the place. Apparently Hannah Dandridge had a good knack for making a house a home. He had no idea what must have happened to the Barnett family belongings, however—not that there had been all that much. His mother had kept a few family mementos, but she'd never been one for a lot of doodads and bric-a-brac. They'd been too busy working to build up the ranch itself. Fixing up the interior always took second place to that. And after his mother's death, the house lacked even her subtle feminine influence.

Juanita used to put little touches here and there, he remembered. She always had chilies and herbs hanging to dry. She made beautiful baskets and positioned them around the kitchen with fruits and vegetables, but otherwise she reserved her creativity for the little house she and Berto shared with their children out by the bunkhouse. He recalled she'd done a beautiful job of setting tiles atop the counters in her much smaller kitchen. He'd often thought of having her do the same for the ranch house.

"Don't forget to set an extra place," Marty called to her brother.

William drew closer to the dining room to watch the children. They were well behaved. Even when his mother had been talking of punishment, Andy had been respectful. William and Lyle had been no different. They'd learned at an early age that respecting one's parents was something God expected. Their mother had been a gentle soul with a heart of gold. In fact, Hannah Dandridge reminded him of her. She seemed like a no-nonsense sort of woman who was used to taking charge of difficult situations. She hadn't had a fit like some women might when they brought the Comanche boy into the house.

"Mr. Barnett?"

He turned to find Hannah looking at him oddly. "Ma'am?"

She continued to study him for a moment, as if trying to size him up. Had she been a man, William might have been offended. Then again, had she been a man, he might not have noticed how blue her eyes were or how her brown hair glinted with golden strands and curled in little wisps around her face.

Hannah pointed to the dining room. "If you're ready, supper is on the table."

William nodded and followed her to the table. He was surprised to see Pablo and Pepita taking a seat. Juanita and Berto soon joined them.

"Thomas is keeping watch," Berto declared. "Him and JD. You don't know JD, but he's good with the horses."

William had seen the young man, but hadn't questioned who he was. On the other hand, he knew Thomas Early quite well. The freed black man had been a tremendous asset to the Barnetts, and William highly esteemed him.

Juanita broke through his thoughts. "I take them and Diego something to eat after we pray."

It seemed strange to have everyone gathered at the table together. William's father would never have had the hired help in the house. He was a firm believer in keeping people in their place. Including his sons. He had ruled his family with a firm hand, always demanding the best they had to give.

"Shall we pray, then?" Hannah asked, bowing her head.

William listened as she offered a short but heartfelt grace. She ended by thanking God for the safe return of Andy and for the fact that the Comanche had chosen not to attack. When she concluded, William opened his eyes to find most everyone looking at him.

He felt uneasy and shifted his focus to the platter of meat in front of him. "Juanita, that looks like your spicy pork."

"Not too spicy," she said with a smile. "The little ones aren't used to it." She nodded toward Marty and Andy.

"I'm sure it's just as delicious," he said, taking a healthy portion.

"You mentioned you were wounded in battle, Mr. Barnett," Hannah said, spooning beans onto Andy's plate.

"Yes, ma'am." He had no real desire to speak about the war or his wounds, but supposed it had to be. "I took a bullet in the leg. Actually, it went clean through but took a bit of bone with it."

"I got shot in the leg once," Marty declared. "Injuns got me."

William looked at the pig-tailed girl and narrowed his eyes. "Truly?"

Hannah nudged the girl. "Tell the truth, Marty, and don't use that word again."

"Well, I fell on a stick once," she said, not seeming to mind at all that she'd been caught in a lie. "It hurt real bad."

William's expression softened. "I'll bet it did. Mine hurt real bad, too. Still does."

"My sister is given to tall tales at times," Hannah told him. "I do apologize."

He looked at the child and then at Hannah. "Your sister? I thought she was your daughter."

Hannah shook her head. "I have raised her since she was born, but no, I have no children nor husband. I live here with my father and siblings. Andy is eight years old and Marty is five."

"Our mama died," Andy said matter-of-factly, "but Hannah takes good care of us. She's just like a ma."

Marty nodded enthusiastically. "She fixes my hair and makes me clothes."

William smiled. "And she does a very good job of it. You're quite pretty."

Marty beamed under his praise. Hannah, on the other hand, seemed uncomfortable being the object of the discussion. She turned to Juanita and requested the grits instead of continuing the conversation. But William needed to know more.

"So tell me about the issues with the ranch." He looked at Berto but hoped Hannah might respond. When no one spoke, he continued. "Look, I know this is a strange situation, but I need to know what happened."

"When you and your father and Mr. Lyle go to war," Berto began, "some men from town come with Mr. Lockhart. They tell me to take care of the ranch, but that you no longer own it. No one lived here for much of the time since you go. Then Mr. Dandridge and his family come."

"I see." William looked to Hannah for further explanation and found that she was now staring at him openly. "And can you expand on that?"

He watched Hannah dab her mouth with a cloth. "My father has been a strong supporter of the Confederacy. I'm not entirely certain how he offered his assistance, but he is a lawyer by trade. He was given this ranch as a reward of sorts. We were told that your family had deserted for the North."

"And you believed that?"

Hannah looked rather surprised. "Why not? Many of the families around here have fled for one reason or another. There are Union supporters just as there are Confederate ones. Three families in Cedar Springs alone left Texas for Illinois because of their beliefs in the Union. Why should your family be any different?"

"Well, perhaps since we left behind workers to run the ranch in our absence, it should have signaled that we intended to return."

"But . . . well . . . you chose a side opposite that which the state supported."

He could see that she was picking her words as carefully as possible. Nevertheless, William felt a sense of indignation rise. "As you said, there were those who supported both sides, all living together in one community. I didn't want this war, Miss Dandridge. I didn't even desire to fight in it. I did so because it was my father's desire."

"So are you gonna live here now?" Andy asked.

William looked to Hannah for that answer. It was clear the question had left her confused. She put her fork down and glanced around the table.

"I'm not entirely sure what is to be done. I can hardly

turn you away in good conscience. If my father were here, it wouldn't even be a matter for me to consider."

"When is your father expected home?" William tried to sound as though the answer were unimportant.

"I can't really say," Hannah replied, her glance darting to the others. "He went to help my sick grandmother. I expected him home by now, and so I suppose the answer is that he's due most anytime. However, that said, it doesn't help us in this situation."

"Miss Hannah," Juanita began, "Mr. Will is a good man. His family love God very much. He is no trouble to you."

William could see that Hannah was weighing Juanita's words carefully. He pushed down his growing irritation that he even needed a defender. This was his home. He knew every inch of this house—every nook and rut on the property. He had worked by the sweat of his brow to build the place with his father and brother. Yet a young, albeit beautiful, woman was now the deciding factor in whether he stayed or had to leave again.

Hannah drew a deep breath. "I can hardly turn you out tonight, Mr. Barnett. The risk is too great, and I won't have your death on my conscience."

"He can sleep in my bed," Andy offered.

"Andrew, that wouldn't be appropriate. We share the loft, and Marty and I can hardly stay in the same room with Mr. Barnett."

Andy seemed to consider this for a moment. "He can stay in Pa's room with the Comanche."

"Sí, that might serve you well, Miss Hannah." Berto looked

to William before continuing. "He speaks Comanche and you'll need someone on guard."

"You speak Comanche?" Hannah questioned.

"Some. Enough," William admitted.

"I need time to think." Hannah frowned and put her linen napkin aside.

William wondered if she'd lost her appetite or if the idea of him under the same roof was so unpleasant she couldn't stomach her supper. He watched as she excused herself from the table and exited the room. She was all grace and manners, but he could see that she was more than a little upset. Well, he was upset, too.

Hannah went to the kitchen and leaned heavily against the counter. What was happening? Mr. Barnett had returned, and Father was still missing. She wondered if Mr. Lockhart might be of use but fretted over the idea of calling him to the ranch. If he knew Barnett was there, he might insist that Hannah leave. Or he might bring the law and cause problems for Mr. Barnett. Either way, Hannah didn't like the choices.

"Are you all right, Miss Hannah?" Juanita asked, joining her in the kitchen. She went immediately to the cupboard and retrieved three plates.

"I don't know what to think of all of this, Juanita. There's a Comanche in Father's bed, a stranger sitting at my dining table, and the ever-present threat of attack. Added to all of this, Father is missing and a war is going on. I'd say things cannot possibly get any worse."

"Miss Hannah, Mr. Will is a good man. You should not

be afraid that he is here." Juanita patted Hannah's arm, then turned back to the counter.

Hannah put her face in her hands. "I don't know what I'm going to do."

The thought of her future terrified Hannah. Perhaps if the war were over she could return to her grandmother's house in Vicksburg. Surely with the gold under Father's bed she would be able to get them back to Mississippi.

She felt Juanita hug her close. The woman had such a kind and gentle nature. She never worried about the differences between them—the fact that she was paid to work on the ranch or that their skin was different colors and they spoke two different languages. Juanita simply saw a need and endeavored to meet it.

"Miss Hannah, God will see you through."

Hannah lifted her face to meet the older woman's dark eyes. "I want to believe that, Juanita. I do. I feel so weak though. I feel as if my faith is an ember about to go cold."

The woman nodded. "Sometimes it is hard. We must trust, even when . . . when very bad times come."

"This is the worst of times to be sure." Hannah let out a heavy sigh and straightened. Squaring her shoulders, she looked beyond Juanita. "I suppose Mr. Barnett could stay in the bunkhouse with the other men. The men could take turns caring for the Indian." She twisted her hands. "I don't know rightly how to even pray about this."

"Ask God to show you," Juanita suggested. "He will."

Hannah tried to put her mind at ease. "I will ask Him."

<hr/>

"Did you have trouble with the Comanche when you were a little boy?" Andy asked William.

"I didn't live here when I was a boy," William told him. "I moved here when I was sixteen."

"I'm eight," Andy declared. "That's half of sixteen."

"Sounds like you're one smart boy."

Andy beamed. "Hannah's been teachin' me since we moved away from town. She's real smart."

"I can well imagine." William didn't want to focus their conversation on Hannah, however. He pointed to the checkerboard. "So you were teaching your sister to play. Are you any good?"

"Pa says I am." Andy sat down by the board. "You wanna play?"

William figured it wouldn't hurt anything and took a seat opposite the boy. The small table was perfect for a game. William wondered if it had been handcrafted for just such a thing in fact. He ran his hand over the smooth edges of the wood.

"My pa brought this table with us when we moved from Mississippi. It's his favorite."

"It's a nice table," William said, moving his checkers into place.

"He had it when he was married to Hannah's mama. She's dead now. Then he got married to my mama."

"And she died when Marty was born, is that right?"

"Yes, sir. I don't remember her." He frowned and pushed back his hair. "Pa has a picture of her, but he took it with him to Vicksburg."

William felt his chest tighten. "Vicksburg?"

Andy made his move then nodded. "That's where we used to live when my mama died. I don't remember living there, but my grandmother still lives there and Pa went to help her. She's sick."

"I see." William tried not to show any emotion. He pushed his checker into place and waited for Andy to move again.

"My mama was real pretty." Andy continued his play. "Where's your ma?"

"She died, too. She's buried here on the ranch. Down by the river."

"I saw it." Andy looked up, rather excited. "It's covered with rocks and has a wooden cross. We put some flowers on it once."

William nodded, remembering the day he and his brother had dug the grave. His mother had succumbed to the grippe, and when she died William felt a part of him had died, as well. He'd only been eighteen, but he missed her more than he could say.

"So did the Indians attack you?" Andy asked, jumping one of William's pieces. He smiled and captured the prize. "I'm winning."

It was William's turn to move and he managed to jump one of Andy's checkers. "Not for long."

"Berto said the Comanche are angry. He said most of the Indians are angry."

"I suppose that's right," William replied. "The way I figure it though, we'd better all learn to get along. If we keep on fighting, we'll kill each other off and then there won't be anyone to take care of the land."

"Mr. Lockhart hates the Indians. He told my pa they weren't

good for anything. He thinks the soldiers should just kill them all."

"Some folks feel that way, but I don't. I think we're all God's creatures and we need to work through our differences."

"But you went to war."

William didn't really know how to explain his thinking to an eight-year-old. "I went because my father wanted me to go. Nothing more."

"So you won't kill Indians?" Andy asked, momentarily forgetting the game.

William grew thoughtful. "If I'm attacked, I will defend myself. But otherwise, I won't seek to harm anyone. I prefer things being peaceable."

Andy nodded. "Me too. I don't like to fight. Hannah says that God isn't pleased when we hurt each other. I like it when folks get along. Pa said there's a big war going on back where we used to live. He said hate is what stirred it up. I don't like war."

Thoughts of battle flooded William with images of death and destruction. "I don't, either," he said, his voice barely audible.

"Mr. William, you come quick. That Indian is waking up!" Juanita called from the archway. "Hurry!"

6

The Comanche boy rallied and quickly faded out again. Throughout the night, William watched the boy and wondered when his people might come for him. He didn't want to upset Miss Dandridge, but there was little doubt in William's mind that the Comanche would track the boy back to the ranch. Of course, if the young man was of value to the band, they might be willing to barter for him. It wasn't likely, but there was a chance nevertheless.

Having been using his nights for travel and days for sleep, William didn't find it all that hard to keep watch. He read a bit, but he felt more on guard than he had in his weeks of dodging soldiers and Indians. He knew Berto and Diego were most likely helping keep watch. They understood the likelihood of the Comanches' return. William and Berto had discussed it in brief and they'd all agreed that given the recent threat, everyone would be better served to sleep under one roof.

William had been glad that Miss Dandridge was the sensible sort. She didn't argue with the suggestion at all. In fact she had taken Juanita and Pepita up to the loft with her and the children. He thought it remarkable that Miss Dandridge didn't separate herself from the hired help. This was the second example he'd witnessed, and he couldn't help but wonder how a young woman so clearly raised among educated, genteel Southern folk could act in such a manner.

William looked at his pocket watch. The sun would be up soon. William wasn't exactly sure what the plan should be. He'd thought by now the Indian boy would be awake—at least enough that he could converse with him and explain they meant him no harm. William had seen more bloodshed than he cared to remember during the war, and the last thing he wanted to witness was the murder of the Dandridge children or Berto's family.

He closed the watch and returned it to his pocket. The timepiece had been a gift from his mother and father on his eighteenth birthday. His mother had died not long after. For the first time in quite a while he allowed himself to remember her and the good days—the days when his mother had been alive and their family had been whole. He knew that in a situation like this, his ma would tell him to pray.

Lucy Barnett could have given lessons in prayer to preachers. She prayed all the time and believed that God heard each and every petition. William had never been quite so confident. He believed in God and had asked Jesus into his heart when he was just a boy at his mama's knee, but as he grew older trust came harder.

Ma had said that was Satan's way of trying to wiggle into a young Christian's heart. Satan liked to attack before a fellow could make his faith strong enough to stand the tests of life. That was why God gave children God-fearing parents and other adults of Christian faith.

"Those who have fought the good fight for longer in life are able to pray and encourage those who are weak," she would tell him.

Then she would touch his cheek and tell him that she was praying for God to strengthen him. Gazing across the small bedroom, William could imagine her standing there, as she might have been when he was a boy. She always made him feel loved and cared about, even when she was busy at her tasks.

"God has a plan for your life, William." Her words were laced with pride and assurance. *"You may not know exactly what that entails,"* she would say, *"but you can rest in certainty that it will be honoring and pleasing to Him."*

William shook his head and thought of the men he'd killed in battle. Was that honoring and pleasing to God? Where was God then?

He leaned back against the wall and tried not to remember the horrors of war. It was nigh onto impossible, though. He could still smell death in his nostrils. Death, mingled with smoke, dirt, and gunpowder. He would never forget the cries of the wounded, the dying. Men who had only moments before been strong and healthy now groaned and pleaded for their mothers, their wives, their sweethearts. Some were just as glad for a complete stranger to take their hand and await death's embrace.

Would the memories never stop tormenting him? Would he ever be able to close his eyes and sleep the rest of the innocent?

He saw movement in the bed and jumped up to find the Comanche boy had awaken. Choosing his words with great care, William spoke the boy's language.

"You are safe here," he told him. "We mean you no harm."

The boy's eyes darted around the room. "Why am I here?"

"Your horse threw you. You landed in the wash—broke your arm and hit your head. You've been resting here all night." William moved closer and the boy cowered. Pain was clearly etched in his expression.

"I mean you no harm. My name is William Barnett. This is my ranch. What's your name?"

The young man watched William for a moment, then answered. *"Tukani Wasápe."*

"Night Bear," William repeated in English.

"My father is He Who Walks in Darkness," the boy said, struggling to sit up. "He will come for me."

"I'm certain he will," William replied. "However, we want no trouble with him or with the *Numunuu*."

"You do not call us Comanche?" Night Bear questioned.

"I respect the People," William said, calling them as they called themselves. "The People have been long in this land and I am not an enemy."

The boy's upper lip curled slightly. "All white men are our enemy. You would see us all dead."

"You don't even know me," William said in his defense. "I do not wish you dead. Would I have brought you here and seen to your care if I wanted you dead?"

Night Bear considered this for a moment. "You brought me here?"

"Yes." William watched the Comanche for a moment. "I was there when you were about to shoot the young boy."

"The white hair," Night Bear said as if suddenly remembering. "His scalp would have been my first. It would have been a good omen."

"No, it would not. That child meant you no harm. When you fell from your horse, that boy came to your aid. He never knew you meant to take his life."

The door opened and Hannah looked inside. "Mr. Barnett, I thought . . ." She stopped in midsentence at the sight of the young Comanche awake.

"This is Night Bear," William said. He looked at the young man. "Do you speak English?"

"I know the white man's tongue," Night Bear replied. "It is evil and full of lies."

"That it is," Hannah said, seeming to forget her surprise. She came to the bed. "I'm Hannah Dandridge, Night Bear. You are a guest in my house. Are you hungry?"

He looked confused for a moment and Hannah asked again, this time gesturing to imitate eating. "Would you like to eat?"

"*Haa*—yes."

"Good. Then I will bring you something right away." She looked at William. "Would you like something?"

"Not just yet," he told her.

Night Bear watched as she exited the room then turned his attention back to William. "She is your woman?" he asked in Comanche.

William shook his head. "*Kee*. No. It's a long story, but let's just say she is a guest—a friend."

Hannah soon returned and placed a tray with a sweet roll and milk in front of the boy. It wouldn't be something the boy was used to eating, but perhaps he was the adventurous sort.

"I'll have some hot food in a little while," she said, straightening.

Night Bear considered the sweet roll for a moment. He poked at it with his finger then looked up. William explained as best he could in the boy's language. This seemed to satisfy him. He picked the roll up and bit into it. The flavor apparently met with his approval, because he wolfed down the entire thing in only a few bites.

"Goodness, you must be hungry. Should I get another one for you?"

"Haa. I eat more," Night Bear declared.

Hannah smiled and William thought it the loveliest smile he'd seen in some time. "I will get you another."

Night Bear drank the milk and waited for her return. William couldn't help but wonder if the boy's father would appreciate the kindness they were showing Night Bear and in turn show mercy. If the warriors returned with a larger raiding party, there was little they could do to defend themselves for long.

"Is your father an honorable man?" William asked in the boy's tongue.

"He is," Night Bear replied. "He is most honorable. He is chief of our band. The Numunuu hold him in high regard. He is wise and just."

"Will he be just with us?" William asked. "We have shown you mercy and cared for you. We did not wish to see harm done to you. Will He Who Walks in Darkness honor our kindness and do us no harm?"

The young warrior seemed to think on this for a moment. "My father hates the white man. He has lost many good people to the fighting. My grandfather and uncles are all dead because of the soldiers at the fort. My father would not agree to the treaties. He will not go to the reservation."

"I can understand his anger, but we are not soldiers and we mean you and your people no harm. My family has lived here for many years and has done so in peace. Even when the Numunuu and Kiowa were fighting the soldiers at the forts, we did not fight with them."

"How did you learn to speak our tongue?" Night Bear asked.

"We once employed a young man who had been raised with the Comanche. He had been traded back to the whites and came to work for us after a time. He taught me your tongue."

Just then Hannah returned with not one, but two additional sweet rolls. "Here," she said, smiling. "This should stave off your hunger for a while."

"*Ura,*" the boy said.

"That means thank you," William explained. "In the Numunuu language."

"I thought he was Comanche," she replied, looking oddly at the boy.

"He is Comanche, but that is not the name they call themselves. Numunuu is what they use. It means the People."

"I see. Well, you are very welcome to the food, Night Bear." She looked to William. "When did he wake up?"

William covered a yawn. "About ten minutes ago. We hadn't been talking long when you came in."

Just then Berto rushed into the room. "The Comanche are back. They are just beyond the pens—on the hill."

Hannah put her hand to her mouth but said nothing. William looked to Night Bear. "It would seem your people have come to take you home."

Night Bear ate the remaining piece of one roll and took up the other in his good hand. "I go to them. I make the peace." He stood, but immediately began to sway.

William rushed to his side. "You have a head injury. You shouldn't move too fast. Let me help you."

Berto came to offer his assistance. "What do you want to do?"

"We will help him walk to his people," William said. "Hopefully, they will see that we are treating him well and perhaps the boy will be able to tell them we are friends."

"Comanche won't be friends with the white man," Berto declared.

William knew it was a long shot, but they had to try. "It's our only choice." He looked to Hannah, but found she was gone. "Where's Miss Dandridge?"

Berto looked around the room. "I don't know."

"I can walk," Night Bear said, struggling against their hold. "I am not a weak woman."

William and Berto let go and waited to see if the boy would fall again. He drew a deep breath, however, and stood his ground. "I will make the peace. You have treated me honorably."

They made their way to the hall and then to the front door. William and Berto walked in support beside Night Bear in case he stumbled or lost consciousness. The one thing that amused William was that the boy never lost his grip on the sweet roll.

To William's surprise the front door was standing open to the world. He stepped forward with Night Bear, fully expecting to find the Comanche waiting in the yard. Instead, the area looked deserted. They walked around the side of the house, however, and that was when William spotted Hannah.

She was walking toward the Comanche as if they were long lost friends. She held out her hands, palms up as if to show them she had nothing that could bring them harm. William and Berto stopped. Night Bear did likewise. The Comanche could clearly see him, but what they thought of the situation was yet to be determined.

William wanted to call to Hannah, but he was afraid of what might happen if he said anything. He watched the breeze play with her long brown skirt as she crossed the open span. What was she thinking?

He caught sight of a horse and rider separating from the line of some fifteen men. The rider directed the ebony horse slowly down toward Hannah. The warrior seemed in no hurry.

"That is my father," Night Bear announced. "Come, we will go to him."

William knew that now would be the moment of decision.

He had no weapon with him. He'd not even thought to take up his rifle. He didn't know if Berto had a pistol or knife, but either way they would be no match for fifteen trained Comanche warriors.

Hannah stopped and waited for the rider to approach her. William couldn't help but admire her bravery. He hoped that the Indian chief would esteem it, as well. People always said that the one thing that impressed the Comanche was shows of strength.

By the time William, Berto, and Night Bear reached Hannah, He Who Walks in Darkness had already stopped just a foot away from her. He fixed Hannah with an intimidating stare. His face was painted black with two red stripes at the forehead and chin. It was a sure sign of war.

"We mean the Numunuu no harm," Hannah said in a loud, clear voice.

The chief stared at her for a moment longer. William and Berto held back as Night Bear moved forward. He began speaking in rapid fire Comanche, gesturing with his good arm. He pointed to his head and then his arm. The sweet roll still remained firmly in his grasp.

"You saved my son?"

William was surprised to hear the chief speak English so well. Hannah stepped forward, seemingly unafraid.

"He fell and was hurt. We did what any good Christian folk would do."

He Who Walks in Darkness looked beyond her to Berto and William.

William held up a hand. *"Maruawe,"* he said in greeting.

It was a traditional welcome and William could only hope that the chief would accept their friendly gesture. He hoped, too, that the man would listen to his son, who was even now defending the whites who had taken him in.

God, if you do still care, William prayed, feeling like a hypocrite, *we could use some help about now.*

7

Hannah could scarcely believe her own actions. Why in the world she had done this thing—this very foolish thing—was beyond her. She hadn't even had time to think when she'd headed out of the house to greet the Comanche. Her only thought had been that if she didn't act fast, her family might well be killed.

She looked into the face of the Comanche leader and tried not to let her fear show. The man was fierce looking with his painted face. She could see his piercing dark eyes slowly assess her. This was a man who had no doubt killed many whites. His only concern at the moment was for his son—just as her concern was for Andy, Marty, and the others.

"We do not wish to be at war with you or the Numunuu," Hannah said softly.

"Your people are always at war with the Numunuu." He did nothing to draw the other warriors to his side but instead looked at his son and spoke in their language.

Hannah couldn't help but wonder what the conversation entailed. When Night Bear extended the sweet roll to his father, Hannah very nearly grinned. The boy had been very fond of the cinnamon-and-sugared roll. His father took the offering and sampled it. He nodded with a grunt and several words that Hannah couldn't understand.

Looking at Night Bear, Hannah could see that his strength was giving out. She turned to the chief. "Your son is injured. He is lucky to be alive—the blow to his head was quite bad."

The Comanche studied her, as if trying to understand all that she had said. William quickly translated. The chief nodded and motioned his son forward. Night Bear extended his right arm and his father pulled him up and onto the horse's back.

Night Bear all but fell against his father in exhaustion. The chief looked at Hannah once again. She smiled, hoping he would see that they were sincere in their willingness to be at peace.

"You are not like most of your people." He held her gaze a moment longer. "We will leave you in peace."

"Ura," Hannah said, barely able to draw breath.

The man smiled ever so slightly and looked past Hannah to William. He spoke in the Comanche language, then turned his horse and headed back to the warriors on the hill. Hannah watched him rejoin the others. They conversed for a moment before turning and heading their mounts to the north.

William came to stand beside her, and Hannah asked, "What did he say to you?"

"He Who Walks in Darkness said you were the bravest white woman he'd ever known." William shook his head. "I think you're the most foolish."

Hannah bristled at this. "I was only trying to help."

"You could just as easily have been killed. The Comanche were here to get the boy. They didn't care who they had to kill to do so. Night Bear is the only son of the chief. He was on his very first raid. They would have killed all of us to ensure that boy's safety."

Hannah put her hands on her hips. Her fear was quickly replaced by anger. "But they didn't. They realized we meant them no harm. I wanted to show them I was willing to risk death in order to prove to them that I meant to be at peace with them." She felt rather smug. "The way I see it, it worked."

"You haven't lived long in this part of the country, and at this rate you won't last long." William shook his head and turned to walk away. "Miss Dandridge, you are a dangerous woman."

Hannah watched him walk away and turned to Berto. "Your Mr. Barnett is a strange man."

"He is a good man," Berto said. "He was afraid for you. The Comanche are not, how you say, peace people. They want back their land—their hunting grounds. They are not happy with the whites."

"But they have made the peace with us," Hannah replied. "That should be an encouragement. That should prove that they are capable of negotiating peace with other whites."

"Miss Hannah, it is not possible, because the whites will not be at peace with the Comanche. Your people hate their people just as much. You know it is true."

Hannah did know this but hated to admit it. She wanted to believe that something special had happened there. Perhaps the start of peace in the entire territory. Wouldn't it be a marvel if that were the case? Wouldn't it be amazing if one act of kindness and mercy led to the settlement of the Indian wars?

To Hannah's surprise, William stopped and came back to face her. He pointed his finger directly in her face. "You were lucky. That's all. It wasn't a matter of bravery or wisdom. What you did was foolish and could have resulted in the death of everyone here. You think yourself clever for having memorized a couple of overheard Comanche words. You probably think you've accomplished something miraculous here."

Hannah wasn't about to let him know that she had been considering that possibility. "God knew what He was doing, Mr. Barnett."

"God did, yes. But you didn't. You just walked out here like you were going to Sunday meeting and expected the entire world to see things your way. Too many people have tried to impose their will on others and have died because of it. You imposed your will and could have seen the death of your brother and sister. Their blood would have been on your hands."

For a moment Hannah actually considered slapping him. How dare this man come into their lives—a total stranger—and dictate to her how she should conduct herself. It hadn't been her desire to meet the Comanche chief. She had simply felt compelled—driven, really—to do as she had. It was God's direction, and Mr. William Barnett was not going to chide her for doing what God had clearly instructed her to do.

"Mr. Barnett, I'm going to overlook your rudeness and mark it down to fear. I will, however, not be judged by you. God is my judge. He alone determines my steps, and if those steps lead me to stand before my enemy, then that is what I will do. Perhaps it's what I am doing now."

She sidestepped him and headed for the house. Her heart was a mix of anger and accomplishment. All of her life men had dictated her directions. Her father, although kinder prior to her stepmother's death, had commanded his family much as a general with an army. When he'd made it clear that Hannah would take care of her siblings, he allowed no room for contradiction or protest. Standing up to William Barnett not only felt good, it felt right. Hannah had defended her choice to follow God's direction rather than man's, and it made her feel liberated.

Inside the house, Hannah found Juanita and the children. Andy and Marty ran to her and wrapped themselves around Hannah as if they were drowning.

"We thought the Comanche got you," Andy declared. "I'm so glad you're safe."

"Did they shoot you with an arrow?" Marty asked, pulling back.

"No. The chief was quite nice to me. He was glad we had taken good care of his son. Because we showed mercy, he showed mercy to us."

"God be praised," Juanita said, hugging Pepita close. "Did they leave?"

The woman seemed to search Hannah's face for any unspoken truth. Hannah nodded and hoped her words would put the woman at ease. "The chief is called He Who Walks in Darkness. He is the father of the boy we cared for. He took his son and they left with the other warriors. He agreed to be at peace with us."

Juanita let out a heavy breath. "I am so glad. Oh, Miss Hannah, we all were so afraid. Why you go out there?"

Unwilling to be reprimanded again, Hannah straightened and looked at the foursome. "I felt God telling me to go. I was only trying to be obedient to God. The Bible says in Romans eight, 'If God be for us, who can be against us?' I believe that God surrounded me with angels of protection." She looked at the clock. "But for now, we need to get you fed and start your studies."

"Pepita and I will get the breakfast, Miss Hannah." Juanita and her daughter headed toward the kitchen.

Hannah looked at her brother and sister and thought again of how close they'd all come to dying. But what should she do now? They had at least a temporary reprieve from Night Bear's people, but did that mean other bands would leave them alone, as well?

"Let's get you two dressed and ready for the day. Come on." She ushered them back up to the loft, where a pitcher of water awaited them. The loft was arranged quite simply. There were three small beds, two chests for clothes, and a small dresser where Hannah kept her things. Walking to the dresser, Hannah picked up her brush.

"Sit here while I arrange your hair," she told her sister. Marty sat obediently while Hannah combed out her long blond hair and plaited it into two neat braids. Next she helped Marty with her stockings and pantalets.

"Now get your dress and apron on," Hannah instructed. She left Marty to check on Andy.

Across the room, Andy was struggling to tuck his shirt into his trousers. Hannah gave him a hand. "Now get your boots on and go do your chores."

Andy looked up at her with a worried expression. "Is it safe now, Hannah?"

She nodded. "Yes. You don't need to be afraid."

"Can we go back down to the wash and see if that steer is still caught in the brambles?"

Hannah had forgotten that she had yet to mete out Andy's punishment for his disobedience. She looked at him with tender affection. "I'll have Thomas and JD check it out. You are not to go down there again unless an adult is with you. Do you understand? Those washes are dangerous places. When the rains come they fill up fast. Night Bear nearly lost his life falling into one. Your disobedience almost cost you your life. Night Bear is a Comanche warrior. He didn't know that you weren't his enemy. Mr. Barnett said that he would have shot you had he not fallen from the horse."

"I'm sorry, Hannah. I know it was wrong. I promise I won't do it again."

She knelt down beside him. "Andy, I believe you. But you will have extra chores each night after supper for two weeks as punishment. Now get going."

He nodded and hurried to secure his boots. Meanwhile, Hannah returned to Marty and helped her do up the buttons and secure her pinafore. The child was hopeless to keep anything clean and the apron was Hannah's best hope for not having to wash clothes for the child on a daily basis.

"Are we gonna sew today?" Marty asked.

"Not today. We have laundry and if there's time, baking. You are going to help me make a cake today, remember?"

Marty's face lit up in delight. "Are we having a party?"

"Remember, it's Diego's birthday tomorrow. We are going to have a cake to celebrate."

The little girl clapped her hands. "I'm so happy. I love cake."

Hannah laughed. "I love it, too. Come on. Let's get your shoes."

When they joined the others at the table, Hannah could feel Mr. Barnett's gaze upon her, but she refused to acknowledge him. The memory of his harsh reprimands echoed in her mind, and she was still at a loss as to what they needed to do about his presence at the ranch.

After grace was offered, however, William spoke up and let her know his plans. "I'll have to go to Dallas one of these days to check on the situation with the ranch. If you would permit me to remain here, I'd be much obliged. I'm certain in time we can figure out the legalities of all of this."

"Perhaps if you start in Cedar Springs with Mr. Lockhart," Hannah said, still not looking at the man, "you will get your answers. Mr. Lockhart is my father's partner in law and real estate. They have a small office in town and I'm certain Mr. Lockhart can assist you in understanding the circumstances." She didn't know what to think about William's request to remain at the ranch. Somehow that didn't seem right, and yet it also seemed wrong to send him away.

"I cannot have you stay in the house with the children and me. It wouldn't be proper," she said, working up the courage to face him. She met his gaze. "However, if you wish to remain here, then I suppose we could make provision for you in the bunkhouse."

She waited for some outburst, but instead William turned to Diego. "You boys wouldn't mind having another bunkmate, would you?"

Diego laughed. "Lots of room out there, Boss."

William turned back to Hannah. "It would appear the matter is settled. At least for now."

She felt a bit of a shiver go down her spine. Somehow she got the feeling that Mr. Barnett was about to change everything. With William Barnett in the middle of her family's affairs, Hannah wasn't at all sure she was any safer than she had been with the Comanche.

"We cannot bake a cake unless we get more flour," Juanita said. "Do you think the store has any?"

Hannah shrugged and passed a plate of ham to Berto. "It's hard to say. The supplies come in so seldom these days. If you can spare me from the wash, I'll have Berto drive me into town and see what's to be had. I need to check in with Mr. Lockhart anyway and see if . . . if he's heard from Father."

"I'll hitch a ride in with you, if you don't mind," William said. "My leg makes walking that distance a bit of a challenge."

Hannah figured this to be a simple way to make peace with the man. After all, it would be a poor example to continue holding him a grudge. It wouldn't be the right attitude to show her siblings.

"You are welcome to ride with me, Mr. Barnett. Perhaps Mr. Lockhart will have answers for both of us."

He nodded and dug into his food without another word.

Hannah meanwhile sipped her coffee and hoped that she wasn't making a grave mistake by involving Herbert Lockhart. She didn't want trouble, and it seemed trouble always had a way of finding her when that man was involved.

∽

In town, William wasn't surprised to find folks rather hostile toward him. Those who knew him and his family seemed unwilling to forget that he'd gone to fight for the Union. At the mercantile, Nelson Pritchard, who had once been a good friend to William's father, barely said two words when William entered the store.

Glancing around the place, William could see that the inventory was low compared to how it had been in the past. Hannah circulated amongst the aisles, picking up an item or two as she went. William watched her, curious. She was certainly feisty.

He observed her hoop skirt sway as she maneuvered through stacks of empty crates. She wasn't dressed all that fancy, but he thought she cut a fine figure of a woman. He stood waiting near the checker barrel and pondered the situation. There had to be some way to remove the hostilities between them. The chiding he'd given her regarding the Comanche was for her own good. She'd been foolish to walk out into the fracas. Still, if he was going to settle this matter with the ranch, he might very well need to appeal to her kindness.

He'd seen that kindness extended to Night Bear. Surely she could spare a little for him, as well.

"William Barnett. I didn't think we'd see you in Cedar Springs again," Mrs. Pritchard said, coming from a back room.

William turned to face the older woman. She offered him nothing more than a disapproving stare. He smiled and gave her a slight nod. "I'm sorry to disappoint you."

She gave a huff and maneuvered by him as though he were diseased. "We figured you'd head north and stay there."

"I'm not a Unionist, Mrs. Pritchard," William said. "I'm a Texan. And I intend to stay a Texan."

"Well, a good Texan wouldn't go off fighting for the Yankees," she said, tying an apron around her thick waist. "Where's your father and brother?"

William grimaced. "They were killed in the war. Killed by Confederate soldiers. I was wounded and left crippled. Perhaps I should allow that to make me feel hostile toward you and the others who have supported the South. But frankly, I don't see that it serves any good purpose."

"Your people were traitors," Nelson Pritchard said, joining his wife. "You are a traitor. You put on that Yankee uniform. You got what you deserved."

"Mr. Pritchard," Hannah Dandridge interrupted, "do you by any chance have flour?"

"We have a bit, Miss Hannah," the man replied, turning away from William. "It's mighty costly."

"Well, I'll take some anyway. We have a birthday cake to make for Diego Montoya."

Pritchard nodded and headed for the flour barrel. "We managed to get some supplies in from some Southern sympathizers out of the Colorado Territory. It's costing us more than it ought to, but these are hard times."

William saw Berto enter the store and turned from Mrs.

Pritchard to join him. Hannah noticed him at the same time. "Was Mr. Lockhart in his office?" she asked.

"No, *señorita*. He was not."

"You lookin' for Herbert?" Mr. Pritchard asked Hannah.

"Yes. We were hoping to speak with him."

"He's gone to Dallas on business. I'll let him know when he returns that you were looking for him."

Hannah flushed and refocused her attention on a bushel of apples. "These look quite good. I'll take a dozen. Oh, and how about cornmeal? I could use a fifty pound sack if you have it."

William noted her embarrassment regarding Lockhart. Then Pritchard moved in close to Hannah and said something that William couldn't hear. She nodded and he spoke again. This time she stepped back and shook her head. "No, it's all right. I'm not worried."

The storekeeper looked at William and then back to Hannah. "I don't want you havin' any trouble."

"Mr. Pritchard, I'm certain Mr. Barnett will be an asset to us. After all, he cares for the ranch just as we do, and as a good Christian man, he will deal with us honorably." She looked at William as if to affirm this, but he said nothing.

Once Hannah finished with her shopping, William and Berto carried the supplies out to the wagon. He allowed Berto to hand Hannah up to the wagon seat, wondering at this woman who burned with angry defiance one minute, then defended him the next. Climbing into the back of the wagon, William said nothing as Berto took the driver's seat once more.

The buildings appeared smaller and smaller as they drove away from town. William watched Cedar Springs pass from sight, soon to be replaced with open range and occasional farms and clumps of trees. Nothing seemed the same; yet he supposed it was bound to change what with time away and the war. He and his father and brother had been gone nearly two years. Two years of blood and guts being spilled in a war he didn't believe in.

"How can you not believe in the sanctity of the union?" his father had asked him shortly before his death.

It wasn't a matter of not believing that the states should stay united. It wasn't even a matter of not desiring to see the slaves set free. William abhorred slavery. No, it was more just feeling that bloodshed and war were not the best resolution to the problem. The entire country was acting like a rebellious child. Why should he be a part of that?

Now he'd returned to all that he loved . . . only to find it, too, taken from him.

He glanced toward the heavens. *Where are you, God? Why did you take everything from me? Why did you forsake me?*

8

Sunday, after morning chores, Hannah and the others gathered in the living room of the main house and did as they had done since coming to the ranch. Despite John Dandridge's loss of his faith, they celebrated the Lord's Day together and Hannah welcomed anyone who wanted to join them. This usually included most of the hands and of course the Montoya family, but today it also included William Barnett.

Dressed in brown trousers and a bib-buttoned white cambric shirt he'd borrowed from Berto, William looked quite handsome. Hannah tried to forget her attraction to him while they read from the Psalms. There was no sense in losing her thoughts over a man who very well might prove to be their ruin. After all, there was still no telling what he would do in regard to the ranch.

Forcing her thoughts back on the verses at hand, Hannah wondered at the psalmist's request. The forty-third Psalm consisted of only five verses. She read them slowly.

" 'Judge me, O God, and plead my cause against an ungodly nation: O deliver me from the deceitful and unjust man. For thou art the God of my strength: why dost thou cast me off? Why go I mourning because of the oppression of the enemy? O send out thy light and thy truth: let them lead me; let them bring me unto thy holy hill, and to thy tabernacles. Then will I go unto the altar of God, unto God my exceeding joy: yea, upon the harp will I praise thee, O God my God. Why art thou cast down, O my soul? And why art thou disquieted within me? Hope in God: for I shall yet praise him, who is the health of my countenance, and my God.' "

Hannah glanced at William Barnett and thought of the psalmist's cry to be delivered from the deceitful and unjust man. But Barnett wasn't either of those things. He might well be the enemy; but then again, he wasn't exactly that, either. Hannah wasn't at all certain what William Barnett was to them. Would he prove to be a blessing or a curse?

Why art thou cast down, O my soul?

She pondered those words, feeling as if God was speaking directly to her. They had known God's mercy in His deliverance from the Comanche. Hannah had to acknowledge God's mighty power in soothing the hearts of the savages toward them. Yes, perhaps she had erred in putting herself in the midst of the matter instead of waiting for the men in her household to handle the situation. But nevertheless, God had blessed them.

After the Scripture reading, they spent some time in silent prayer, as had become their custom. Hannah knew that they each had a different background where religious training was concerned, but she believed that if a person acknowledged

God the Father and accepted His Son, Jesus, as Savior, many of the other issues could be easily worked out.

When the mantel clock chimed twelve, Hannah lifted her head and said amen.

Marty scratched at the lace around her collar. "Can I change my clothes now? This itches."

Hannah took pity on her sister. "Yes. You and Andy can change into your play clothes. Pepita, can you go help Marty with her buttons?"

Pepita nodded and reached out for Marty's hand. "I will help."

Andy beat Marty to the loft ladder and shot up before she could even protest. Hannah very nearly laughed at the scene. Her siblings were not much for dressing in their Sunday best. She supposed it had to do with them being raised on the frontier. In her own childhood there had been many occasions for dressing up—supper alone had been a daily reason for putting on one's best clothes. When they'd all lived together in Vicksburg, the dinner table was a place for socializing, and that required a certain decorum.

Things were far different here in the wilds of Texas, however. Washing clothes was an arduous task and fine silks were inappropriate for ranch work. Not realizing this, Hannah had brought a trunk full of useless fashions that remained packed at the foot of her bed. She sighed, thinking of the world she had left. What was the sense in bringing out such finery here? She could hardly wear them to work in the garden.

She felt someone touch her arm and glanced up to find William Barnett by her side. "Yes?" she asked, startled that he would be so bold as to take hold of her.

"I asked if I might have a moment to discuss something with you. You didn't seem to hear me."

Hannah looked away in discomfort. "I'm afraid I was lost in my thoughts. Of course we can speak." She glanced around the now-empty room. "Would you care to remain here, or should we speak outside?"

William inclined his head toward the door. "Let's take a walk."

She nodded and followed him outside. The temperature had cooled considerably in the last couple of days. Hannah thought that perhaps it might even turn cold. Since coming to Texas she'd experienced snow twice and thought it quite marvelous.

"Look, I asked to speak with you so that we might exact a sort of truce between us," William said without waiting. "I'm not your enemy."

Hannah stopped and fixed him with a serious gaze. "Neither am I yours."

"I'm glad we're able to establish at least that much," he said with a hint of a smile. "I also want you to know that no matter what the situation turns out to be with the ownership of the ranch, it is not in my nature to turn out women and children to fend for themselves."

Hannah bristled for a moment. How could he suggest that the ranch's ownership was in question? She felt confident that once he spoke with Mr. Lockhart, it would all be resolved. He would see that the property had been confiscated as spoils of war, and that he and his family had forfeited any possible possession.

Still, there was no sense in making matters worse by pointing this out. Hannah drew in a deep breath. "I appreciate your concern, Mr. Barnett."

"I would ask that you extend the same consideration, if possible."

She nodded. "I would not throw you to the mercy of the Comanche nor to the people of Cedar Springs. Apparently they are not yet able to understand your choosing to fight for the Union."

His expression hardened. "It wasn't my choosing. It was my father's. I was simply being the obedient son."

"Well, that is something I can well understand," Hannah replied. "Perhaps not being a son, but being obedient. My father is the reason I am here. It was not my choosing."

"So maybe you can understand my situation."

She gave the briefest of nods, then folded her hands against the blue calico dress she'd chosen. It wasn't her finest by any means, but it was nicer than most of the skirts and blouses she wore for every day. She also thought it did wonders for her eyes. Suddenly she had a terrible thought. Had she worn this gown to impress Mr. Barnett? Was she trying to attract his attention?

"I intend to earn my keep. If you will give me permission to do so, I would like to take over the running of the ranch. Berto is good at what he does, but there are certain things my father had planned for the ranch—things I would like to implement and continue."

His request seemed reasonable. After all, it was free labor for the betterment of the property. When her father returned, he would probably be grateful for the innovations and improvements.

"I see no reason you should not continue with those plans already in place," Hannah replied.

Just then Andy came flying out the open door. "Thomas Early said we could go look for steers in the wash after dinner. If you said it was all right."

Hannah smiled. "I think that would be fine. Just promise me you'll stay with Thomas and not wander off on your own."

"I promise." Andy looked up at William. "You can come, too, if you want."

"I'm afraid my leg is giving me trouble today, so I might take you up on that offer another day."

Hannah looked at the man's leg and then quickly returned her focus to his face. "I didn't realize your leg was bothering you. Is there anything I can do for you?"

"No," William said uncomfortably.

"My sister is the bravest in the world, don't you think, Mr. Barnett?" Andy asked, hugging his arms around Hannah's waist. "She faced those Comanche all by herself. Well, she said there were angels with her, but it was still brave."

"It was foolish," William replied before Hannah could speak.

She had thought to tell her brother her actions had been folly, but William's comment made her angry. *So much for our truce*, she thought.

"Hannah, can I go with Andy?" Marty called as she joined them. "He said he's going to the warsh with Thomas." Her drawl mimicked that of the cowboy.

"I know his plans, but no, you may not go." She turned back to William. "I would appreciate it if you would keep your opinions of me and my actions to yourself. I can explain myself to my brother and do not need your reprimand."

"It wasn't a reprimand. I was merely setting the boy straight. I would hate for him to live by your example."

Andy pulled away from his sister. "Don't be mean to Hannah, Mr. Barnett. She's real smart, and Pa says she's about the strongest woman he's ever known."

Hannah startled at this. She'd never known her father to say anything of the kind. Had he truly told Andy such a thing?

"I don't doubt that your sister is smart in some things," William said. "And I'll agree with your pa that she's a strong woman, but what she did with the Comanche was not smart. Nor would she be strong enough to stand up to them should they have decided to attack. I would hope you would never do anything so foolish."

"I feel," Hannah interjected, "the Bible is correct in Corinthians where it says, 'But God hath chosen the foolish things of the world to confound the wise; and God hath chosen the weak things of the world to confound the things which are mighty.' It has been my experience, Mr. Barnett, that often God's calling appears foolish to those who have no true understanding of His direction. Perhaps you should pray for guidance."

William's eyes narrowed. "Perhaps you should pray for wisdom."

"I was brave," Marty declared in the midst of their standoff. "There was an Injun . . . Indian once who wanted to steal one of our horses and I told him no."

Hannah looked to her sister and shook her head. "Martha Dandridge, you must stop these tales. You cannot tell such falsehoods without punishment. Go to the loft and stay there until dinner. Go to your bed and spend the time thinking about why it is wrong to lie."

Marty's lower lip quivered, but she did as she was told and walked with slumped shoulders back to the house. Andy seemed to understand that Hannah was no longer in a good mood and took that as his cue to leave.

"I'm gonna find Thomas and tell him you said it was okay to go after we eat." He took off at a run, as if fearful that Hannah would change her mind.

Hannah had no desire to make Andy unhappy, however. She was more focused on putting William Barnett in his place. But that, she realized, would have to wait, for the sound of an approaching rider drew her attention to the road beyond the ranch.

She sighed. "It would seem Mr. Lockhart has learned of your desire to speak with him."

They waited in silence as the horse and rider drew closer. Lockhart seemed to frown as he recognized the man at her side. Hannah didn't know what kind of problems might exist between the two of them, if any, but she had no desire to be in the middle of their discussion.

"Mr. Lockhart, what brings you our way?" she asked as he dismounted. She knew what his answer would be but couldn't think of anything else to say. She didn't want to suggest that she was happy to see him, for that would be a lie. Then it dawned on her that he might have word of her father. "Have you heard something about my father?"

"I've had no more information on him." Lockhart tied

off his horse and came to where they stood. "I heard, however, that Mr. Barnett was back and had business with me." He narrowed his eyes. "I do hope you haven't caused Miss Dandridge any trouble."

"Well, I must be excused," Hannah said, not wanting to remain. "I need to see to helping Juanita with our dinner. Would you care to stay and eat with us, Mr. Lockhart?"

He broke into a broad smile. "I would cherish the opportunity."

Hannah nodded and turned to go. "If you two wish to remain out here for your discussion, I'll send Marty for you when the meal is ready."

William wanted to say something more to Hannah, but her retreating figure made it clear that she had ended their conversation. He didn't like leaving matters as they were. He knew his attitude had put her off once again, and her preaching at him didn't help him to relent.

Instead, he turned to Lockhart. The man wasn't a complete stranger. Lockhart had been in the Cedar Springs area off and on prior to the war, and while William had relatively little to do with the man, he knew him nevertheless.

"Lockhart," William said with a nod.

"Mr. Barnett. I can't say that I expected to see you in these parts again."

"And why not? This is my ranch now that my father and brother are dead."

"I beg to differ," Lockhart replied, squaring his shoulders. "The law of this land would say otherwise."

"The Confederate law?"

"Exactly so. Texas is a part of the Confederacy." Lockhart smiled. "Even if you and your family thought otherwise."

"Look, I'm not here to discuss the politics of the day. I simply want to know why it is that the Confederacy thought it acceptable to rob me of my land. I intend to fight this as far as I need to in order to see the matter set straight."

Lockhart sputtered a bit and cleared his throat. "The Confederacy gave this property over to John Dandridge. It was in payment for legal work he did for the governing entities. You have no more claim to this land than the Comanche do."

"Well, like the Comanche, I'm not easily dissuaded." William looked out across the ranch yard and shook his head. "I helped to build everything you see here. I worked alongside my father and brother to build a place we could be proud of—a valuable, working ranch to support our family. I won't allow you or the Confederacy to strip that away on a whim."

"It was hardly a whim, Mr. Barnett. Your father deserted the South. He forfeited his rights to property here in Texas when he chose to fight for the Yankees."

"My father chose to fight for the unity of the States. He did not support the existence of slavery, but neither did he concern himself with issues of individual states' rights. He believed in the sanctity of the union. I, too, believe that to be the best possible situation for our country. However, I did not go to war with that on my mind. I went only as an act of support for my father's wishes and those of my brother. They paid for their choice with their life's blood. I will not allow you to exact the price of this ranch, as well."

"You have little to say on the matter," Mr. Lockhart replied. "Those men who govern this great state have made that decision."

"Then I will have to do what I can to change their minds." William could see that Lockhart was not at all pleased with this response. No doubt he had planned to come and demand William leave the premises and obey the dictates of the Confederacy.

"You will find that very difficult to do. As you probably realized, folks in Cedar Springs aren't exactly friendly toward traitors."

"I wouldn't know, since I'm not a traitor," William countered. "Look, it doesn't matter to me that folks understood my father's decision. God knows I didn't completely understand it myself. But what I do understand is that my family put blood and sweat into this land, and I won't let you or anyone else just snatch it away."

"That really won't be your decision," Lockhart said, his tone smug. "The land was taken in a legal manner. My partner—Miss Dandridge's father—was a strong supporter of the Confederacy, and this ranch was given to him as a reward for his faithfulness."

"But this ranch wasn't anyone else's to give." William took a step toward Lockhart but kept his balled fists at his sides. "I won't let you or anyone else steal it away. This is my home and I intend to remain here."

"Mr. Barnett, Hannah says to come eat now," Marty called from the doorway.

William held Lockhart's gaze only a moment longer, then turned and smiled. "We're coming, Miss Marty."

Conversation at the dinner table was rather stilted. Lockhart seemed highly offended that Berto and his family, as well as the ranch hands, should be in their company. He looked as if he might say something, then seemed to think better of it. Maybe he wasn't as stupid as he appeared, William thought.

"It's been some time since I've had fried chicken," William commented. "I must say this is a real treat."

"We have whole bunches of chickens," Andy replied. "They lay a lot of eggs and we kept a bunch of the chicks. Now they're big enough to eat."

William smiled. "And I'm mighty glad they are. I don't recall that there were that many chickens when I went away from here."

Andy shook his head. "Nope. We brought a bunch with us. Pa likes eggs for breakfast every day."

"I like 'em, too," Marty declared.

"I couldn't agree with you and your pa more," William replied. "I'm quite fond of eggs myself. My ma used to have a few chickens. She liked to cook up all sorts of things with them. I like bacon, as well. Used to be my mama would fry up big old pans full of bacon and potatoes. Mighty filling." He smiled at the memory.

Marty nodded with great enthusiasm. "I love bacon and potatoes, too. Hannah sometimes makes them for us."

"Me too," Andy agreed. "Hannah says we're runnin' out of bacon though. When Pa comes back we're gonna go hunting for wild boar. It's real dangerous."

"That it is," William said. "I have only done it a couple of times myself. Maybe I could go hunting in your father's absence and help to restock the larder."

"Then when Pa gets back, maybe we could all go hunting together," Andy said with great enthusiasm.

"I hate to remind you," Lockhart said after taking a portion of cheesy grits, "but the chances of your father's return are slim to none."

Hannah's hand went to her mouth, and Andy looked in confusion to Lockhart. "What do you mean?"

"I mean exactly what I said," he replied.

"That's enough," Hannah said, barely able to get the words out. "Would you care for corn bread, Mr. Lockhart?"

He shook his head. "Do you mean to tell me that you haven't yet told these children of their father's capture? The man may well be dead—probably is. You shouldn't have kept such a thing from them."

Marty began to cry. "Hannah, is Papa dead?"

Andy's face was etched in fear. "Is he, Hannah?"

William could see the anger flicker in her expression. "Mr. Lockhart, I would appreciate if you would keep your thoughts to yourself." She turned to the children. "Our father has been taken by the Union to answer questions about his trip to see Grandmother. We do not know anything else, so stop fretting."

"Well, that's hardly the full truth, Miss Hannah," Lockhart continued. "I believe it's best to be honest with the young ones. They need to recognize that their father may well not return . . . at least not anytime soon . . . maybe never."

Marty fell into Hannah's lap, crying. "I want Papa to come home."

Andy bowed his head, but William could see that he was fighting back tears. "I believe," William said, turning to Lockhart, "you should shut up."

Lockhart's expression seemed to challenge William's

authority. "Sir, I will have you know that as the partner of Mr. Dandridge, I am responsible for seeing to the welfare of this family. John Dandridge's last words to me before leaving for the East were asking that I care for his children in his absence. I take my responsibility seriously. The fact that their father is most likely dead is nothing to hide from them. The sooner they accept the truth, the sooner they will be able to move forward with decisions regarding their future."

William got to his feet as Andy began to sob quietly. "I think you'd better leave."

Lockhart stiffened. "I do not believe it is your place to request my departure."

Shaking his head, William pushed back his chair. "I'm not requesting anything. I'm telling you to go."

9

"Do you think Pa is dead, Hannah?" Andy asked.

Hannah thought he sounded even younger than his eight years. "I don't know, Andy. The war has taken the lives of many, and it is possible, since Papa went to a place where the fighting was quite fierce. However, it's also just as possible that our father is safe. We must pray for him and ask God to show us the truth."

Andy shook his head and fixed Hannah with a worried look. "What if he is dead? What will we do without a pa?"

Hannah had asked herself this question many times over but hadn't allowed herself an answer. "I don't know." She hated to sound so defeated. She wanted answers as much as he did.

Glancing across the yard, Hannah felt a sense of relief that William was occupying Marty. She had cried for some time but had calmed when William took her in hand. It surprised Hannah, but at the same time she didn't resist his actions. If

Marty could be comforted by Mr. Barnett, she would count it a blessing.

"Will we have to leave Texas?" Andy asked.

Again, Hannah had no answers. She thought of Mr. Lockhart's offer of marriage. If all of her family were dead, what else could she do but marry someone, and do so quickly?

Hannah pushed back Andy's hair. "I don't know, Andy. I plan to seek counsel and to pray. I hope you'll pray, as well. God has the ability to take this situation and work it out to His glory. I don't know where that will take us, Andy, but we have each other."

"But you could die, too. You could have died when the Comanche came. Mr. Barnett said it was foolish."

Hannah held her opinion of Mr. Barnett's comments and gave a sigh. "It was foolish, Andy. But I felt compelled to do it. I suppose it was one of those things that if I'd had time to think about, I would never have done it." She knelt in the dirt and took hold of his forearms. "But you don't have to worry, Andy. I'm not planning to die anytime soon."

"But nobody plans to die, Hannah." Andy frowned. "It just happens. You said so yourself when you were talkin' to me about Ma. You said sometimes these things just happen. I remember it."

Hannah nodded. "And so they do. But, Andy, please don't live in fear of such a thing. I can't promise that I'll never die, but I do promise to make certain there is provision for your care and Marty's. You don't need to be afraid that you'll be left alone."

She wasn't at all sure how to fulfill that promise, but Hannah intended to get an answer to that problem right away. If all else failed, she would marry Mr. Lockhart. If only for the sake of Andy and Marty.

The last thing I ever wanted was a loveless marriage, she thought, then shook her head. No, the last thing she wanted was for any harm to come to her siblings. She was determined to protect them at all costs, even if that meant marrying a man she didn't love . . . and probably never would.

⤺

Herbert Lockhart seethed. How dare William Barnett interfere in his plans? How dare he demand Lockhart leave the ranch? He wasn't the owner—he had no say there. Yet Hannah had let Barnett order him about.

He pounded his fist on the desk. "I've worked too hard to have this fall apart now."

The paper in his hand was proof of that. He had worked hard to forge John Dandridge's signature, but the result was worth the effort. Looking from the forgery to the original, Lockhart had to admit he couldn't tell the difference.

Each page bore the title of "Last Will and Testament," and each revealed the supposed wishes of John Dandridge. The only difference was that Herbert Lockhart had manipulated the document for his own benefit, rather than that of Dandridge's children. He couldn't help but smile at the thought of Dandridge's ranch and monies coming to him. If he played his cards right, he would have it all.

The front door to his office opened, and Lockhart was surprised to find Nelson Pritchard. "Nels, what brings you here?" Lockhart asked, quickly putting the pieces of paper in a drawer.

"You hear that William Barnett is back in town?"

"I did. I also saw it with my own eyes. I was out at the ranch just yesterday. He's out there acting like the cock of the roost."

"He's awfully high and mighty for a traitor. I tried to warn Miss Dandridge, but she didn't seem overly concerned."

Lockhart leaned back in his chair. "What do you suggest we do about it?"

This question seemed to surprise Pritchard. "Well, I don't know. What can be done?"

"Seems to me the man is trespassing. Maybe he's coerced Miss Dandridge into allowing him to take up residence at the ranch. It's difficult to say, since he doesn't seem to leave her alone for long."

Pritchard nodded and took a seat across from Lockhart. "I thought that, too. Seemed he was just a bit too friendly with her."

Lockhart let out a heavy breath. "Perhaps it's a matter for the sheriff."

"Do you suppose so? What kind of charge would you put on Barnett?"

"I'm not entirely sure. I'll have to give it some thought." Lockhart wanted to figure something out that would get Barnett out of his hair permanently. Pity he couldn't pin Dandridge's death on him.

"Folks around here aren't going to be too sympathetic to Barnett. His father was a traitor, pure and simple. Ain't gonna tolerate that."

"I agree, Nels. I completely agree. This republic . . . state . . . wasn't created with folks making allowances for such things.

Now with the Comanche problems worse than ever, we need to present a united front and stand together. William Barnett and his kind would do better to head north and stay there. Once the war is over and we've won the right to govern ourselves, we'll have an easier time throwing folks like that out of the state."

"Can't come soon enough for me," Nelson muttered. "I don't abide cowards or traitors. Seems to me there's a lot of both."

"You're right, but it's a necessary evil that we'll have to tolerate for the moment. Half the local army is made up of men who didn't want to take a stand in the war. At least they're here to kill Indians, but that doesn't mean we'll need them once our good men return."

"No, sir. We won't have use for them at all."

Lockhart considered the man for a moment. "You know, you would be within your rights to refuse him service at the store. If everyone acted accordingly, Barnett wouldn't find it so easy to remain in the community."

"That's a good idea, Herbert. A good idea. I'll get the word out to folks. There's no sense in encouraging him to stay. Once he sees we all feel the same way, he'll have to go."

Smiling, Herbert Lockhart nodded. "Sounds like the start of a plan, Nels."

❧

Hannah stood in the storeroom just off the kitchen and took inventory of their supplies. Things were getting harder and harder to come by. The blockades in the Gulf and along the Mississippi, not to mention the fact that the Comanche now controlled the Santa Fe Trail, had left Texas struggling to get by. There was plenty of beef, but it was too warm most of the time to keep the meat from spoiling. It didn't salt as well as pork, although it could be jerked, and smoking it didn't keep beef as long as it did pork.

They did have the blessing of gardens, and the state was full of fruit trees. It wasn't all that hard to get oranges up from the south or pears, apples, and figs from nearby. Pecans grew wild down by the river and wild hogs were plentiful, especially to the east of them. Hannah supposed they suffered far less than most in the South. Texas offered a wide variety of benefits within its own borders, and if they could hold the Union Army at bay, they might survive the war with less difficulty than the rest of the country. Sadly, Hannah knew that folks east of the Mississippi were truly suffering. She read about it whenever a newspaper made its way to the ranch, and she feared that if the North had their way, the entirety of the Confederacy would be starved out.

The very thought made her all the more determined to work hard to put aside food for her family. Throughout the summer, Hannah had helped Juanita and Pepita to garden and can what they could. They had managed to raise a nice variety of vegetables, and those would surely see them through the winter months. Even so, other things like flour and salt were going to be harder to come by.

She stepped from the storeroom and closed the door behind her. She continued to study her figures as she took a seat at the kitchen table. If they were careful, they would get through until . . .

"Until what?" she wondered aloud.

Until Father came home? Until the war ended? Until she knew whether or not she'd be forced to marry a man she didn't love?

"You all right?"

She looked up to find William Barnett watching her from the back door. "I'm fine. Why do you ask?"

"It looked like you were scowling. I figured either you were thinking of me or something was wrong."

This actually made her smile. "I wasn't thinking of you. I was taking an account of our food. When Father left, he didn't intend to be gone more than a few weeks. We worked hard to can and preserve what we could for the winter, but I need to make sure we can get through for however long it takes. I was just realizing that I didn't know how long that might be."

William nodded. "The uncertainty makes it difficult for everyone. I hope you know that I mean to help provide. Berto and I were talking about hunting a couple of wild boars and smoking the meat. We have the supplies to make repairs to the smokehouse and I can see to those myself."

"Too bad you can't hunt down an animal made of sugar or coffee."

To her surprise he laughed. He was always such a serious man that it was rather pleasant when he did so. Hannah motioned to his leg. He was rubbing it, and she couldn't help but wonder at the problem.

"Is it paining you more than usual?"

William glanced down and then stopped rubbing his thigh. "Yeah, I suppose it is."

"Berto said to figure on rain," Hannah offered. "My grandfather had terrible joint pains that always grew worse when it was about to rain. Maybe that's why your leg is hurting more."

"Could be." He didn't offer anything more.

Hannah put aside her ledger. "I want to thank you for what you did for us the other day. I should have told the children about our father's disappearance. Mr. Lockhart had no way of knowing that I'd kept it from them."

"Even so, he should have held his tongue once he realized the truth."

She couldn't have agreed more. "That's why I'm grateful that you asked him to leave."

"I didn't really ask," he said, limping to help himself to a cup of coffee.

"No, I suppose you didn't. But in any case, I am grateful."

William poured the coffee and leaned back against the counter. "Lockhart never cared much for my family, and in turn I never cared much for him. Seemed to me he was always trying to swindle someone out of their land."

"I suppose some folks might feel that way. As a manager of real estate he could give that impression. I know people suggested the same of my father. I don't think they truly mean to cause harm, however."

"You're gracious to say so."

William sipped his coffee and seemed to stare right past her. Hannah felt uncomfortable, but didn't know what to say or do. She looked back at the closed ledger and let the heavy silence settle over her.

"So your people were from Vicksburg?" William asked.

Hannah looked up. "Yes. I was born and raised there. My father, as well. My grandparents had a very nice place near town. We all lived together and some of my best memories are of those days."

"How was it your father decided to come here?"

"He was lost in grief. My stepmother, Andy and Marty's mother, died giving birth to Marty. Father was beside himself. A friend wrote to encourage him to move to Dallas, and that convinced my father. He was desperate to leave Vicksburg and all that reminded him of what he'd lost. My grandmother encouraged him to allow us to remain behind with her, but for reasons I still do not understand, Father insisted otherwise. He wanted all of his children to accompany him, but my brother Benjamin refused. He remained with my grandparents."

"Is he there still?"

Hannah swallowed the knot in her throat. "No. He died during the battle. My grandfather, too. My grandmother took ill shortly thereafter, and that is why my father was making his way back. He figured to either bury her or get her well enough to return to Texas with him."

"And you've had no word on his whereabouts?"

"Only what Mr. Lockhart was able to find out. We knew it would be a grave risk, but we had figured that since Father wasn't a soldier and had planned only to care for his mother, perhaps the Yankees would leave him be."

"Perhaps Mr. Lockhart's information is incorrect."

Hannah looked up to find him watching her. "I suppose that is a possibility. I tell myself that at least a few dozen times a day.

Even so, there has been no word, and it isn't like Father to be gone all these months without getting us even a brief message."

"Unless someone was headed this way, it would be hard to get word through. The lines of communication aren't exactly in good working order. The mail routes were all canceled, many of the telegraph lines have been disabled, and the South has had to focus on the war efforts rather than repairs. I had a difficult time getting down here myself."

"I hadn't thought about that. I suppose it was very hard trying to make your way with a wound as bad as yours."

He shrugged. "The wound had healed as much as it could. The limp and pain will always be with me. Still, it was harder than I figured it'd be. Probably the worst of it was speaking with a drawl in Northern country and avoiding the conflicts between the two."

"Berto said you made your way through part of the Indian Territories."

"Yes. I traveled mostly at night the entire length of my journey, so it seemed as reasonable to pass there as to try and make my way through Arkansas and Louisiana."

"Were you in grave danger?" Hannah asked.

"There were a couple of times when I was nearly found out," he admitted. "I had taken up camp near a river and an entire band of Kiowa happened to come there for watering. I hid in the brush for over an hour while they refreshed themselves and their mounts." He blew out his breath rather loudly. "It was probably the hardest thing I've ever done. Kiowa and Comanche can hear a mouse running across an open field. I figured for sure they'd hear me breathing."

Hannah shook her head, trying to imagine such a frightening experience. "I suppose hiding from the army would be much the same."

"Not exactly. Those boys aren't trained that way. Some of the best officers are great at strategy and planning, but they have lived a life of ease otherwise. They've either never been trained to live off the land or they've forgotten what they knew. Then you have the enlisted men, a hodgepodge of farmers, bankers, clerks, and students. No, I found it far easier to avoid army encounters."

"I had hoped my father would have the same ability, but he wasn't raised to live off the land, either. He grew up with a lawyer for a father and followed in his footsteps." She bit her lip for a moment, wishing she'd not said anything about him.

"Well, some men have good instincts. Your father must have had a great deal of wisdom to bring you all here and settle in Texas. It's about the best place in the world, you know." He smiled. "Lockhart probably has it all wrong. I wouldn't fret overmuch about it until you hear something reliable."

"I'm sure you're right." Hannah got to her feet and tried hard to control her wavering emotions. She thought she might start to cry if she thought too much longer on the hopelessness of the situation.

"Do you have other family?"

"No. I suppose that's why this all seems . . . I . . . it's . . ." She buried her face in her hands, no longer able to hold back the tears. It was terribly embarrassing to break down in front of this man she hardly knew. But it was even worse when he took hold of her and pulled her into his arms.

Hannah wanted to push him away but found she couldn't. It had been so long since anyone had offered her comfort and reassurance. For so long she'd been required to be strong—to resolve problems and issues that weren't hers to solve. She slumped against him like a wanton woman and sobbed. What was she to do?

"It'll be all right," he whispered against her ear. "You aren't alone in this."

She felt him stroke her back, and the warmth of his touch left her feeling rather breathless. She pulled away and looked into his face.

"I want to believe that everything will work out," she murmured. His face was just inches from hers, and Hannah couldn't help but notice the fullness of his lips.

"Miss Hannah?"

Hearing Juanita's voice, Hannah dried her eyes on the edge of her apron. If the housekeeper hadn't interrupted them just then, Hannah wondered if she might very well have kissed William Barnett.

She tried to offer Juanita an explanation. "I'm sorry. I was a bit overcome by thoughts of Father."

Juanita's look was compassionate. "You have a heavy burden to bear, Miss Hannah. Best to let God bear it for you."

"I know. I'm trying to do that," Hannah admitted. She looked to William, who was already back to drinking his coffee. Apparently the moment had meant little to him.

"I need to go check on the children. Hopefully they've finished their arithmetic." Hannah left without another word. She hoped that she hadn't made too big of a fool of herself.

The last thing she needed was for Mr. Barnett to think her a silly woman given to tears at a moment's notice.

She heard Marty's screams before she could see what had caused them. When Hannah entered the living room, however, she was unprepared for what she saw. Andy had pinned Marty to the floor and was sitting on top of her.

"What in the world is going on?" Hannah asked, crossing the room. "Andy, get off of her."

"Not until she takes it back," Andy demanded.

Hannah looked to Marty, who'd stopped screaming by this time. "Takes what back?"

"She said our pa was dead. That she saw his ghost."

Hannah rolled her eyes and yanked Andy up by the arm. "Marty, is that true?"

"True that I said it," Marty replied, jumping to her feet.

Hannah shook her finger at the girl. "You know very well that telling such tales is a lie. God does not look favorably on lying, Martha Dandridge."

Marty's lips puckered. "I'm not lyin'. I saw it when I was sleepin'."

"So you dreamed it?" Hannah questioned. "Dreams are not the same as real life. A person can dream about a great many things that never come to be. In the future, if you should have any more dreams of our father, perhaps you should share them with me first. Then we'll decide if they need to be told to Andy."

She looked to her brother. Hannah could tell by the set of his jaw that he was still quite upset.

"Andy, if you're done with your sums, I could use a hand," William said from the archway.

Hannah glanced over her shoulder at the man and then back to her brother. "You can help him if you'd like."

Andy nodded. "I wanna help."

Once again Hannah was grateful for Mr. Barnett's interference. He seemed to have a way with the children. She sighed and pulled Marty close. "Come on. I'll read you a story."

10

Hannah was less than delighted when Herbert Lockhart showed up with the sheriff at the Barnett Ranch. Rain had softened the hard-packed dirt, and Hannah and Juanita had been busy tilling a new area of land that they hoped to put into garden come spring. With another bank of clouds moving in fast, Hannah had hoped they might get the ground dug up before the rain started. Now it looked like that effort would be for naught. Wiping her hands, Hannah left Juanita to continue the work while she went to see what the men wanted.

"Good morning, Miss Hannah. You know the sheriff, of course." Herbert Lockhart tipped his hat and the sheriff did likewise. They climbed down from their horses in unison and tied them off at the post.

"To what do I owe this visit, gentlemen?" She continued trying to clean her hands on her apron. "As you can see, I've been quite busy. We're making plans to double the garden and had hoped to finish before the rains set in."

"A wise decision given the way the war is going," the sheriff replied. He was an older man whose dark eyes seemed to take in everything at once. "Of course, there's also the Indian wars."

Hannah nodded. "We seem to be faring all right for the time." She looked at them both, wondering again why they had come.

"We need to speak with Mr. Barnett," Lockhart said, looking around. "Is he here?"

"I'm afraid most of the men are working at their chores, and Mr. Barnett has gone from the ranch to hunt."

"When will he be back?" the sheriff asked.

"That I cannot say. He and Berto have gone to see about bringing us home a wild boar."

"When did they go?" Lockhart asked.

"Yesterday. Can you maybe tell me what this is about?"

Mr. Lockhart came closer. "Perhaps it's just as well he is gone. I have my concerns that he has imposed himself upon you here. I brought the sheriff along so that we could force him to leave. He's trespassing here, and there is no need for you to feel obligated to take him in."

Hannah felt a wave of anger course through her as it usually did when some man tried to tell her how to live her life. She stiffened and put her hands on her waist. "I haven't felt obligated in the least, Mr. Lockhart. Mr. Barnett is here because, frankly, we found his presence useful to us. He is working as an extra hand, you might say."

"So you aren't being coerced to endure his presence? He hasn't forced you to allow him to live here?" the sheriff asked.

"Not at all," Hannah assured him.

"And he hasn't tried to take back the ranch?" Lockhart pressed.

"No. He has made it known that he believes the land to have been stolen from his family—wrongly taken as spoils of war. He has never desired to be anything but a Texan, and therefore he believes his loyalty is and always has been with the state."

"He fought for the Union," Lockhart all but spat out.

"He fought, because his father insisted. It wasn't his desire to go off to war, Mr. Lockhart. And because of that, I can't help but believe he has a good point." She hated to admit this—and she wasn't at all sure that she would say as much to Barnett himself. But for the sake of putting Mr. Lockhart in his place . . . Well, in this instance she had no trouble.

"If his point is valid," the sheriff replied, "you will be the ones trespassing. Are you prepared to leave the property should Barnett find a way to regain control?"

Hannah knew the question was inevitable. "Yes, I am considering several options, Sheriff. However, Mr. Barnett assures me that he has no desire to see my family out of a home. We have each agreed to work with the other and see this matter through until my father returns."

"And when is that expected?" the sheriff asked.

Lockhart was the one to answer this. "We can't be sure he will return. My sources suggest that he may even be dead."

The sheriff looked at him as if this were news. "What sources are those?"

Hannah wondered what Mr. Lockhart had said or done to get the sheriff of the county to make a trip all the way out to the ranch. Perhaps he had lied or touted his concern for her safety. She wasn't surprised the sheriff would question Lockhart's news about her father.

"I have men who are, you might say, spies for the Confederacy. They travel extensively, and when they pass through, they are good to give me information. For a price, of course."

The sheriff nodded. "Of course. And these men suggest to you that Mr. Dandridge is dead?"

"I'm afraid so." He looked at Hannah. "We can't be certain yet. I've paid one of the men to investigate further. Mr. Dandridge was supposed to attend his mother in Vicksburg, but he never made it there and there has been no word from him since."

"Is that true?" the sheriff asked Hannah.

She could see that his question irritated Mr. Lockhart, but she didn't care. "The only information I've had at all has come through Mr. Lockhart." A few sprinkles of rain began to fall. "Why don't you gentlemen come inside? It would appear we're due for another storm."

"This is a fine place you have," the sheriff commented as they moved into the house.

"Thank you. The Barnetts worked hard to put the ranch together, as I'm sure you know. I've only done what I could to add personal touches here and there. If you'll both take a seat in the front room, I'll excuse myself to wash up. I'll have Juanita serve you some refreshments, as well. Do you prefer coffee or tea?"

"Coffee for me," the sheriff answered, "if you have it. The war's put an awful hold on things I took for granted. Coffee is one of those things. If we weren't able to get it smuggled in from Mexico, I doubt we'd have a decent cup to share amongst us."

Hannah had never really taken a liking to the strong liquid, but her father loved it. She always tried to keep a pot on when he was at home.

"Yes, coffee sounds good," Mr. Lockhart replied.

Hannah nodded and smiled. "I'll be right with you."

She went to the kitchen and found Juanita just stepping inside as the rain began to pour in earnest. "I check the children," she said, slipping off her shoes at the door. "They are with Pepita in the barn cracking pecans."

"Sounds like a good thing to keep them busy. The sheriff and Mr. Lockhart are in the front room awaiting my presence. I wonder if you might bring in some refreshments."

"You want I should serve them dinner?"

Hannah glanced at the clock. It was nearly noon. "Oh, I hadn't realized how late it was getting. Yes, I suppose we must offer them something substantial. I don't want the children to have to endure Mr. Lockhart's comments about Father, however. Would you mind giving the children a picnic in the barn? I'm sure they'll find it to be great fun."

Juanita smiled. "I will. I have frijoles and tortillas ready, you want that I should open some cans of peaches and maybe fry some ham?"

"That sounds fine. The gentlemen would like coffee, so after I finish washing my hands, I'll take them each a cup. That should hold them until you announce the meal."

"I will be quick."

Hannah dried her hands and poured two cups of coffee. She hoped they liked it black. Mr. Lockhart generally asked for his that way, so she took a chance that the sheriff would do likewise.

"Here we are," she said, entering the living room. "I have told Juanita that you will stay for dinner. I hope you won't make a liar out of me." She handed the sheriff his coffee first and added, "Besides, by the time we finish with our meal perhaps the rain will have moved on."

"That's mighty kind of you, Miss Dandridge. I reckon I would be much obliged."

"Dinner sounds fine." Mr. Lockhart gave her a smile. "All the more time to spend in your charming company."

Taking a seat, Hannah motioned the men to do likewise. "Juanita will come for us when dinner is ready. In the meanwhile, Sheriff, perhaps you have some ideas on how I might get additional information on Father."

"I will certainly do what I can. When I return to Dallas I can send a telegram. Some of the lines are down, of course, but we might luck out. I can wire Shreveport and see if we can confirm he made it at least that far. As headquarters for the western troops of the Confederacy, there will be checkpoints there that could very well afford us some information."

"I already have my man checking into this," Mr. Lockhart assured them. "There's really no sense in going to the extra effort. My man will return soon enough with information or he'll wire it to me should it prove necessary."

The sheriff looked at Lockhart and voiced exactly what Hannah was thinking. "It can't possibly hurt to have additional questions asked—especially by law officials. I have friends in Shreveport who will definitely be a boon to our search."

"Thank you so much," Hannah said, nodding. "I'm desperate to learn the truth. It isn't easy for the children. . . . You can well imagine how it is to be so young and worry about your safety and security."

"Indeed."

"I have begged Miss Dandridge to move to Cedar Springs and forsake this place," Mr. Lockhart began. "I have, in fact, asked her to be my wife. Although she has not yet given me an answer."

Hannah looked at the man with a pasted-on smile. "Why, Mr. Lockhart, such topics are generally not discussed in the presence of others. I do believe that given my circumstance, it would be quite wrong of me to entertain proposals of marriage while Father's welfare is uncertain. I believe I told you this once before."

The man realized the rebuke and clenched his jaw. With the slightest nod of his head, he fixed Hannah with a hard stare. "I do apologize for my uncivilized manners."

"You are forgiven," Hannah said, turning back to the sheriff. "You mentioned something of the Indian wars earlier. Is there any news related to this?"

"Well, there have been some positive changes. Governor Lubbock has reorganized the Frontier Regiment to be a more formal military unit. The men have elected Major J. E. McCord as the new leader. His thought is that the regular patrols are ineffectual. He has replaced this idea with intense scouting. He wants to use surprise to the army's advantage."

"Surprise?" Hannah asked. "In what regard?"

"In regard to attacking. They are hoping to seek out Indians wherever they may be and eliminate their threat."

"By eliminating the Indians?" Hannah asked.

"Yes. Their plan is to show the Indian they have no business here on the frontier—that the only place of refuge will be the reservations."

Hannah thought of He Who Walks in Darkness and Night Bear. They would no doubt be up in arms for sure if the army tried to force them to a reservation.

"Otherwise," the sheriff continued, "the state is pushing for the Frontier Regiment to become an official part of the Confederate government. That way Richmond will pay the bills, and not our fair state."

Hannah thought about this for a moment. "But wouldn't such an alliance also create problems with the soldiers and where they served? I mean, if they become a part of the Confederate Army and that army should need them to fight in the East, won't that leave our area depleted of protection once again?"

The sheriff smiled. "You're a smart young woman, Miss Dandridge. That is exactly the argument that has been posed. I suppose we'll see what happens. They are supposed to be making a decision before Christmas."

"Miss Hannah, the dinner is ready," Juanita announced from the hall.

"Well, gentlemen," Hannah said, getting to her feet, "I suggest we take our conversation to the dining room."

Herbert Lockhart was none too happy with the way this trip had turned out. He sat at Hannah's table and that in and of itself was a good thing. However, he had made no progress in seeing Barnett put off the ranch. In fact, Barnett wasn't even there to be confronted by the sheriff.

He ate in silence for a few moments and tried to figure out how he might alienate Hannah from Barnett's charms. He didn't like knowing that the man was at the ranch, where he could influence Hannah, and do who knew what else to win her over to his side. The man was young, and some might say handsome. Lockhart knew that was not something he could boast for himself. A life spent working indoors had made him soft—even a bit round. He knew his balding pate was also no match for the full head of hair Barnett boasted. Women seemed to put a great deal of store in such things.

"This is a mighty fine lunch, Miss Dandridge. Your hospitality is truly a blessing. I had in mind to chew on jerked beef for my noon meal." The sheriff rubbed his mustache and smiled. "This is well worth the long ride."

"Thank you, Sheriff. I'm glad you're enjoying the food."

"And the company," the man added.

Lockhart became tired of the insipid small talk. "You know, there still is quite a lot of danger here." He looked at Hannah. "The Comanche and Kiowa are raiding throughout the area to the west and north. You really need to reconsider my invitation to move to town."

"I have considered it. I suppose I should tell you both that we had a bit of an episode here. A young Comanche warrior was injured and my brother and Mr. Barnett brought him here to recover."

"Here?" Lockhart looked to the sheriff. "See, I told you there were threats to the area."

"Well, there are no more immediate threats to this ranch," Hannah replied. "I met the boy's father, the chief of this particular band. He has promised us peace in return for having helped his son."

"Those savages won't keep their word. Look at the way they've already broken treaty upon treaty," Lockhart declared.

Hannah raised her hand. "Mr. Lockhart, I believe further exploration of the matter would show that our government has also broken treaties. But, that aside, I feel confident that I have earned the chief's respect and that he will honor his word."

"That is naïve of you, Miss Dandridge," the sheriff countered. "Mr. Lockhart is correct in saying that the Indians won't keep their word. They can't be trusted. They have attacked settler after settler. They have wreaked havoc on the Santa Fe Trail—a long utilized trade route that is now cut off to us."

"I understand there are those who are warring. I didn't mean to imply that I had somehow single-handedly set matters aright. I merely state what happened to show you that we have made an arrangement for ourselves that seems to be working quite well."

"They aren't the only band of raiding Comanche," Lockhart said, putting aside his fork. "You cannot hope to believe that the agreement you have with one band will modify the actions of the entire Comanche Nation. Not to mention the other warring tribes."

"No, I suppose I can't." Hannah looked to the sheriff and then back to Lockhart. "But I am praying it will be so."

Herbert Lockhart wanted to shake the woman until she changed her mind. He had hoped that by moving her into town, they could strengthen their relationship. Perhaps if she stayed in his home and didn't oppose his being there, as well, their relationship might become somewhat intimate.

To his surprise, the sheriff changed the subject. "I understand Mr. Barnett was wounded in the war."

Hannah nodded. "Yes. His father and brother were killed in battle, and he took a bullet through his leg. It has left him somewhat lame."

"And where did this occur?"

She frowned. "I don't seem to recall."

"I can answer that," Lockhart said, barely able to contain his delight. "It was at the Battle of Vicksburg."

He tried to pretend the announcement was unimportant, but he could see by Hannah's response that William Barnett had not been forthcoming with the information. "Yes, as I understand it, he and his brother and father were on the frontlines of that battle almost from its inception."

"That was a terrible battle," the sheriff added. "I heard that the siege caused much suffering for the townsfolk."

Lockhart felt a rush of pleasure upon seeing Hannah's pale face. He turned to her. "I find it amazing that you are so tolerant of having a man on your property who might well have caused the death of your dear family members and friends. You are quite the forgiving Christian, Miss Hannah."

Putting her napkin aside, Hannah got to her feet. "Please do not get up, gentlemen," she said as Lockhart and the sheriff started to rise. "I need to check on my brother and sister. I hope you'll excuse me."

"Of course," the sheriff replied. "I'm going to help myself to another one of these peaches while you're gone."

She nodded. "I'll have Juanita bring more coffee."

Lockhart wanted to say something more but decided it just might benefit him to remain silent. He'd obviously upset Hannah enough that she needed to take her leave. With any luck at all, she would allow her shock to become rage—and then hopefully she would throw Mr. Barnett from the ranch.

He smiled to himself and watched her leave. Perhaps things were starting to look up. Now if he could just steer the sheriff's attentions in another direction to keep him from concerning himself with Dandridge's whereabouts, everything would be perfect.

11

Wild boar was some of the best eating Texas had to offer, and William was more than happy to labor over the dead beast in order to provide for the ranch. It wasn't his first boar to butcher, but the arduous task was not one he looked upon favorably.

"We're nearly done," he told Berto, putting another piece of the hog in salt.

"This will see us through for many months," Berto said.

William assessed the meat and nodded. "The men did a good job fixing up the smokehouse. I'm sure we can get most of this meat hung and cured in good order. Where did Juanita want the fat taken?"

"She said to leave it here. She will come and tend to it." Berto straightened and wiped his messy hands on a towel. "I can finish this. You still going to start breaking that black today?"

The horse in question had been green broke and nothing

more. The men had questioned William about even attempting such a feat with his injury. In the days before the war, however, William had been the best at breaking, and he meant to see his reputation continue. He had plans for turning the black into a fine cow horse, but there would be a great deal of work to contend with first. The animal was very nearly as stubborn as Hannah Dandridge. William smiled to himself. Nearly as stubborn, but not quite.

He cast aside the heavy butcher apron and washed his hands. "I might spend some time getting reacquainted. I'll get to that though after I have a cup of coffee. This cold spell is chilling me to the bone."

"Hopefully it will not last long." Berto declared.

William nodded and made his way to the house. He passed the area where the summer kitchen was situated. Here Juanita and Hannah worked on the laundry throughout the year, keeping a pot of hot water going almost all the time. He stopped for a moment and warmed his hands over the steaming liquid. His leg was hurting him something fierce, and the thought of a nice long soak in a hot bath sounded far more inviting than breaking a horse.

"Oh. I didn't realize you were here," Hannah said, seeming startled. She stepped from the back door with a small pot in hand. "Is the butchering done?"

Turning back to the boiling water, William rubbed his hands together. "We're pretty much finished. Now we'll get to smoking it. Should have enough meat to last through the next few months."

"That's a relief to know." She began to draw water from the

pot. "I suppose you already know this, but we'll need to have more water brought up from the river. The sledge barrels are nearly empty, and since the well has nearly dried up we don't have any other choice."

"I'll get JD on that. Andy can help him if you don't mind."

"Not at all." Hannah's tone seemed rather stilted, but was nonetheless polite.

Since his return from the hunt, William thought Hannah had been acting rather cool toward him. There was no accounting for how a woman might act at any given moment, but Hannah Dandridge definitely remained a mystery to him. One minute she was holding off Comanche and the next she was bawling her eyes out. Still, he didn't know what to make of her. She almost seemed hurt, and yet he knew he'd neither said nor done anything that should merit such a response.

He watched her ladle out water. She was by far and away the most beautiful woman he'd laid eyes on. Her thick hair, pulled back from her face and pinned into a serviceable knot, begged his touch. He could almost feel the strands between his fingers. She seemed to sense him watching her and glanced up.

"Yes?" she asked, as if he'd posed a question.

He was at a loss for something to say. "Umm . . . is there coffee on the stove?"

"I believe so."

"Great. I was just making my way there when the warmth of this fire caught my attention."

Hannah looked at the glowing embers for a moment. "I should add some more wood." She hung the ladle back on its nail and went to the woodpile. William watched her select pieces of pine as though she were choosing fabric. Hannah seemed to calculate each piece's value before returning to the fire with her choices.

When she finished she picked up her pot of hot water. "You won't forget about filling the barrels?"

He shook his head. "No. I'll see to it right away. Guess we need to check into drilling another well, too."

"Thank you." She left without another word, and William couldn't help but feel that something was wrong. She wasn't acting at all like herself.

He decided against the coffee and went in search of JD and Andy instead. Once he instructed them to retrieve the water, William went to see the black. He had dealt with a hundred green-broke horses in his day, but this time was different. With his war wound, he could only wonder if he'd be able to sit upon the horse properly and endure the pain. Riding a well-broke horse had been less painful than trying to walk, but breaking a horse required a great deal of muscle and strength. Especially in one's legs.

Walking to the pen where the black was corralled, William studied the gelding for a long while. The horse came to him after a few moments. He was seeking a treat, and William didn't disappoint him. He reached into his pocket and drew out a piece of apple.

"So you remember me, do you?"

The horse had just started his training when William went away to war. That had been over two years ago. The now five-year-old gelding had known very little training since that time. Berto had attempted to keep working with the animal, but as he told William, the gelding seemed destined to belong to one man and one man alone. William.

The sleek black horse had been sired out of a match with one of Theodore Terry's stallions and a Barnett mare. Ted lived about seven miles away on a ranch that had been established long before William's family had come to Texas. The Terrys weren't a part of the original three hundred who had come to Texas, but William figured their lineage could no doubt be included in the next one hundred who populated the territory.

"We'll have to get you properly broke in so we can take a ride over to see Ted and Marietta and let them know what a good mount you turned out to be."

The horse nickered softly as if understanding the compliment. William smiled. "Well, we aren't getting it done standing here jawin'."

He headed to the barn to retrieve the horse's tack when he spotted riders approaching. There were at least five mounted men, and from the looks of them, they were Confederate cavalry. William bristled. What did they want? Had they come to cause him trouble?

Remaining by the barn door, William's hand went to his thigh. The very sight of the soldiers caused a dull ache to rise up in his leg. The memories associated with that uniform—with any uniform—were far from pleasant. However, as the riders drew closer, William thought he recognized the man in front. He forgot about the tack and went to greet the visitors.

"Will, is that you?" the rider said, pulling his mount to a sharp halt. He jumped from the back of the horse and dropped the reins. "It is you! Well, I'll be."

Tyler Atherton pushed back his forage cap, grinned, and extended his hand. "Last time I saw you, you were headin' off to be a Billy Yank."

The two had been friends since William's family had first come to Texas. He was rather surprised to find Atherton still speaking to him after his family's well-known decision to fight for the North. William noted that the other mounted men didn't seem as friendly. They watched him with great apprehension.

"And you are still a Johnny Reb, I see." William shook Tyler's hand and offered him a grin. "Have you brought the war to Dallas County?"

"In a way, but we can discuss that in due time. I wonder if you might have feed for my men and horses."

William didn't want to explain the situation with the ranch and neither did he want to impose five hungry men on Hannah's dwindling supplies. However, given that he'd just returned from killing two boars, William figured he could extend an invitation.

"If you want to wash up at the bunkhouse, I'll see what I can get Juanita to feed you."

Tyler turned to the men. "Dismount and wash up. We're gonna have some grub."

The men's somewhat standoffish countenance changed to acceptance. They dismounted and tied off their horses before joining Tyler and William. "Men," Tyler continued, "this is my good friend Will Barnett. This is his family's ranch, so treat it with respect."

"Actually, the ranch is . . . well . . ." William realized he wasn't going to get out of an explanation. "Since my father decided to fight for the North, the ranch was given to a family more supportive of the Confederate cause." He looked at the men before him. "I want you each to know that I do not consider myself a Yankee, nor do I want to put you ill at ease. My convictions . . . my desires are with Texas, and that is where they will remain."

"As part of the Texas Third Cavalry," Tyler answered for them, "our loyalty is first with Texas, as well. So therefore we meet on common ground."

William could see in the expressions of a couple of the men that they didn't support Tyler's words, but they said nothing. The front door opened at that moment and Hannah stepped from the house.

"Well now, if that ain't a ray of sunshine," one of the men declared.

Tyler turned to William. "You'd best introduce us."

Hannah looked at William and then to the soldiers. "Mr. Barnett, is there a problem?"

"This is my good friend Tyler Atherton," William announced. "These are his men. We haven't had a chance to discuss why they've come." He turned back to Tyler. "This is Miss Hannah Dandridge. Her father took over the ranch."

"Miss Dandridge, it's a pure pleasure to meet you." Tyler offered her a teasing smile. "I can see why Will is stayin' close to home."

Hannah blushed, but looked to William for answers. Her quizzical stare made it clear that she was waiting for an explanation.

"I'm wondering if it would be all right with you if we gave these men and horses food and maybe a bed for the night."

Hannah glanced back at the men. "You're willing to let Confederate soldiers stay here?"

William frowned. "Of course I am. This man is my friend. He and his men are hungry and tired. I wouldn't begrudge anyone food and rest."

She seemed to consider this only a moment before turning to Tyler. "Your men are welcome to stay, Mr. Atherton."

"You can call me, Tyler, Miss Dandridge."

"That would hardly be appropriate, Mr. Atherton. I do see, however, you are a soldier."

"Yes, ma'am. A lieutenant in the Texas Third Cavalry." Tyler's gaze never left Hannah's.

William felt a strange sense of jealousy wash over him when Hannah offered Tyler a smile.

"Then perhaps you would allow me to call you . . . Lieutenant."

Tyler laughed and gave a sweeping bow. "You can call me anything, ma'am, so long as it ain't late to the dinner table." His men laughed, as well, and even Hannah appeared amused.

"Well, I'll leave it to Mr. Barnett to show you where you can wash up and make yourselves comfortable. I'll see to your meal."

She turned and walked away, pausing only a moment at the door to glance over her shoulder. William wanted to think she was looking at him, but he figured she was probably more interested in his friend.

William decided to let it drop. There was no telling what Miss Dandridge might be thinking. "Come on, boys. We can put your horses up back here."

Hannah wasn't accustomed to being so popular. The men in the lieutenant's company were more than happy to entertain her with stories and even some music. One of the men, a Private Bierman, played a lively harmonica while another private sang.

The soldiers seemed to find it pleasant to be in the company of children, and Andy and Marty were delighted by the attention. Two of the men actually got on the floor to shoot marbles with Andy, while Private Bierman showed Marty how to blow into the harmonica.

Had it not been for the very sad circumstances that had brought them there, Hannah might have found the entire visit a delight. Instead, she was considering everything that the lieutenant had discussed over lunch.

The Confederate soldiers were desperate for food. The entire South was suffering. The scenes depicted by the lieutenant and his men were not ones Hannah wanted to dwell on for long. When they spoke of the siege at Vicksburg and people even eating the dead horses, she thought she might well be ill. She was glad Juanita had fed the children separately in the kitchen.

Tyler Atherton and his men had come to see if they might get William's help in moving some cattle east—smuggling them past Union troops in order to feed the South. They hoped to at least get them past the Mississippi River, at which point they could turn the herd over to other Confederate troops.

"I hope I didn't upset you overmuch," the lieutenant said, coming up behind Hannah.

She jumped and turned so quickly that her boot caught in

the rug. She would have fallen had the lieutenant not taken hold of her.

"There now. I do apologize. I didn't mean to sneak up on you." He smiled, and she liked the way his eyes seemed to twinkle.

"That's quite all right. I was watching the children have fun with your men. They seem so carefree in these moments that it's hard to imagine the war is really going on at the same time."

Atherton nodded and his expression turned serious. He let go of his hold on Hannah. "It's goin' on all right. That's why I'm hopin' you'll agree to help us with the cattle."

"I can't imagine it not being the right thing to do," Hannah said. "Even the Bible tells us to feed the hungry. I can understand the Yankees wanting to keep the Confederate soldiers weak, but how can they even begin to live with themselves when they think of starving out innocent women and children?"

She looked up to find William had entered the room. Her mind immediately went to what Herbert Lockhart had said about William and his family being at Vicksburg from the start of the battle. Had he allowed her family to starve? Had he approved the methods used for bringing the town and the soldiers there to their knees?

"I have no idea of how you will manage this cattle drive without the Yankees knowing what is happening, but you have my blessing," Hannah said. "And I'm certain my father would agree . . . were he here."

"Well, we have some ideas on gettin' those steers to the Mississippi. We have friends all along the way to help us. That was part of what we've been doing these past months. See, we were cut loose just before the battle at Vicksburg."

"You were at Vicksburg?" she asked.

"My men and I were sent out just before the Yankees descended on us. We've been establishin' stops along the way while workin' to get this far west. It hasn't been easy, but I believe that God has been on our side."

"Both sides like to believe that, Tyler," William said, interrupting the conversation, "but I don't think that God is paying much attention to this war."

The room went silent at this declaration. The lieutenant's men left off their play with the children and got to their feet. Hannah could feel the tension build. She knew if she didn't do something, there might very well be a fight.

"Gentlemen, I am of a mind that God loves all of His children equally," Hannah said. "No doubt He is grieved by this war and weeps, just as I have, over the loss of life." She hoped William would say nothing more and allow the matter to drop.

"Of course you're right, Miss Dandridge," the lieutenant agreed. "War is a despicable thing, and we should not even be discussin' it in your presence. We will, if you would so graciously allow us, depart for a time of rest. My men and I have long been in the saddle and we're a mite weary from our endeavors."

"Most certainly you may go, Lieutenant," Hannah replied. "I will see to it that you have everything you need."

The handsome man took hold of her hand and bowed over it. Hannah thought him quite gallant—a true knight in shining armor. Only this armor was poorly made wool and tattered cotton. The mix-matched uniforms all looked as though they'd seen better days.

Atherton led his men from the house, but Hannah didn't

miss the scowls on their faces as they passed William. She was afraid if words were exchanged again, the men would most likely come to blows—and she didn't want to see that happen in front of her brother and sister.

"I wonder if I might have a word with you, Mr. Barnett."

William seemed to understand the seriousness of the situation and stepped back. "Perhaps you might accompany me to the smokehouse. I want to check on the fire."

"Can I come, too?" Andy asked.

"No," Hannah replied. "I need you and Marty to get back to your studies. I will be with you shortly to check on your work."

"Aw, do I have to?" Marty moaned and picked up her doll. "All I ever do is read and write. Doing school is hard."

Hannah suppressed a smile. "You must be educated, Miss Martha. Now get your slate and practice your alphabet while I'm gone."

She didn't wait to see if they heeded her command, but rather led the way through the house and out the back door. William Barnett followed her a few paces behind, but once they were outside, he came alongside her.

"I would appreciate it," she began, "if you and your friend would refrain from discussing the war further—at least around the children. I have no desire to watch you brawl and bring the war to this house."

"There's no desire for that on my part, either, Miss Dandridge. I assure you." William stopped and turned to face her. He continued to study her. "Is there something else you wish to discuss?"

Hannah wanted to ask him about his part in the Battle of

Vicksburg, but decided she should follow her own advice and say nothing more regarding the war. "I just want to protect the children. They shouldn't have to hear or see the ugliness associated with this war."

"I couldn't agree more. No child should have to." He turned and looked away. "Now, if you're finished, I need to see to the wood."

"Certainly," Hannah said, unable to think of anything else to say.

She felt her loyalties being torn in two different directions. Her family had suffered greatly at the hands of the Union Army. William Barnett had been a part of that army, and perhaps, as Mr. Lockhart said, was among the very soldiers who put an end to the lives of her grandfather and brother.

Yet even with that in her thoughts, Hannah knew that Mr. Barnett was a good man. She'd heard him talk of his regrets in going to war. She knew that he only served out of obedience to his father . . . and wasn't she there for the very same reason? How could she fault a man for that?

Still, the stories of Vicksburg and the siege haunted her. The idea that William Barnett might well have fired the shot that ended her brother's life was more than she could bear. Without another word, Hannah turned and hurried back to the house. She needed to distance herself from William Barnett and all that he represented.

Now, if her heart would just cooperate.

William and Tyler worked together to bring in four longhorn steers. They'd found them down by the river and decided to drive them into one of the holding pens until the men could take them east. The real work would come in another day or two, when they set out for rounding up the rest. They would probably be gone for at least a week, depending on how far out the animals had spread on the open range. Allowing cattle to graze at will was both a wonderful blessing and an exhausting curse to the rancher.

Riding an older reliable mare his mother had once owned, William was glad for the chaps he'd tied on. The brush was dry and much of it dormant as the colder months were upon them. His legs would have taken a real beating had it not been for the leather protection. Tyler had borrowed a pair of chaps from Berto, but he didn't seem nearly so roughed up. He'd let William do most of the hard work of getting the steers onto open ground.

"So tell me more about Miss Hannah. Is she your gal?" Tyler asked.

"Hardly. She's no one's gal that I can see. She's her own woman through and through."

Tyler laughed. "I haven't seen anyone so pretty since leavin' to join up."

"Which brings me to a question of my own," William said, throwing Tyler a sidelong glance. "Why didn't you head out to California like you talked about? Last thing you told me was that you had no mind to join up."

"Well, those plans were made before the Comanche burned us out and killed Pa. You weren't here when it happened. I think you'd been gone maybe a month." He squinted and pulled the brim of his forage cap down to block out the sun. "The rest of the family was with me in Dallas because Pa was worried about a raid and wanted Ma and Lenore safe. When word of the attack came, my ma and sister were grief-stricken beyond words, but Grandpa Venton and I were mad. We made the women stay in Dallas and rode out with a handful of men to see what was left of the ranch and Pa. There was nothing but burning stubble and the dead." Tyler shuddered and stared out across the landscape. "My pa and the hands put up a good fight, but not good enough. Only a couple of the men survived. My pa . . . died."

William could see the man's thoughts had clearly taken him back to that day. "I'm sure sorry about that, Tyler. I hadn't heard about the attack."

"I didn't even try to write you—I knew it would be too difficult to get word across the lines."

"I appreciate that you even thought of trying. You were about the only one who remained on speaking terms with our family. You and your family."

Tyler shook his head. "None of us wanted this war. I was praying that Texas would choose to stay out of it. My pa felt just like yours. Even Sam Houston wanted no part of it and folks . . . well, they used to listen to him. I guess this was bigger than all of us though."

"I guess so," William replied. "I'm almost glad I got shot when I did."

"Where'd you catch it?"

"Vicksburg."

Tyler turned in the saddle and fixed William with a look of disbelief. "Does she know that?"

William knew he was talking about Hannah without needing to hear her name. "No. I haven't been able to bring myself to tell her. It's bad enough she thinks of me as the enemy. Partly because of my father's stand in the war, and partly because this has become her home and now I'm here to reclaim it."

"And will you?"

"What? Reclaim it? I'm trying to. I went into Dallas the other day and spoke with an old friend of the family. He's a judge and believes we were wronged. He's trying to get the place returned to me."

"And what will happen to Miss Dandridge and her family if he does?"

"I don't know. I haven't figured anything much further along than helping you with these cattle."

"And what of Miss Dandridge's father? She said he's gone missing."

William considered this for a moment. "I fear it may be more than that. She's had no word from him in months. By her own account, it isn't like her father to remain out of touch. He has the means and intelligence, even a good number of connections with the Confederate government. If he wanted to get a message to his family, I doubt he'd have any trouble."

"So you figure he's captured or dead."

"That's about the size of it. As much as I hate to admit it, I tend to agree with Lockhart's belief that the man is dead."

"Herbert Lockhart? Don't tell me he's still around to cause trouble. He's pestered my ma with letters wanting to buy the ranch. She told him it was my decision, but Lockhart keeps askin'."

"He settled in Cedar Springs full time. He and Miss Dandridge's father were partners in law and in the real estate market."

"Was Mr. Dandridge as corrupt as Lockhart?" Tyler asked.

"I somehow doubt it," William answered. "I never knew Lockhart all that well, but didn't like him just the same. Strangely enough, he seems to think of Hannah—Miss Dandridge—as his own personal property. He keeps telling her that her father wanted them to marry."

Tyler laughed at this. "I can just bet he does. A fella that old with a young beauty like Miss Dandridge would be quite the match. Did her father really want Lockhart to marry her?"

Shrugging, William maneuvered his horse to the right to get around one of the steers and encourage him to get back in step with the others. "I don't know much, but the way she talks, I can't imagine her father made those wishes very clear—if he mentioned them at all."

"I can't imagine any man hatin' his child so much that he'd want her to marry a weasel like Lockhart," Tyler added.

They rode in silence for a few moments before William asked, "So why did you join up to fight?"

"I wanted to make my grandfather and ma proud. I know Ma didn't want me to go, but Grandpa Venton said it was our duty. Once the fighting began in earnest, Grandpa said that was enough of that. He felt like the North was stickin' its nose into our business. He would have gone, too, if they'd have had him."

"They probably would now." William shook his head. "The South has to know it's going to lose. They lack the industry they need to hold out forever."

"You want to know something, Will? I believe that's the truth of it. I had thought at one time the North might just let us slip away and be done with it. But now it's a fight of pride as much as anything else. The North isn't going to let the South off easy, no matter what. In fact, even after this war is over, I've no doubt we'll be payin' for our actions for a long time."

"Yeah, I think you're probably right."

They had reached the edge of the yard and William rode ahead of the steers to open the gate at the pen. The cows were surprisingly docile and plodded one by one through the opening. William secured the gate behind them and turned to smile at Tyler. "Now just another fifty-six or so to round up."

"You won't regret this, Will. I'll make sure our side knows about your help. In fact, I have a favor to ask of you."

"What's that?"

"I want to set out three herds of twenty steers each. That's a small enough number so as not to arouse too much suspicion. Three men can easily handle that many . . . in fact two men can do it. I thought maybe you and me, we might make up one team."

"You want me to help you drive the cattle east?"

Tyler nodded. "I figure to send the other two groups to the north and south of us. Like I said, we tried to arrange places along the way where folks would help us. We have a good plan, but I'd feel a whole sight better if you would ride with me. Private Bierman isn't much of a cattleman. He rides well enough, but his father bought his way into the cavalry. I think the boy only worked in his pa's store prior to that. I'll put him with two of the other men and that will just leave another two-man team. If you'd join us, I'd make sure the Confederacy knew of your help. Maybe give you a clean record in their eyes."

"I don't want to help any army," William replied. "I'm doing this for the sake of feeding the hungry. I would just as soon see civilians receive this food as feed the Confederate Army. If you hate me for that, I understand, but it doesn't change my heart."

"No, I don't hate you, Will. We've been friends too long for that. This war has given all of us hard choices. Do it for whatever purpose you choose, but I really need your help. At least as far as Shreveport. I can probably pick up another man or two there."

"I'll think on it. First we have to get enough steers to make it worth your while."

Tyler laughed. "Just being here with the beautiful Miss Hannah Dandridge makes it worth my while. I much prefer scavenging for food in the company of pretty gals over killin' men." He sobered and rubbed his chin. "Yes, sir, I prefer just about anything to killin'."

"Well, I wish you luck with Miss Dandridge. You will most likely find a battlefield easier to manage."

⚬⚬⚬

After supper that evening, Hannah worked with Marty and Andy to clean up the kitchen. She'd sent Juanita and her family away, giving them the rest of the night to themselves. She did this at times just to enjoy a quiet house and to do her own chores instead of having a servant do them for her.

She felt it was also important for Andy and Marty to learn responsibility. Hannah figured the sooner they learned, the better off they'd be. She'd come to Texas having to learn most everything for herself, and it hadn't been easy. Fancy sewing, playing the piano, and painting teacups had done very little to help her on the frontier.

Marty yawned and stretched to reach one of the cups Hannah had just washed. "I'm tired of dishes," Marty declared. "I dry two hundred dishes every day."

"Is that so?" Hannah asked her sister.

Looking up, Marty appeared only slightly chagrined. "No, but sometimes it feels that way." She looked back at the cup in her hand. "I really hate cups. They got handles and are all curvy with little places that stay wet. I don't mind plates."

Hannah smiled. "I feel the same way about washing them, but they have to be done. And look, we're nearly finished."

Andy returned just then to put the salt and pepper on the stove. "Table's clean."

"Thank you." She took pity on Marty. "Why don't you and Andy go play a game of checkers. I'll finish up here and then I'll read you a story before you go to bed."

Marty didn't need to be asked twice. She put the cup down none too gently and threw the dish towel aside. "I'm gonna beat you," she told Andy.

"Ha. I taught you how to play. You can't beat me." They continued the discussion as they left the kitchen and headed down the hall.

Hannah couldn't help but smile. Her heart swelled with the love and devotion she felt for them. She wanted them to be safe, protected. Perhaps that was why she'd been giving more and more thought to what she would do if her father was proven to be dead.

"Miss Dandridge?"

She turned to find the lieutenant standing at the back door.

"I wonder if you might have a few minutes to walk outside with me. It's real nice outside—a little chilly, but the stars are out." He grinned. "I know it might not be in keeping with proper etiquette, but I'd like to talk to you for a few minutes."

Hannah smiled. "At times the rules of proper society get only a head nod on the frontier. I think we can make an exception. Let me grab a wrap." She dried her hands but didn't pull off her apron. Instead, she went to where the lieutenant stood and motioned behind him. "My shawl is just there, if you'll allow me to get it."

"Here, let me." He took hold of the brown wool shawl and helped Hannah to adjust it around her shoulders. "There."

"Thank you, Lieutenant." She allowed him to open the back door and escort her outside.

The stars shone brilliantly overhead, just as the lieutenant had mentioned. The skies were a piercing black with thousands upon thousands of pinpricks of light. Hannah had oftentimes enjoyed coming outside to just stare up at the glory of God's heavens. Tonight was certainly no different.

"Have you ever seen anything so lovely?" she asked, her gaze fixed on the sky.

"No, ma'am, I haven't."

She turned to find the lieutenant watching her. Hannah felt her cheeks grow hot and looked away. "My mother used to remind me that the Psalms speak of how the heavens declare the glory of God. She said that all of creation was designed to bring glory back to the Creator." She drew a deep breath of the chilled night air and smiled. "Are you a man of God, Lieutenant?"

"Well, I'm not opposed to Him," Tyler replied casually.

Hannah didn't expect such an answer and turned to study him. It was too dark to see him clearly, but she could tell he was returning her gaze. "Exactly what is that supposed to mean, Lieutenant?"

"I guess . . . that is to say, I figured God gave me strength to make my way in the world. He expects me to go about my business and do the right thing."

"And how do you determine what the right thing might be, Lieutenant?"

He said nothing for a moment, and Hannah wondered if she'd upset him. Men were funny creatures when it came to discussing God. "I suppose that you believe as Benjamin Franklin stated—that 'God helps those who help themselves'?"

"I thought that was a Bible verse, to tell you the truth."

"Not at all. God does indeed call us to go about our business and do the right thing, but I believe our business is to know Him better, and that the right thing can only be determined by studying His Word."

"Whoowee, Miss Dandridge, you sound like a regular Sunday preacher. But I didn't ask you out here to talk about God."

"And so what did you wish to discuss, Lieutenant?"

"You. I figure you're about the prettiest gal in all of Texas. Do you have a beau?"

Hannah hadn't realized this was the direction Lieutenant Atherton had figured to take. "My father's partner has proposed marriage," she replied. "However, with my father missing, I cannot even begin to think of courtship or proposals."

"Your father's partner is Mr. Lockhart, is he not?"

"That's right. Do you know him?"

"Enough to know he's not a good choice for you. He's old enough to be your pa. Most likely he just wants what he can get from you—money and property and such. He's that kind of a man."

Hannah bristled. "I see."

"Well, I didn't mean it to sound like you weren't prize enough. It's just that someone like Lockhart is always thinking of his own needs, and if your pa is . . . well . . . if he's not coming back, then Lockhart probably figures to get this ranch for himself."

"Well, thank you, Lieutenant Atherton, for sharing your opinion with me."

"On the other hand, Miss Dandridge, I admire you for your-self. I think you're a fine woman."

Hannah shook her head. "You are kind to say so, Lieuten-ant. However, if you would excuse me, I promised my brother and sister I would read to them."

He reached out to take hold of her arm. "I'm sorry if my boldness offended you. It's just that I don't have much time, and I thought I should make my interest known. Will said you weren't anything to him . . . I mean . . . Well now, that sounded bad. He just told me that you two weren't a couple or . . ."

Hannah didn't know why it hurt to hear him say that she wasn't anything to William Barnett. She didn't want to be anything to him, but at the same time it stung her heart that he would tell his friend that she was nothing.

"Thank you for the compliment you are paying me, Lieuten-ant Atherton, but I have no interest in seeking a beau. And Mr. Barnett is quite correct. We are nothing to each other." With that she left the lieutenant and made her way into the house.

13

"The cows, they give good today," Juanita said, setting two pails of milk alongside the two Hannah had just placed on the table.

"They did indeed. And the chickens laid well, too. We're in high cotton, as my father would have once said. It's a blessing, too, with all the extra mouths to feed."

"Sí. Those men, they get hungry."

Hannah nodded. "I'm just glad that they appreciate ham and beans. It's probably more than most Confederate soldiers are getting."

"You are good to share with them, Miss Hannah," Juanita said, placing a cloth over the pails.

"It's our duty to feed the hungry," Hannah replied. She shaded her eyes and looked out across the yard to the sloping hills and prairie. The men had gone out early to round up steers close to home. She had no idea of when they would return, but given her agreement with He Who Walks in Darkness,

Hannah felt somewhat confident her family would be safe enough here at the ranch.

"Mr. Will tell me they should be back by supper. Tomorrow they will travel much farther. I will make them food to take, but what would you like for us to eat tonight?"

Hannah considered it for a moment. "Why don't you make that spicy pork he likes so much?" Truth be told, it was a favorite of hers, as well. "We'll have that with rice and corn bread. And since we have plenty of eggs and milk, would you make us some flan, as well?"

"Sí, that will be a very good treat." Juanita smiled. "Mr. Will like flan very much."

Hannah didn't reply. She wasn't looking to please Mr. Barnett. Her heart was still troubled by Mr. Lockhart's declaration that William had fought at Vicksburg. She tried to put it from her mind—had prayed that God would give her peace about the matter—but still the horror of it all lingered in her mind.

"Miss Hannah, you must know Mr. Will is a good man. I know him for a very long time now. He was always good to his mama and she love him very much. I think he was her favorite. Mr. Lyle, he was more like their papa. But they were all good people."

"I'm sure they were, Juanita." Hannah tried to put aside her thoughts of Vicksburg. "After all, they brought you here and kept you on to run the place. I'm so glad for our friendship." She looked at the woman and smiled. "I honestly wouldn't have gotten through these last months without you, Juanita. You have been a good friend."

"I'm glad we are friends. Mr. Barnett, he did not like to be friends with his workers."

"You're speaking of the father?"

"Sí. He like your father. They are men who keep orders."

Hannah wasn't sure she understood. "Keep orders? What do you mean?"

"They are the boss. They work to run the ranch."

"Oh, you mean they order people about? Yes, that's true. My father comes from a long line of men who give orders."

"Give orders. Sí." She paused and nodded her head. "This is what I mean."

"I grew up in a house where everything was well managed," Hannah said, remembering her childhood. "My grandparents owned three slaves and the slaves cared for the house. My grandfather and father were lawyers—*abogados*," she added, using the Spanish she'd learned while in Dallas.

Juanita smiled and nodded. Hannah liked being able to learn some of the woman's language, though it was completely foreign to Hannah. She'd not known a single person of Mexican descent until coming to Texas.

"As lawyers, they made good money and we shared a large house. So having people to do the household work was something I always knew. That's why it was so hard for me to come here. Even in Dallas we had a housekeeper. I've had to learn so much living out here. Especially about taking care of children."

"It is a hard life here," Juanita agreed. "You have been a good mother to Andy and Marty. They are most lucky to have your love."

"I can't imagine my life without them," Hannah admitted.

Movement on the horizon caught Hannah's attention. She squinted and put her hand to her forehead as a single mounted rider drew closer. The rider was clearly Comanche, but she didn't recognize him until he'd come nearly halfway to the house.

"It's Night Bear," Hannah said in surprise. She noted that he still wore the splint and sling she'd put on his arm.

She and Juanita stepped to the edge of the yard to greet him. "Night Bear, you are welcome here," Hannah said with a wave of her hand.

The young man halted his horse. "We have great sickness in our village and need your help."

"What seems to be wrong?" Hannah questioned, walking closer. "Describe what the sickness is."

"My father sends me to you. He does not know what this sickness is. There are little sores all over the faces, the hands of our people. They have fever and much pain."

Hannah looked to Juanita. "It sounds like smallpox, but I can't be sure." She turned back to Night Bear. "Where is your village from here?"

He pointed back and to the northwest. "A day's ride. I stopped along the way to rest, but must return now. Will you come with me?"

"Of course," Hannah said without thinking.

Juanita put her hand on Hannah's arm. "Miss Hannah, you cannot go. Mr. Will would never want you to do this."

If anything, Juanita's words only served to make up Hannah's mind. "I am going to go and help these people. They've come to us in need. To do otherwise wouldn't be Christian. Let's gather some food and medicine, and I will go and do what I can. When the men return, you can tell them where I've gone and that Night Bear is seeing to my care."

She could see that Juanita wasn't at all happy with this plan. "Night Bear, I must get some things, but I will come with you to the village. Have you eaten?"

He nodded. "But I would like more of your sweet bread." He smiled. "It was very good."

"I don't have any sweet rolls made," Hannah apologized. "But we have cookies. You can have some with milk if you like while you are waiting for me, and then I will take some extra with us for the road."

He threw his leg over the head of the horse and jumped to the ground. "I come."

Half an hour later, Hannah rode out from the ranch with Night Bear. She felt apprehensive now that she'd had time to really consider what she was doing. White women had been taken hostage by the various tribes in the area—some were returned and some were never heard from again. She prayed she was making the right choice. She knew Mr. Barnett would never approve.

"Why did your father send you for me?" she asked Night Bear.

"He said you were good with my healing. Our medicine man is dead. Most of our older people, too. Almost everyone has the sickness. We are very weak."

"But you aren't sick."

He looked at her and for the first time Hannah noticed he seemed more than just tired. "You are sick, aren't you?"

"I am not so sick yet. I do not have the sores. I just feel much pain in my head."

"Oh, Night Bear, I am so sorry. Can you make it back to the village? You said it would take us all day."

"It will be night when we reach my people. We are hidden in the rocky places far beyond. I will be able to ride there."

As the journey continued, however, Hannah could see Night Bear growing weaker and weaker. She tried to make certain he drank plenty of water, and at one point insisted they brew some willow tea for him to drink. The tea seemed to help and as they continued out across the vast unmarked land, Hannah couldn't help but wonder if they might come across some of the ranch hands or soldiers who were rounding up cattle. But the farther they traveled the less likely that possibility seemed.

The sun set early, as was the pattern with the coming of the winter months. Hannah was only a little afraid. Her fear of wild animals was second only to her concern about renegade Indians. Night Bear didn't seem to mind the darkness, and as the sky once again filled with stars, Hannah found that she didn't fear it so much herself.

There was a real sense of peace in her spirit. God had sent her here. He had sent Night Bear to her for such a time as this.

She knew her healing skills were only average, but her mother had taught her much—her grandmother, too. Juanita had added to that knowledge with frontier skills that were necessary to endure life in Texas. But if God had sent her to these people, then God would also send her the wisdom to deal with their illness. If it was smallpox, there wasn't a great deal she could do for the Numunuu, but see to their comfort.

She had no idea of the hour when they finally reached a series of ravines and rocky crags. Night Bear maneuvered them along a narrow path until finally they were well hidden in the canyon. Before long, they came upon the village without Hannah even realizing it. Only the fact that Night Bear had halted his horse and was dismounting told her that they'd arrived.

A faint glow of light came from across a small circle of darkness. Hannah strained to see and thought she could trace the pattern of several tepees.

"You can get down. We will go to my father first."

Hannah did as she was told, surprised to find that there were two other men who had silently joined them. Night Bear spoke swiftly in his native tongue and the men replied with what sounded like grunts to Hannah.

"They will take care of our horses and bring your things. Come. We will speak with my father."

Pulling her coat close, Hannah prayed that God would show her what to do. She thought only momentarily of how angry Mr. Barnett and the lieutenant would be when they realized she was gone.

Night Bear pulled open the flap to one of the tepees and motioned her inside. Hannah's senses were assaulted with the stench of sickness and unwashed bodies. A small fire had been made in the center of the room, but it was dying out. Along the walls of the tepee, Hannah could see two people lying on the ground.

Moving to one side, Night Bear knelt and spoke to his father. Hannah remained standing, not knowing what else she should do. The young warrior motioned her over.

"My father would like to know what this sickness is."

"I will need light," she told Night Bear. "Build up the fire. I have some candles in my bags. Have them brought here quickly."

He did as she instructed while Hannah knelt beside the chief. "I was sorry to hear you were sick," she told him.

The Comanche looked up at her with a glazed expression. His black hair splayed out wildly around him. "My people are dying—many are dead."

She nodded. "Night Bear told me. It sounds like smallpox, but I will need to see better before I can be certain. Even then, I've only seen it once before. I've had medicine to prevent my getting it, so I should be able to help you without taking sick."

"Here are your things," Night Bear said, motioning the two men into the tepee. One brought Hannah's supplies while the other stoked the fire and added wood. The room brightened considerably and Hannah realized she didn't need to worry about the candles.

Studying the sores on He Who Walks in Darkness, Hannah's suspicions were confirmed. It was smallpox. She glanced at Night Bear, who stood swaying slightly to her right. "You need to get to bed," she told him.

He Who Walks in Darkness looked at her in question. "Your son is sick with the smallpox, just as you are. I presume most of the village people are ill?"

He nodded, but spoke in Comanche to Night Bear. Hannah heard the boy reply "Haa—yes." Then he went to a pallet and sank to the ground.

"Can you cure us?"

Hannah looked at the chief and shook her head. "No, there is no cure for this. I can, however, help to make you comfortable. The strong will survive this, but the weaker ones will most likely die. I will not lie to you—it is a horrible disease."

He closed his eyes. "It is good you do not lie. Ura."

"You are welcome," Hannah replied. "Now rest. I will get some willow bark tea brewing and check on the others." She looked to Night Bear. "I'm sorry, but I suppose I will need your help a bit longer. I do not wish to alarm your people. They will need to know that I am not here to harm them."

Night Bear nodded. He got to his feet. "I will show you to the others and explain."

Hannah drew a deep breath. This wasn't going to be easy no matter how she looked at it. Smallpox had swept through the village—probably brought to them by diseased blankets or some other trade goods. Now that it was here, however, it wouldn't just go away without exacting a huge toll.

❧

"It was mighty fine of you to take us in for the night," William told Ted Terry and his wife, Marietta. "I figured to make it back to the ranch, but we've had some issues rounding up a few of the steers. Headed about ten of yours back this way."

"Thanks, but what are you wanting with them this time of year?" Ted asked.

The two men exchanged a look. "I suppose," William began, "it would be better if I didn't tell you. At least that way you won't have to lie about it later."

Terry eyed him with a raised brow. "Lie about it? I think you know me better than that."

"I do, and that's why I'd probably best not speak of what we're doing with the cattle."

Tyler nodded, but Ted Terry was no man's fool. "Might this have something to do with the war efforts?" he asked.

"It might," William said. "Then again, it might not." He smiled. "Seriously, I wouldn't want you to get in any trouble for our doings."

Ted nodded as his wife came into the room with fresh coffee. "I thought you boys could use something to warm you up. I'm having the cook fix you something to eat."

William smiled at the woman. She was, as they often said in Texas, a handsome woman. Marietta's eyes still held a sparkle of life usually reserved for the very young, even though her brown hair was heavily salted with gray. William hadn't seen her for years and yet she hadn't seemed to age a day. A very unusual thing for women on Texas ranches.

She put the tray on a table near her husband. "Do you want me to pour or would you boys rather go back to talking and pour for yourselves?"

"We'll get it, darlin'," Ted told her. "You've done more than enough. Thank you."

She kissed the top of his head, then turned to Tyler and William. "I'll come and get you when the food is ready."

Ted was already pouring the coffee by the time she exited the sitting room. William turned back to his host and took the offered cup. "Thank you. Like I said, we hadn't intended to travel so far. But it is good to see you again."

"And you," Ted said, handing Tyler a cup. "But I still want to know more about this venture of yours. I'm not afraid of what the future holds. You know God has a purpose in bringing you here, and I don't intend for you to deny me my involvement in it."

William chuckled. "Well, when you put it that way, I suppose I shouldn't hesitate."

"Are you serving the Lord, William?" Ted asked quite seriously.

"I . . . well . . . I can't rightly say that I am. God and me got a little bit separated during the war."

"I reckon you know that wasn't by His doing?"

William knew the older man wouldn't cut him any slack when it came to God. "I suppose I do. Still, whether this is a mission for God or not, the war makes it impossible to keep from offending someone."

The man nodded. "You're always bound to offend someone in life. Best you realize that early on." He smiled. "Even so, whatever you're up to . . . I want to help."

14

"She went where?" William didn't usually raise his voice to anyone, but he was certain he couldn't have heard right.

Juanita gave a quick glance at Pepita before answering. "Miss Hannah go with Night Bear to his people. They are sick and Night Bear's father sent him to get help."

"Of all the stupid, ridiculous ideas! It wasn't enough she marched out to meet the Comanche on horseback—now she's gone to visit them in their camp." He shook his head and slapped his hat against his aching leg.

William motioned to Berto and handed him the reins to his horse. "He's played out. Would you saddle up the sorrel for me?" William pulled his saddlebags from the horse.

Berto nodded and took off for the barn. William looked at Tyler. "I'm going after her."

"You want us to come with you?" Tyler asked. "My men and I could—"

Holding up his hand, William shook his head. "No. We

can't go storming into a Comanche village and not expect things to go horribly wrong. If I show up there with a bunch of soldiers, they aren't going to take it as a friendly move."

"Going alone isn't the best idea you've ever had, either. What if another band of Comanche or Kiowa come your way?"

"That's why I'm taking the sorrel. He's the fastest horse we have. He can outrun any Indian mount." William looked back to Juanita. "Would you pack me some supplies? I'll head out as soon as they're ready."

Juanita nodded and hurried with Pepita into the house.

"I should have known she'd do something like this," William said.

"You couldn't know that Night Bear would show up or that his people were going to get sick. I'm surprised they would even seek help from a white woman. They must be sufferin' something fierce."

"I'm sure they are." William gazed off to the north. "Miss Dandridge is going to do a bit of suffering herself. Living with the Numunuu won't be an easy thing. They are a nomadic people and they aren't exactly set up for comfort."

Tyler laughed. "Sounds like you're worried—maybe you have feelings for Miss Dandridge."

Narrowing his eyes, William scowled. "You're the Romeo, not me."

Tyler studied him for a moment. "Not this time. You look a mite lovesick, if you ask me."

"Well, I'm not." William wasn't about to reveal how close Tyler was to guessing his confused feelings. "She has a brother and sister to care for. Their pa is missing. Her place is here.

Her responsibilities and loyalties should be here—not risking her life to smallpox."

"How do you plan to find her?" Tyler asked, sobering.

"I'll track them. I've been able to hone my skills in the war."

"Mr. Barnett!" Andy came running from around the back of the house. "Mr. Barnett, Juanita said you were going to find Hannah. Can I come with you? Please?"

His breathless pleadings touched William. "I'm sorry, Andy. I need to travel fast. Besides, I need you to stay here and take care of Marty and your guests. You're the man of the house now. Can you help me with this?"

Andy seemed to actually grow taller. He looked at William and then Tyler. "I can take care of them."

"Tyler will be here if you need his help."

"That's right," Tyler said. "You just let me know what I can do."

Andy nodded then frowned. "Will the Indians hurt Hannah?"

William didn't want to lie to the boy, but neither did he want to frighten him. "Well, I don't figure they sent Night Bear here to hurt her. Juanita said the Comanche are sick and that the chief asked for Miss . . . for Hannah to come tend them. So I figure she's all right."

"Then why are you going after her?" he asked, his eyes never leaving William's face.

"Because she will probably need help."

Andy considered this for a moment. "I reckon she will."

William opened his saddlebags when he saw Juanita approaching with a handful of items. Pepita followed with a bulging flour sack.

"I put in more herbs for Miss Hannah. I put in tortillas and meat for you."

He took the cloth-wrapped food and stuffed it into one side, then put the herbs in the other. Pepita handed him the flour sack.

"We tore up old sheets to make cloths for washing and bandaging," Juanita explained. "We put in vinegar, too. Miss Hannah took some, but she will probably want more. It help with the itching and wounds."

"Thank you. I'm sure Miss Dandridge will be grateful for these."

Just then Berto returned with the sorrel. "He's ready."

William hung the flour sack around the horn, then threw the bags on behind the saddle. Grabbing the reins from Berto, William hoisted himself up into the saddle, ignoring the pain that shot through his thigh. There wasn't time to favor his injury, and William wasn't about to let on that he was hurting.

"Here, take this," Tyler said, tossing up a canteen. "It's full. I filled it in that stream we crossed about a mile back."

Taking the canteen in hand, William gave Tyler a nod of thanks. "I'll track out to the north. Since Juanita said they didn't expect to reach the village until late in the night I have a feeling I know where they've gone."

"Tierra del Diablo?" Berto asked.

"That's my guess. A lot of good hiding places are in the Land of the Devil, and it's one of the Comanches' favorite places because the buffalo like to wander through there from time to time."

"How long do you think you'll be?" Tyler asked. "Should we come lookin' for you if you aren't back tomorrow?"

"No. Like I said, if you show up there, the warriors may see it as an aggressive act. If they will allow me to enter and help, I'll do what I can before I return with Miss Dandridge. Andy, take good care of your little sister."

"I will, I promise."

With a nudge of his heels, William moved the sorrel out across the yard. His anger faded in light of his growing concern. What in the world had Hannah been thinking to go off to a Comanche village on her own? No doubt she felt sorry for the Numunuu. But even if that was the case, she could do very little in the face of smallpox. And what if she took sick? Had she had the cowpox vaccine? The army had seen to it that he had. He'd suffered through with a mild case of fever and blistering, but nothing like the full force of the disease.

William forced himself to focus on tracking. At the top of the hill he dismounted and studied the ground, looking for signs.

The trail was easy to pick up. The ground had been fairly soft when they'd gone out, but since there'd been no other rain, the tracks remained. William remounted and headed out. At this rate he would have an easy time of following the two horses. One shod. One shoeless.

His mind raced with thoughts of what he'd say and do when he found Hannah. He didn't want to cause problems with the Comanche. If they were suffering a small pox epidemic that would be trouble enough. Even so, it was no place for a gentle-born woman like Hannah Dandridge, and he intended to rebuke her for this nonsense. William ran a hand through his hair. Good grief, the woman needed a keeper. Her life and responsibilities were just as he'd said—there on the ranch looking after her brother and sister.

Hannah's image filled his mind. China doll features with hair the color of rich earth. Blue eyes surrounded by sooty black lashes. And her rose-colored lips.

William kicked the horse harder than he'd intended, as if he could throw off the disturbing thoughts by pushing the animal to run.

Hannah Dandridge was unlike any woman he'd ever known. Juanita said she learned quickly and showed limitless endurance. Not only this, but Hannah had formed a friendship with Juanita, disregarding her status or race.

"Miss Hannah she no complain," Juanita had told him one night after dinner. *"Her papa is hard to live with, but she good to him. I see her heart hurting when he is in his anger, but she never say anything bad to me. She love him very much."*

"She sure doesn't have any problem speaking her mind with me," William muttered. Except of late.

He frowned and slowed his horse lest he lose the trail. Hannah had been guarded with him in their last encounters. Before, she had been feisty and strong willed, but the last time he'd talked to her had been different. She'd held herself aloof and her comments were stilted and to the point. What had caused the change? More troubling still: Why did it bother him so much?

By the time darkness washed over the plains, William felt confident that Tierra del Diablo was the right destination. He knew there would be no way to discern the trail without light.

Navigating the narrow sloping path wouldn't be easy, yet he hesitated to dismount. By the time he reached a fork in the trail, William knew he'd have to do something.

He brought the horse to a halt and listened. He could hear the ripple of water—nothing too big—just a small creek most likely. He knew further beyond the rocks there was a river and most likely the camp would be somewhere in that vicinity. He just needed to figure out which way to go.

Hannah moved from tepee to tepee. Many of the Numunuu had already died—mostly those who were older or very young, and therefore less capable of fighting the disease. The younger warriors were holding up better, as were some of their women. Even so, a band that had once been over seventy in number was now only thirty or so. Her presence in their camp brought surprise and scowls at first, but as the people grew progressively sicker, Hannah's ministerings were welcomed. She bathed the sick over and over using what vinegar she had. Diluting it with more water than she would have normally used had allowed it to go further, but now that meager supply was gone. So, too, the willow bark, herbs, and her food.

The same two men who had helped her the night of her arrival seemed somehow immune to the disease. Red Dog and Running Buffalo spoke very little English, but through a series of hand gestures, Hannah was able to make her requests known. It puzzled her as to why they'd not taken the illness. Perhaps they had taken the vaccine at some point or perhaps they had some sort of natural immunity. Either way, she was grateful for their help, especially since they were doing women's work. Night Bear had explained the situation to her and in turn, Hannah instructed him to let the men know that in doing these tasks they would be heroes—saviors of a sort to their people. The men seemed to accept this, although their apprehension of Hannah was still apparent.

Smallpox symptoms took anywhere from one to two weeks to appear after exposure. The entire camp had apparently received their original exposure a couple of weeks earlier, because most were in the stage of the illness where blisters were forming. Once these filled with fluid and then pus, Hannah knew it could take weeks for the sores to all scab and fall off. Until then, the Numunuu would be contagious.

Hannah tried to figure out what she should do about getting word back to her family. She obviously couldn't leave to do it herself. She had no idea of how to get back to the ranch. On the journey with Night Bear, Hannah had tried to keep landmarks in her mind, but the last part of the journey had been dark and she couldn't really trust that her memory would serve her all that well. She'd been exhausted when they'd arrived in camp, and that had only increased by immediately going to work to help the sick. She had managed a brief nap that afternoon, but otherwise she was just forcing herself to stay awake through the evening.

He Who Walks in Darkness was in the pustule stage of the pox and was running a fever again. His body was working to fight the infection, but Hannah wasn't at all sure he would live. His wife, Little Bird, was almost certain to die. She showed no signs of fighting the disease, and every time

Hannah checked on her, the woman seemed to be losing ground. Night Bear, although ill, seemed to have a very mild case. He was weak and had begun developing blisters, but they were few and smaller. Hannah prayed that he might have an easier time of it.

Coming to the chief's tepee, Hannah entered with a basin of warm water and a towel. She moved first to check on Night Bear. He was sleeping soundly on his pallet. The fire had recently been stoked due to Hannah's insistence that the warmth of the enclosure be maintained. Red Dog and Running Buffalo kept the fuel and water supplies stocked. They also managed to bring in food. At first Hannah refused. She had some of her own supplies left and that was enough to satisfy her needs. However, she'd run out of food earlier in the day, having eaten the last of her tortillas.

"Have many died?" He Who Walks in Darkness asked.

Hannah knelt beside the chief. "Yes. Over half the people are dead. Many of the others are sick and may well die."

He closed his eyes and grimaced. Hannah washed him with the warm water and wondered at the Comanche's spiritual convictions. Did they believe in God? Or did they worship creation? She'd heard that some tribes honored a long list of spirits.

"Might I ask you a question?"

The chief opened his eyes. "Haa."

Hannah smiled. "I wonder if you would tell me about your beliefs in God."

"God? The white man's God?"

She shrugged. "Or any other that you esteem."

"I've no time for gods. I am a warrior—my life is war. We are . . . strong."

"But what of this? What of dying? Do you believe in life after death?"

He Who Walks in Darkness seemed to consider her question. "There is a life after death, but it is no good to die like an old woman. My men should die in battle—I should die in battle."

"I believe in Jesus," Hannah told him while continuing to bathe his sores. "I believe that God—the one true God—sent His Son, Jesus, to save us from our sins."

"What are sins?"

Hannah was surprised that he would hold any interest at all in what she had to say. She tried to pretend it was a normal question. "Sins are wrongdoings. Things that we do that go against what God wants us to do. Like stealing or killing. Those are sins."

"Those are my ways," the sick man replied.

She offered him a slight smile. "Unfortunately, we all have sins. We are sinful people. We do whatever pleases us rather than working to please God."

"The spirits look for strength in a man. Not white man's . . ." He seemed to struggle for the right word. "White man's . . . religion."

Pausing in her work, Hannah tried to think of how she could share her heart. The language barrier was a bit of a problem, but not as great as it might have been. She thought of how she might speak to Marty or Andy—not in a way to belittle them, but rather to make the concept simple.

"Do you know what the Bible is?" she asked.

"White man's God book."

"Yes. It is a collection of God's wisdom and teachings to us. The Bible shows us who God is and how He wants us to live." When He Who Walks in Darkness said nothing, Hannah continued.

"The Bible says we have all sinned. We've all done things that go against what God would like for us to do. We hurt each other and do things that cause great pain. That isn't what God wants. He wants us to love each other, because He loves us." She picked up the towel and began to wash him once again. "God says that payment for sin is death."

"Every man will die," He Who Walks in Darkness countered weakly.

"Yes, in the body," she agreed, "but there is also the death of the spirit. Without being clean from our wrongdoing, we cannot please God. We cannot enter heaven. I don't want your people to die without knowing God's Son, Jesus. Jesus came to earth to save us from our sins. He died a horrible death as a sacrifice for our sin. If we believe in Him and ask Him to be Lord of our life, then we can be set free from the penalty for our sins."

"White man's stories."

She looked at the chief and shook her head. "No, it's so much more. I am here because I felt God wanted me to help you. I came to care for you and your people, as if I were caring for Jesus—my Lord. I know that must seem strange to you, but I speak the truth. I told you earlier that this disease is very bad. I told you I would not lie to you. I'm not lying now."

"The white man has his ways. The Numunuu have their

ways. The white man's God would not want the Numunuu, just as the white man does not want us. So we will fight. We will make war on your people until we are gone from this place."

Hannah felt a sadness overwhelm her. Perhaps if she spoke the Numunuu language, then she would be able to convince this very sick man that God truly did love him—that the color of his skin was not important to God.

Seeing that the chief was exhausted from their conversation, Hannah finished his care and got up to go. "I will pray for your people. I will pray to my God for you, He Who Walks in Darkness. I will pray that you will find a way to walk in the light."

Leaving him, Hannah went to the small tepee Night Bear had shown her to the night before. The place had belonged to two older women whose husbands died early in the epidemic. The women also died shortly before Hannah had come to stay with the Comanche.

She slipped off her boots and took her place on a pallet she'd made earlier. Fearful of disease, she had boiled the blankets given to her that morning. It had taken all day to dry in the humid air, but tonight they felt useable. Hannah wrapped up in the blankets and had just drifted off for a few minutes of sleep when she heard a commotion outside. Straining to hear what the problem might be, she was startled to recognize William Barnett's voice.

Hannah jumped to her feet and ran out of the tepee in her stockings. She saw Red Dog confronting a man just beyond the fire.

"Mr. Barnett?" she asked.

"It's me," he replied. "I'm trying to convince this man that I'm no threat to him."

She drew closer and could see that Red Dog had a knife drawn. She put out her hand and touched the warrior's forearm. Shaking her head, she smiled. "Mr. Barnett is a friend." Red Dog continued to eye Barnett suspiciously, but he lowered the knife. Hannah was glad that William could speak the language. "Would you please tell him that you are a friend and you've come to help?"

"I've been trying to tell him that," William all but growled.

Red Dog looked to her and Hannah reached out and took hold of William's hand. Patting the top of it while smiling, she repeated the word *friend* while William gave him the Numunuu word.

"*Haits. E-haitsma.*"

This seemed to appease Red Dog. He grunted several words to William before leaving them. Hannah waited for a translation.

"He says I am to share your tepee."

15

Hannah hadn't thought it would be possible to sleep. Mr. Barnett put his gear inside the tepee, but quickly assured her that he wouldn't risk her reputation by sleeping inside when she was there. Instead, he built a very small fire just outside and placed his bedroll there. Hannah felt bad for him having to endure the cooler night air without a shelter, and when she heard rain falling against the thin leather skins of the tepee, she felt it her duty to bring him inside.

"Mr. Barnett, I believe the space is large enough to accommodate us both," she told him from the opening of her shelter. "With this rain, I cannot in good faith allow you to get sick from exposure."

"I've camped out in worse, Miss Dandridge. Rest assured, I'm capable of sleeping in the rain."

"Perhaps." She stiffened and replied, "But I think it unwise. I hardly need for you to fall ill, too. We will neither one be in any state of undress, and anyone can walk in at any time to see that we are above reproach. I hardly think it will compromise either of us."

Barnett looked at her for a moment, and then with slow, determined actions he got up from the fire, gathered his things, and followed her into the shelter.

Hannah pretended it didn't bother her to see him stretch out on the ground across the fire from her. She tried to rationalize that he had followed her there only because of his anger at her traipsing off without his permission. Her heart had very nearly stopped at the sight of him, however.

Attraction to the enemy was something Hannah knew was surely warned against in the Bible. For this reason alone, she didn't want to think of William Barnett, but the sound of his soft breathing kept leading her mind to dangerous places. She wrestled with her thoughts of this man and his Union affiliation, and it was with those thoughts that she finally fell asleep.

When she awoke hours later, it seemed as though she'd only just closed her eyes. She looked over to the place where William had been and found his bedroll empty. Sitting up, Hannah wondered at the time. She pulled on her boots and did up the laces as quickly as her fingers would move, feeling a sense of urgency to learn where William had gone and why.

Exiting the tepee, Hannah shivered at the cooler temperature. The ground was still wet, but the rain had stopped. Although her first concern was William's whereabouts, Hannah made her way to the chief's lodgings. Entering, Hannah found things about the same. Little Bird was still clinging to life, but barely. Hannah found herself praying for the woman's soul. What if no one had ever told her about Jesus? What if she died without knowing that she could be saved for all eternity? The thought saddened Hannah. How many people died every day without knowing that God loved them and had given them a free gift of eternal life?

He Who Walks in Darkness was sleeping rather peacefully. Hannah was glad that the urgency of the illness was passing for him. He would no doubt recover, but his skin would be horribly marked. Knowing the Indian beliefs, he would probably just see the pox scars as a mark of victory.

Hannah slipped over to Night Bear and to her surprise found him awake and watching her. "I'm sorry if I woke you," she told him. "How are you feeling today?"

"My head is much better. It doesn't pain me like before."

"Good. That's a very good sign." She surveyed his blisters. They weren't nearly as numerous or severe as the pox on some of the others.

"Do you feel like taking some broth?"

Night Bear nodded, then reached out to touch her arm. "I have questions."

"I will try to have answers."

"You spoke to my father about the white God." His dark eyes searched her face. "Did you speak truth?"

Hannah smiled. "I did. God is—"

"I thought I might find you here," William Barnett interrupted.

Hannah glanced over her shoulder. "I see you are well." She held herself aloof. "Could you please bring some broth for Night Bear?" She tried not to notice how his rather disheveled appearance only served to draw her attention. His brown hair seemed a little more wavy than usual, and the top of his bib shirt was unbuttoned and folded back to reveal a hint of dark chest hair. She looked away quickly, lest her thoughts betray her.

"Certainly," he replied. Then without another word he was gone.

Hannah turned back to Night Bear and smiled. "God is love, the Bible says. He is also faithful. He will forgive you your sins if you ask Him to."

"And He will keep me from death?" Night Bear asked, struggling to rise a bit.

"Spiritual death, yes. As I told your father, everyone dies a physical death."

"I do not know your God." Night Bear closed his eyes as if suddenly weak. He fell back against his pallet. "Would you tell me of Him?"

Feeling her heart skip a beat, Hannah nodded even though he couldn't see her. "I would happily tell you about God and His Son, Jesus. God is the great Father of all. He created the world and all that is in it. But He saw that man was given over to sin and needed a savior. Because of this, He sent His Son—Jesus. Jesus came to earth as a man, even though He was God."

Night Bear opened his eyes and looked at her. "This Jesus is here now?"

"In a way," Hannah said. "You see, in those days it was necessary to have a blood sacrifice for sins—wrongdoings. The people would offer up an animal, and by shedding its blood they were forgiven their sins."

"Your God requires blood?"

"Yes. At least He did until Jesus came. Jesus offered mankind a way free from his bad behavior. Jesus shed his own blood in order to give man a connection to God. His blood covers the sins of the world, and we no longer need additional blood.

"You see, Jesus knew that we could not help ourselves, so He willingly gave His life to help us."

"He does not sound like a warrior," Night Bear said. "The Numunuu are warriors. Our God would need to be a warrior."

Hannah smiled. "Jesus is definitely a warrior. He loves His people, but He fights against Satan and his demons."

"Who is this Satan?"

"He is the enemy of God and God's people. The devil, or Satan, as he is named, tries to steal people away from God." She considered the life of a Comanche in order to better explain. "Satan goes out and looks for people to steal from God. When a person doesn't have Jesus for their Savior, Satan tries to trap those people into a life that serves him. God protects His people, however. God has promised to never leave us."

"But I do not see Him here," Night Bear said, looking around the room. "You said your Jesus was here."

"And so He is," Hannah said, putting her hand to her heart. "He lives within me, within all who accept Him. He is here beside me and all around me. I cannot see Him in the flesh, but He makes His presence known by giving me the Holy Spirit."

"A spirit—a ghost spirit?"

"The Holy Spirit is often called the Holy Ghost. He is the very essence of God's heart. When Jesus returned to heaven, where Father God awaited Him, He promised to send the Spirit to us. He knew we would need help."

"To fight this devil?"

"Yes. And for a time God has allowed Satan to cause

problems, but He won't let it go on forever. He is coming back to put an end to Satan."

"He will kill him?" Night Bear asked.

"Yes. He will put him in the lake of fire for all time."

"Where is this lake of fire?"

"I don't suppose I know, but I do believe it exists . . . or will when the time comes."

Hannah hadn't heard William return, but when she looked up he was standing there listening to her. She reached up for the bowl of broth and ignored any thought of trying to explain. Perhaps he thought her foolish, trying to save the Numunuu.

"I've checked on the others. Two died in the night, and I've helped Red Dog prepare them for burial," William told her.

Hannah hadn't even thought of the burial rite. "Is there a ceremony?"

"Yes, but the ritual hasn't been honored in full. There isn't time and there aren't people to participate because they're either dead or sick."

She nodded and turned back to help Night Bear drink a bit of the broth. "Thank you," she told William.

When she finished with Night Bear, Hannah made her way outside, only to find Mr. Barnett waiting for her.

"We need to talk," he stated.

"I suppose you are angry that I've come here, but before you rebuke me, know this: I came here to aid dying people. I don't care that they are Comanche or dangerous. They are human beings and they needed help. I am tired of people telling me that I must go here or stay there when God clearly has other plans for me."

Mr. Barnett said nothing, so she continued.

"Furthermore, He Who Walks in Darkness apparently trusted me enough to send for me. That kind of trust should be honored, and so I came. I do not fear my own death, Mr. Barnett."

"William."

She looked at him oddly. "What?"

"Stop calling me Mr. Barnett . . . please. Call me William."

With great hesitancy she nodded. "Very well. William. Now if you'll excuse me . . ."

"No, I won't." He reached out and took hold of her arm. "What you've done here is not at all wise. In fact, it's probably the most foolish thing I've ever seen anyone do."

"Once again, Mr. Barnett . . . William . . . 'God hath chosen the foolish things of the world to confound the wise.' "

"Meaning exactly what?" he asked, refusing to release her.

Hannah glared at his hand. Mr. Lockhart was generally good enough to recognize his mistake and remove his inappropriate touch, but not so William Barnett. When Hannah returned her focus to his eyes, he only fixed her with a hard stare.

"I mean that obviously you believe yourself much wiser than anyone else."

"Wiser than you, to be sure," he interrupted.

"Be that as it may, you give no credence to the possibility that I was following direction from a higher authority."

"So God told you to risk your life and come here?"

"The risk was minimal compared to the need, wouldn't you say?"

He shook his head, his expression dark. "No, I wouldn't say

that at all. The risk was great. What if you had been taken by another band of Indians or even another tribe? What if Night Bear had gotten sick before you reached camp? You didn't even know where he was taking you."

"That's true, Mr. Barnett." She didn't care that she'd reverted to formalities. "But God did. Surely you are not going to discount the fact that God often led people to places that were unknown. To Abraham God merely said, 'Get thee out of thy country.' He told him to leave his kindred and his father's house. Why should it surprise you then that He directed me to do likewise?"

William looked at her for a moment longer before replying, "Because as far as I can tell, Miss Dandridge, you don't wait to get direction from anyone."

"This is where you are wrong, Mr. Barnett. I've been taking orders from people all of my life—particularly the men in my life. I have come to learn over time that only God directs me in ways that are worthwhile."

"Maybe that's because you've been listening to the wrong people." He dropped his hold on her. "But be that as it may, you have a responsibility to Andy and Marty. If you die out here, what are they going to do?"

Hannah swallowed down her guilt. She had already asked herself that question a hundred times. "I suppose that God will watch over them as He has me. Truly, Mr. Barnett, do you imagine me so daft that I would not consider these things? I have had the sole care of my siblings since they were very small—in fact since Marty's birth. She is like my own child—Andy, too. Do you honestly imagine me forgetting their needs?"

"It would appear that you have in this matter."

"Well, that only serves to prove to me that you do not know what you're talking about. I made provision for my brother and sister. I arranged for their welfare, so you needn't worry."

"I suppose you set something up with Mr. Lockhart," William said in a snide tone.

Hannah felt a rush of embarrassment. She couldn't imagine why Mr. Barnett would suggest such a thing, or why it should cause her such feelings of humiliation.

"I see no reason to continue this conversation. I need to check on the people."

"I just did that before coming to see you," William answered. "What you need is to face the truth. You are headstrong, Miss Dandridge. Headstrong and dangerous—not only to yourself, but to others."

With that he left her, stalking off toward the far end of camp. Hannah watched him, unable to turn away. Why was it that his comments should so thoroughly offend and wound her? It wasn't like she cared what Mr. Barnett thought. He was nothing to her—he'd said as much to the lieutenant.

But it did bother her. It bothered her a great deal.

Not knowing what else to do, Hannah returned to the chief's tepee. She hoped she might be able to continue her discussion about God with Night Bear, but she found him sleeping. She sighed. Perhaps she had planted the seeds of the gospel deep enough that they would take root and grow. She smiled at the sleeping warrior. Not really a man, but certainly not a boy. She thought of Andy and tried to imagine him trekking out across vast distances to get help. The Comanche raised their children to be self-sufficient, whereas she had raised Andy and Marty to be dependent. Perhaps it was time to reconsider her manner of parenting. No doubt that would please Mr. Barnett. The frontier of Texas was a harsh land in which to raise children, but Hannah was willing to admit she could benefit from the advice of others. Just not from Mr. Barnett. His advice didn't interest her at all.

She clenched her fists and then forced herself to relax. There was no sense in allowing William Barnett to control her or make her feel bad for her choices. Her mother had always told her that the person who riled your anger was, in that moment, in control of your heart and mind.

Hannah drew a deep breath and let it out very slowly. She would not allow Mr. Barnett to monopolize her thoughts. She would focus on God and what He desired of her. That was enough—that was the right way, as far as she could tell.

Two more days passed, bringing the death of several more Comanche, including Little Bird, Night Bear's mother. When William carried the woman's body from the tepee, Hannah couldn't help but see how much it had upset Night Bear. She went to him and did her best to offer comfort.

"I know how much this hurts, Night Bear. I lost my mother when I was fourteen. It was the saddest day of my life."

"She was a good mother," he said, his voice husky with sorrow.

"I prayed for her, as I have for all of your people," she said. "I prayed that God was able to speak to her heart. He is not a cruel God. He is just and fair and desires that each and every person know of Him and His gift of life."

"But your God did not save her from dying." Night Bear fought back tears. "If your God is all powerful, then why was He not strong enough to keep her from death?"

Hannah brushed back the boy's black hair. "Remember what I told you: We must all face a physical death at some point in our life. God saves us from a spiritual death. Our bodies will grow old—they will get sick or injured, and we cannot stop such things from happening. But if we trust in Jesus, then we never have to die a spiritual death."

"Have you prayed for me?" Night Bear asked.

"I have. I've asked God to heal your body and give you strength to recover if it be His will. But I've also asked God to help you to understand who He is and to see that He is the one true God of all." She stroked the boy's fevered brow. "I believe God has plans for you, Night Bear. I believe you came into my life for the purpose of hearing of His love. Perhaps one day you will accept His gift of eternal life, and then you will help your people to trust Him, as well."

"My people are dead. So many are gone. . . . We will not be able to exist on our own and will have to join with another band in order to survive."

"Then they will become your people, true?"

He nodded ever so slightly. "I think we might all pass from this earth if the white man has his way."

"Perhaps you will find a way for the white man and Indian to live together in peace," Hannah said, encouraging the young man to think beyond the moment. "Perhaps one day we will live side by side."

The young warrior looked at her for a moment before shaking his head. "Your people will not let us live . . . in Comanche way."

"Maybe you could change. Maybe if you tried our way of living, you would find it a better way."

"What if our way is better?" he asked.

Hannah frowned. She had lived several days in a Comanche camp and she could tell this boy that his way was not better. How could he possibly see it as better to sleep upon the ground in shelters comprised of nothing more than hides? How could he favor a life of wandering from one place to another—of killing and stealing? Then again, had she grown up with this way of life, might she not also believe it the best?

She leaned back and stood. A thought came to mind. "We are always convinced that our way is the better way," she said. "But only God's way is perfect. If you seek Him, Night Bear, He will be found. And in finding Him, you will also learn the best ways to go."

A quick glance at He Who Walks in Darkness assured Hannah that he was resting as comfortably as possible. William's meager ration of supplies had allowed Hannah to offer the chief comfort and some relief from the itching and pain, but now those supplies were gone.

She longed to get word back to her family—it had been uppermost on her mind since she realized it would be impossible to just up and leave these very sick people. Seeking William, she left the tepee and wandered through the camp. Hannah spied him pouring water from a pot by the fire.

"We need to send someone back to the house," she said, coming alongside him. The warmth of the fire and sight of the steaming water made Hannah yearn for a bath. She had worked herself to a state of exhaustion over the last few days and was certain she was dirtier than she'd ever been. She reached inside her apron pocket and drew out a piece of cloth. Dipping it into the hot water, Hannah gingerly squeezed out the excess.

"Did you hear me?" she asked when William said nothing.

"I heard. I just don't believe I have a solution. I'm not leaving you here, and I doubt that you want to go home just yet."

"It's not a matter of want, Mr. Barnett." She wiped her face with the cloth and felt slightly revived. "I believe my family and the others will worry about our welfare. I do not wish to grieve anyone. Therefore, I believe we should write a letter and perhaps we could get Red Dog or Running Buffalo to take it."

He looked at her in disbelief. "Do you honestly think either of those Comanche are going to want to risk their lives in such a journey?" He stood, leaving the water beside the fire. "I think the fact is, we've done as much as we can here. It's time to go home."

Hannah glanced around the camp. "How can you say we've done as much as we can? There are still many sick people. Those who are recovering are weak and cannot help those who are still so terribly ill."

"And you propose to remain here until everyone is back up and raiding? Is that it?"

She grew angry at his condescending manner. "I propose that I remain here and help the sick. You can go wherever you like, but I'd prefer it be back to the ranch so that at least my family won't worry about my safety."

William stepped closer. "Shouldn't you have considered that before gallivanting off with a Comanche for parts unknown?"

She put her hands on her hips. "Will you take a message back to the ranch?"

He shook his head. "I'm staying if you're staying."

He was only inches away and Hannah couldn't help but notice the small scar on the right side of his jaw. She found herself wondering why she hadn't seen it before. What had caused it? It was only an inch or so long and rather faint. Perhaps it had happened when he was young and over the years time had faded the reminder.

"Well?"

Hannah realized with much embarrassment that she'd been staring at William's face. Shaking off her thoughts, she turned to walk away. "I will ask Red Dog to take the message."

"And where will you get the paper and pen for such a message?"

She glanced over her shoulder and kept walking. "I have a pencil and paper, Mr. Barnett. I'm not the complete idiot you believe me to be."

∼

Herbert Lockhart rode to the Barnett Ranch fully intending to speak his mind. He had a folded letter in his pocket, which he had spent some time concocting. The letter told Hannah how in the event of his death, her father desired her to marry Lockhart. It also told of how under Texas law, Lockhart would be the one to inherit the ranch because he was a co-owner.

He was rather proud of himself for the piece of work. The information given was worded exactly as he'd heard Dandridge speak. The man's very presence could be determined in the comments about his children and their welfare.

As for Martha and Andrew, it is my desire you would not be burdened with them for the duration of your life. I have allocated monies for them to be sent away to school, where they might receive a quality education and free you to enjoy your new life with Herbert Lockhart.

Smiling as he remembered the words he'd written, Lockhart was more than a little pleased. This would no doubt compel Hannah to yield to his desires. It was all so very logical. He would tell Hannah that he had confirmed her father's death and that because of this, he had opened her father's last will and testament. In there, he'd found this letter that addressed his desires for the future.

The ranch seemed unusually quiet when Lockhart arrived. Dismounting, he tied off the horse and bounded up the well-worn path to the front door. With a loud knock, Lockhart announced his presence.

When no one answered, Lockhart knocked again. This time his impatience betrayed itself in the length of time he pounded the door with his fist. After another minute or so, Juanita came.

"Señor Lockhart," she said, sounding surprised.

He smiled at the woman. She wasn't a bad-looking sort for a Mexican. He rather liked the way her white peasant blouse seemed to make her brown skin all the more prominent. She was well kept and clean, unlike many of the poor Mexicans who continued to live in Texas. Once they might have owned the entire state, but not now. And their welfare had suffered.

"I've come to see Miss Dandridge," he explained.

"She is not here, señor."

He frowned. He'd just ridden out on the only road to town, so he knew she wasn't there. It was possible she'd gone visiting, but he happened to know she wasn't very well acquainted with the folks at the neighboring ranches.

"Where is she?" he finally asked.

Juanita's expression turned guarded. She looked to be hiding something as she focused on the ground. "She is with Mr. William."

Lockhart's head began to throb as anger took control of his thoughts. "I see. And where have they gone?"

"I cannot say," she replied.

"Can't or won't?"

Juanita looked confused. "If you come to the back, you can talk to Berto. He is sharpening knives."

Herbert followed the woman around the side of the house to the area they referred to as the summer kitchen. Here, Berto had put a grinding stone under the canvas canopy. He sat bent over the stone working to sharpen the edge of an axe.

"Señor would like to know where Miss Hannah and Mr. Will go," Juanita explained.

"They are helping the sick," Berto explained. He got up from his seat and put the axe aside.

"What sick are you talking about?" Lockhart demanded.

"The Comanche," Berto answered. "They sent a rider to ask Miss Hannah to help them. They needed care."

Herbert barely held his rage in check. How dare this man tell him such an outrageous story. "You lie! Miss Dandridge would not go off to an Indian camp to help the sick. Where is she?"

Berto looked puzzled and turned to Juanita. In rapid-fire Spanish the two dialogued for a moment. Herbert was more than a little annoyed. He couldn't speak the language and hadn't any idea what was transpiring between the husband and wife.

Finally Berto turned back to him. "Juanita say that Miss Hannah wanted to help them. Night Bear—the chief's son who she cared for here—he come to her and beg for help. Miss Hannah—she go. When William find out, he go after her."

"When was this?" Herbert asked, finally allowing for the possibility that the Mexican was telling the truth.

"Six days now."

"Six days?" Herbert questioned in disbelief. "She's been gone for nearly a week and you didn't send for me? Where is this Indian camp?"

"I don't know. William—he think they camp in the Tierra del Diablo."

Lockhart was familiar with the phrase but not the area. He seethed to imagine Hannah being used by the Comanche or William Barnett. She would have no defense—no ability to keep them from doing to her whatever they wished. Chances were better than not she'd be no use to him at all when they were through with her.

The sound of a rider approaching caused all three to turn. Coming down the gentle slope of the hill, a single Comanche warrior was waving something in the air. Juanita moved closer to Berto, but Herbert reached for his gun.

It was only a derringer, not powerful enough to shoot from this distance, but he would put a bullet between the eyes of that dirty savage as soon as he came close enough. Berto turned and saw the gun. He put his hand over the weapon.

"No, señor. He come in peace. He is alone."

"I don't care," Lockhart said, trying to pull the gun away from Berto's grip.

Berto held fast. "Señor, he may bring word from Miss Hannah. Let me go to him, and I will see what he say."

Lockhart drew in a deep breath. The Comanche had halted his horse just beyond the main yard. "Very well, but if he kills you, that will be the price you pay."

Juanita threw her husband a worried glance, but said nothing as he walked out to meet the Comanche. The two exchanged greetings with raised hands and then the Comanche handed Berto the very thing he'd been waving. Without waiting for Berto to reply, the brave kicked his horse into action as he wrenched the animal's neck hard to the left. In a flash, the pony and rider climbed over the hill and were gone. Berto opened what looked to be a letter and studied it for a moment before heading back to his wife and Lockhart.

Lockhart put away his gun and held out his hand. "What did he give you? Hand it over."

Berto put a letter in Lockhart's hand. "He say this is from Miss Hannah."

"It's probably some sort of ransom demand," he said, opening the folded paper. Scanning the note quickly, Lockhart could hardly believe what he read. The Comanche were suffering from smallpox. Hannah was helping the Indians and intended to stay on until they were on the mend. William Barnett was there assisting her and they were both well. She wanted to let the family know so they wouldn't worry should the two of them be absent for some time.

"What does it say?" Berto asked. "I cannot read English."

Herbert shook his head and threw the letter to the ground. "Maybe you should learn."

He stormed out across the yard and rounded the house as Andy Dandridge came out the front door. "Hey there, Mr. Lockhart. What are you doing here?"

"Apparently wasting my time," Lockhart replied in a clipped tone. He grabbed the reins of his horse and climbed into the saddle. His anger kept him from saying another word. Instead, Lockhart kicked the side of his mount and raced back down the road. He would deal with this matter in the only way those savages could understand. He knew where the local militia was and how he could garner their help. Those Comanche would rue the day they put his plans in jeopardy.

By Hannah's best guess it had to be nearing December. She had spent at least two weeks in the Comanche camp if her figures were correct. It was easy to lose track of time since her focus had been on the sick. William had worked nonstop to bury the dead with Red Dog and Running Buffalo and a few of the others who had recovered from their sickness.

Tradition normally would have dictated more ceremony, but they did well to create a plot for each body on the west side of the village, despite the rocky ground. Hannah was most grateful. The stench of death lessened considerably as the bodies were cared for, and she couldn't help but believe this would help the overall health of the camp.

For days Hannah had watched the burial process with a strange interest. The Comanche tradition was to bring a person's knees to their chest, arms on either side of the chest and head bent forward. There was generally a pit where the body was laid along with their weapons. The latter were broken first, Night Bear said, to indicate that the warrior's fighting days were done. However, He Who Walks in Darkness had told Hannah that he intended to go on warring in the afterlife, so it seemed beliefs were varied.

Generally a warrior's saddle and other belongings were buried with him, as well, so that he would have plenty of things for his life beyond this world. The Comanche fearlessly confronted the living, but the thought of spirits returning to wreak havoc due to improper burial was terrifying. Once again, superstition had a stronghold over the people.

It hadn't been easy to dig plots big enough for the bodies, much less all of the accompanying properties, but Mr. Barnett had been intent to see it done as best he could. Hannah was grateful that William was willing to help with this duty. She did what she could to prepare the body prior to its burial, but her time was needed with those still living.

The sounds and smells of life in a Comanche camp permeated even her dreams, though she longed for home and her brother and sister. But even so, Hannah had the strangest peace that she was doing exactly what God wanted her to do. Away from the responsibilities of the ranch, with nothing but time and isolation, she'd thought a great deal about who she had become while living on the Texas frontier. The girl she'd been back in Vicksburg would never have taken on such an endeavor. That girl was forever gone.

After a restless night, Hannah forced her eyes open and wondered at the time. William was gone, but that wasn't un-usual. He had taken to sleeping outside the tepee most nights, and only shared the confines of the shelter when the weather was bad. Hannah knew that normal circumstances would have made such an arrangement a great scandal, but Mr. Barnett had handled himself in a most gentlemanly manner. She could not fault him for his actions.

What she did fault him for was his past choices. She couldn't shake from her mind the fact that he'd been at Vicksburg—that he'd taken lives there. She knew that war required many sacrifices, but losing her brother and grandfather were not ones she easily accepted. Now perhaps her father had been imprisoned or killed, and that would be one more thing the war had taken from her.

Yawning, she forced herself to get up. She put on her boots, then rebraided her hair in a single plait. Her back ached from sleeping on the ground so long. She couldn't imagine how the Numunuu endured such a life. They did everything seemingly on the move. Horses were their pride and joy. Hannah had seen a good number of Indian ponies positioned just beyond the camp. Horses were used for trade and bartering as well as war, and the more ponies a warrior owned, the more respected he was. Hannah thought it rather an imbalanced life. Horses were important, but stability and proper houses were not.

Without warning, she heard shouts from outside and then blood-curdling yells filled the air. Gunfire followed, causing Hannah to jump to her feet. She hurried to see what was happening amidst the chaos and had just reached the flap of the tepee when someone came crashing through. Falling backwards, Hannah clung to the person who somehow seemed to roll to one side and take the impact of their fall.

It was then that Hannah saw that William Barnett was the man holding her. "What's happening?" she demanded.

Bullets zinged around them, cutting through the hide of the shelter. William pushed her head down against his chest and covered her.

"Soldiers," he managed to tell her above the din. "We're under attack by the Frontier Army."

Hannah felt a chill wash over her. How had the soldiers found them? Would they kill everyone or were they merely trying to frighten them?

"Hannah, listen to me," William said, taking hold of her face. "We need to get out of here. The ground slopes down to the river just behind the tepee. I'll cut our way out. Stay down on the ground and move toward the river once we're outside."

"But why? Why do we have to leave?" she asked. "They'll see that we are white and not harm us."

"They won't stop long enough to check skin color," he replied. "If you're living here, they're gonna figure you to be Comanche or else soiled by association. Now, come on." He released her and crawled on his belly toward the back of the room. Taking a knife from his boot, Hannah watched as he stabbed the hide and pulled downward.

More bullets passed through the tepee and the unmistakable smell of smoke left Hannah no doubt that the soldiers were setting fire to anything that would burn. Tears filled her eyes. This was murder, plain and simple, just as it was murder when the Comanche did it to the whites.

"Come on. Move." William motioned her toward the back. Hannah crawled as she'd seen him do and was soon at his side.

"I'll go first, then you follow right behind me. Keep moving and don't look back."

Hannah found it impossible to speak. She bit her lower lip to keep from crying out in fear amidst the screams and gunfire. All around her the world seemed to be coming to an end. Sharp rocks bit into her palms as she dragged herself through the opening. The ground sloped sharply nearly five feet from the tepee, and brush and rocks lined the edge of the ravine. She saw William slide over the edge and disappear. Had he fallen? She reached the place where he'd gone and found him waiting for her. He pulled her over the side without consideration of the terrain. Hannah cried out as her ribs hit the rocky wall.

William pressed her against the rock and held her there. But despite the measure of comfort she felt in his protection, fear enveloped her. She felt faint and worried about whether she might pass out.

After a few moments the gunfire slowed to only occasional shots. There were no more screams, and Hannah could only surmise that the Comanche were all dead. She couldn't stop her tears and hung her head so that Mr. Barnett would not see them.

As the gunfire ceased altogether, Hannah heard the bellowed orders from one of the soldiers. "Round those savages up. On the double-quick. Find the white hostages."

Hannah raised her head at this. "Hostages?"

William shook his head. "They most likely concern themselves with hostages anytime they raid a village. Even so, we'll try to make our way back into camp without getting shot and let them know that we aren't here against our will."

Hannah noted the warmth of his body as he held her. She liked the way he made her feel safe—as though nothing in the world could hurt her. When he released her to survey their surroundings, she felt a palpable loss. Why did she have feelings for this man—this man who confused and vexed her?

Helping Hannah back to the top of the ridge, William called out to the soldier's leader. "Captain! Captain, hold your fire!"

They stepped forward as a mounted officer moved toward them. "We're here to rescue you."

"We didn't need rescuing," Hannah said, pulling away from William. "These people are sick with smallpox. You had no need to ride in, guns blazing. You've surely killed innocent people."

"Beggin' your pardon, ma'am, but there is no such thing as an innocent Comanche."

She wanted to tell the man exactly what she thought of him, but William pulled her back in step with him. "Captain, Miss Dandridge is right. This village is sick with smallpox. Your men have risked their lives coming here."

"A soldier risks his life wherever the trail takes him," the man replied. "And who might you be?"

"William Barnett."

The man's eyes narrowed. "Heard tell of some Yankee sympathizers called Barnett. Seems they up and joined the Union to fight against Texas."

Hannah put herself in front of William at this point. "Sir, I wonder if you might have any water. I'm feeling faint." She put her hand to her forehead in the manner she'd seen many a young lady do in order to gain attention.

The captain jumped from the horse's back and pulled free his canteen from around the horn of his saddle. William, meanwhile, took hold of Hannah from behind to steady her.

"Here, take a drink," the captain ordered.

Hannah did just that. "Goodness," she said, lowering the canteen and her eyes. "The excitement has been just about too much for me." She reached out to the captain. "I am sorry for making such a fuss." She cautiously cast a glance toward William, whose raised brow and expression let her know that he was on to her game.

"Now, ma'am, why don't you sit for a moment and rest. I have to get back to the detail of rounding up these savages." He took the canteen and remounted the horse. "I'd appreciate it if you'd stay right here so that my men can do their job."

Hannah started to speak, but Barnett tightened his grip on her. Once the captain was far enough away, Hannah felt William loosen his hold. She turned and looked at him for a moment. The expression on his face was rather puzzling.

"Are you all right?" she asked.

"I'm fine."

"Well, I'm not. I cannot let those soldiers further harm the Numunuu." She started for the camp, but William pulled her back.

"Hannah, listen to me."

It was the second time he'd called her Hannah, and her heart was beating faster at the realization. She waited for him to continue.

"Those men aren't going to be sympathetic to your concern for the Numunuu. I think it best if you went on playing the sweet helpless belle for now. You're really rather good at it."

"You sound sarcastic," she said, "but it saved your neck."

"You have a very low opinion of me, Miss Dandridge."

Hannah ignored his tone. "What are they going to do to the survivors?" she asked. "What are they gathering them together for? Will they kill them?"

William shook his head as he looked back to where the soldiers were working. "I don't know." He turned back to face her. "But you cannot stop whatever they have planned."

"Well, I can't stand by and let them be murdered." She walked away from him, but William quickly caught up to her.

"Look, I don't know what happened, but I get the feeling these men are here because someone told them we were here."

She stopped and looked at him. "What are you saying?"

Barnett looked to where a handful of warriors were being forced to stand. Night Bear was at the front of the group. "I think someone found out about our being here and didn't much care for the idea. I think they probably told the soldiers we were being held captive."

"Who would do such a thing?"

"I don't know," he said, "but I intend to find out."

❧

Seeing that their hands were filled with the remaining Comanche, the captain gave only a token protest when William told him they were returning home. A few hours later, William and Hannah rode up to the Terrys' ranch house. They were both dirty and exhausted and neither had eaten since that morning. William helped Hannah from her horse and feared she might well crumple to the ground had he not held her fast for a moment.

She rallied and straightened. "I've heard of the Terrys, but I've not yet met them."

"Well, it's high time you did. They're good folks and your closest neighbor." William secured the horses. "We'll stay the night here if they don't mind, and knowing Ted and Marietta as I do . . . I'm pretty sure they won't."

He led the way to the front door. Ted Terry had spared no expense in the latest renovations of his home. Each time William visited, the place seemed more inviting than the last. When he'd been a boy of seventeen, the house had only been a small four-room building. Three years later Ted added a larger living room and kitchen. Five years later he gave Marietta an entire second floor. Having only been here a couple of weeks earlier, however, things were the same. The front porch wrapped around the house in white-washed welcome. The chairs there seemed to beckon a fellow to take a load off his feet and rest a spell. William had done that very thing, visiting with Ted and Marietta on many occasions prior to the war. Those days seemed so long ago.

He didn't get a chance to knock. The door opened and Ted Terry stood with lamp in hand. "Will, I didn't think to see you again so soon. Who have you brought with you?"

"Ted, this is Miss Hannah Dandridge. She's the one I told you about."

The older man smiled. "Welcome, Miss Dandridge. You two look done in. You'd best come inside and tell me what's happened."

William nudged Hannah toward the house and was glad that she didn't offer protest. Once inside, William explained their circumstances and why they'd come. Ted listened with his customary consideration, until his wife appeared.

"Goodness, Mr. Terry, why haven't you asked these folks to sit?" she questioned. She took one look at Hannah and frowned. "Child, you look positively spent. What does our Will mean by dragging you out here?"

"This is Miss Hannah Dandridge," William interjected. "She's the one staying at my . . . at the ranch." He looked to Hannah. "This is Mrs. Terry."

"Now, now. No sense in formalities. Call me Marietta."

"Marietta, Will was just tellin' me that they were up at Tierra del Diablo helping some sick Comanche when soldiers came in and slaughtered most of the living."

"There was a Comanche village that close by?" she asked with a shudder, then sobered even more. "And you two were up there? I can see there's a long story to be told, but not now. Miss Hannah is all but weaving on her feet. I'm going to put this child in a warm bath and then to bed."

William smiled at the motherly woman. "You'd better feed her, too. She hasn't had a whole lot to eat in the last two weeks."

Marietta shook her head and gave a *tsk*ing sound. "Well, we will see about that."

Hannah willingly went with the woman while William remained with Ted. He knew the older man would be able to offer some objective thought on the events of the day.

"Why don't you come with me to the kitchen, and we'll round you up something to eat and drink while you tell me about the parts you left out. This story seems a bit more complicated than you've let on."

"It's very complicated," William said, frowning. He followed Ted to the kitchen and sank into an offered chair. "I think someone sent the soldiers because of us, but I can't be sure."

"Why do you say that?" Ted motioned the cook to his aid. An older Mexican woman stepped forward and awaited instruction.

"*Hola*, Teresa," William greeted wearily.

"Hola, Mr. Will." She beamed him a toothy smile. The years had taken their toll on her body and face, but her teeth had remained intact and were her pride and joy.

"We need a plate of food and some hot coffee for Mr. Will. The missus is going to want a plate for our other guest, as well."

She nodded and went quickly to work as Ted pulled out the only other chair at the small table and took a seat. He looked to William, awaiting further explanation. William continued.

"Miss Dandridge went to help the Comanche when that wounded boy I told you about came to the ranch, asking her to come. I tracked them out to Tierra del Diablo and when I saw the mess, I stayed and helped, too. Many of the Numunuu were dead and needed burying. Several days ago we sent a letter back to the ranch letting them know where we were and that we were safe. The soldiers attacked the village at dawn today, and we were caught in the crossfire. Even so, once the commotion settled down, I heard the captain instruct his men to find the white hostages."

"Meaning you and Miss Dandridge?"

"That's what I think."

Teresa placed a cup of steaming coffee in front of him. William took a long drink before continuing. "It was almost like they knew who they were looking for. I know they always look for white hostages anytime they attack an Indian village, but this made it sound like they knew we were there."

"But who would have sent the soldiers? Your people wouldn't have done that, would they?"

William took another drink and nearly finished off the contents. "No," he said, putting the cup down. "They wouldn't have."

"Maybe the soldiers had been tracking that band. You know they are working to quell the uprisings. There are so many bands out there wreaking havoc on the settlers that the army had to step in and put it down."

"I know that, but we were well hidden."

"Yet you found them," Ted countered. "You aren't the only one who can read tracks."

He let out a heavy sigh as Teresa place a plate of food in front of him. "Gracias." She picked up the cup and went to refill it as William continued. "So you think this was just some coincidence?"

"Now, Will, you know I don't believe in happenstance. God has a plan for everything. He knows where we're going to be at any given time, and He has foreknowledge of all that will happen. You were there for a reason, and those soldiers came for a reason. God alone knows what those purposes were."

"Sure wish He'd let me in on it," William said, picking up his fork.

"You stop fighting Him and surrender, and He just might," Ted said with a mischievous smile. "You think He doesn't know that you're angry with Him right now. You think you're somehow keeping God in the dark—that He hasn't a clue what's in your heart, but He knows it all, William. He knows why you're fighting Him and He knows just what it's going to take to bring you back in line. And, in time . . . you're going to know it, too."

"That's what I'm afraid of," William said, stabbing a piece of beef steak. "That's exactly what I'm afraid of."

Marietta kept Hannah company as she ate her supper in bed. The older woman had insisted it be done this way, and Hannah was too tired to argue.

"You're very fortunate to have someone like Will around to help you," Marietta said, working with a crochet hook to make a shawl.

Hannah watched the woman's nimble fingers quickly manage the blue yarn. She considered her words carefully. "He is rather . . . imposing."

Laughter was not what Hannah had expected from Marietta Terry. The woman looked up from her work and shook her head. "I've heard William Barnett called devoted and responsible, but never imposing. Why don't you tell me why you feel that way?"

Again, Hannah wondered just how much she could say. The Terrys were, after all, good friends of William's family. They were also her closest neighbors, if a person could call seven miles away close.

"He just strikes me as . . . determined. Perhaps that's a better word. He knows what he wants and believes his way to be best."

Marietta nodded. "He's a smart one, that Will. Even as a very young man he seemed to understand this land better than his pa or his brother. Their ma, God rest her soul, doted on him. I think that was because the older boy was his father's shadow. The two sons were quite different. William was always so considerate . . . you might even say softhearted. I've seen him go out of his way many a time to offer some kindness. Before this war broke out, I don't think the man had an enemy at all. Folks knew him to be reliable and helpful, and out here, that's more valued than gold."

Hannah thought for a moment about Marietta's statement. William Barnett had been quite helpful to her, and she supposed he was reliable, as well. "Why did he go off to war?"

With a frown, Marietta ceased her crocheting. "His pa had it in his mind that it was their duty to go. Ted tried to tell him that sending one son to fight was more than enough, but Jason Barnett never did anything by halves. He said not only would Lyle go to fight, but William and he would go, as well. They would make a formidable trio—at least that's what he told Ted. Poor Lucy would have been beside herself, had she still been alive. I think it was the only time I've ever been glad she was gone. She was a dear friend and I miss her more than I can tell you. We only had a very short time together, but that woman packed a lot of love into those two years."

"How did she die?" Hannah asked.

"She took sick one winter. I think it was early December. Some sort of grippe. Will's pa and brother were off dealing with some calving cows. They'd left Will to break some horses, but instead, he was with her the whole time. She died with him at her side—holding her hand."

Hannah could well imagine Mr. Barnett—William—sitting beside his mother, trying his best to nurse her back to health. "My mother died when I was fourteen," she murmured. "I was there when she passed on. My brother was, too. He was twelve. The doctors said she had a 'poor constitution.' I think it was their way of saying they didn't know what killed her."

"How long ago was that?" Marietta asked.

"Ten years—1853."

"Why, that's the same year that Will lost his ma. You two have a great deal in common."

Not wanting to hear about common ground with William Barnett, Hannah hurried to change the subject. "The Barnetts fought for the North. Wasn't that rather strange?" Hannah nibbled on the corn bread Marietta had slathered in butter and pretended the answer wasn't important.

"It isn't so strange considering folks in Texas can be pretty diverse when it comes to where their loyalties lie. Mostly folks here are for the preservation of Texas. Those that have been here as long as Ted and me remember when Texas was its own country. If you take a good look around, you'll see that there are a good number of people supporting the Union. Some quite boldly and others in a more covert manner. Sometimes whole towns are favoring the North rather than the South."

"My father definitely supported the Confederacy. Of course, now he may be captured or even dead."

"Will mentioned that on his earlier visit. I've been praying for your father ever since."

"I have no idea of what I'll do if he's dead." Hannah shook her head. "Especially if the ranch goes back to Mr. Barnett."

"Well, it is his ranch. The state had no right to take it from the family. I think once this war is settled it will be set right again."

"That's what I'm afraid of, too. And if my father is gone, that leaves me with my brother and sister to raise. I have no way to support them." Hannah had no idea of why she was telling Marietta Terry, very nearly a complete stranger, all of this information. Somehow the woman just put her at ease and it felt right.

"Mr. Lockhart of Cedar Springs has proposed I marry him. He said he would take care of us, but I don't love him."

"You shouldn't ever marry a man you don't love. Hard times come in every marriage, and if you don't have love to hold you together you're going to have a bad time of it."

"Mr. Lockhart has implied that my father had approved him as suitor and husband. I couldn't say if that was true or not. My father changed a great deal after the death of my mother, but even more so after my stepmother died. A kind of bitterness overtook him, and the man I knew was suddenly more demanding and far less kind. Even my grandparents were shocked by his behavior and choices. I don't think I knew him at all these last few years."

"Death can certainly change a man," Marietta replied. "I

know losing his mother was hard on Will. He bore a heavy sorrow in her passing."

Hannah nodded. "It must have been hard for him, especially if his mother was the one who truly understood him."

Marietta put aside her crochet work, tucking it into a small basket at her feet. "William needs a good woman in his life. The war was hard on him. He had no heart for it."

Hannah frowned. "I suppose no one really has a heart for it."

"But Will less than others. He's always been a man of peace. He wasn't given to fighting and drinking with the other men. His father and brother could be quite the ruffians when they chose to be, but not Will. He always seemed far more sensible. I think his father worried this made Will soft, but I think it just made him considerate. And that goes a long ways with me." She shook her head. "The War Between the States has separated a lot of good families from their loved ones. I'd expect you've probably lost someone, as well."

"My brother and grandfather were killed defending Vicksburg."

Marietta gave her a sympathetic smile. "You have endured so much for one so young."

Hannah finished with the tray and leaned back against the pillows. "It amazes me still that you can have both Yankee and Confederate support in the same state. I was born in Vicksburg and they were most decidedly in favor of the South. I thought— and upon reflection I can see the naïveté in my thinking—but I presumed if a state sided with the Confederacy, the people would also."

Marietta picked up the basket at her feet, then hoisted up the tray and smiled. "That would be logical thinking in most states, but Texas isn't most states. We're still more like a country all our own. If you stick around, you'll learn that for yourself." She smiled. "You get some rest now. I'll check in on you later and make sure you're warm enough."

"Yes, ma'am."

"And Hannah," Marietta said, pausing at the door, "don't be marrying someone just out of fear for the future. You need to remember that God will provide. You and your brother and sister can always come here and stay a spell with Ted and me. We like having folks around. Our children are all grown and living elsewhere now, so your little family would be a welcome addition."

Hannah could hardly believe that this woman would extend such an invitation to a stranger. Marietta's kindness touched Hannah's heart and gave her a reassuring peace that defied words.

"Thank you."

Marietta nodded, then blew out the lamp and, juggling her basket and the tray, managed to close the door as she left.

Hannah slid further down and felt the warmth of the quilt wrap around her like loving arms. It had been so long since she'd slept in a bed. With a sigh, she closed her eyes and thanked God for being clean and fed and warm. Then, with a memory of the soldiers marching the Comanche off to the reservation, Hannah frowned.

I wish I could have stopped them. I wish I could have done something to save the Numunuu. O God, she prayed silently, *Night Bear looked so weak and betrayed. Father, please strengthen him and help him to understand that we didn't want this any more than he did.*

The memories of the battle were almost more than she could handle. The scenes replayed themselves out over and over, and when it was all done there were no more than eight living souls who survived the attack, ten counting Mr. Barnett and herself. What would happen to them now?

"What will happen to any of us?" she whispered in the dark.

⁂

William was glad to be home at last. He'd felt a sense of unrest ever since the attack the previous morning on the Numunuu camp and longed for the solitude of the ranch. Tyler and the soldiers had also recently returned from collecting cattle, and were more than a little anxious to begin their trek east with the animals.

"Now that you're back, we need to leave as soon as possible," Tyler told him. "It's getting more and more dangerous, and if this is going to work, we need to get a move on."

"I know. I was already figuring that. What I can't understand is how the soldiers found the Numunuu camp."

"Well, it's good riddance, I say." Tyler's lip curled in anger.

"I can't figure out how they knew we were there in the first place," William continued. "They didn't call us by name, but they knew there were white people in that village. After the fight, the captain told his men to find the white hostages. I heard it myself. Later, when the captain learned our names, he wasn't surprised by it or wondering where we'd come from. Instead, he tried to bring up how my family fought for the North."

"What did you do?"

"Nothing. Miss Dandridge interceded by pretending to have the vapors or whatever it is women have when they faint dead away."

"She fainted?"

"No, but she gave a good impression of heading that way." He smiled. "She really is something else."

Tyler laughed long and loud. William saw Berto headed their way and elbowed his friend to quiet down. "I don't want to have to explain to Berto what it is that's amused you—especially seeing as how I'm afraid to know the reason myself."

"We are glad to have you returned," Berto told William. "We were not able to read your letter in full, until Mr. Tyler come here. Mr. Lockhart, he would not tell us what you said."

"What do you mean?" William asked.

"It seems Lockhart was here when the letter arrived via your Comanche messenger," Tyler interjected. "Berto told me he read the letter, threw it to the ground, and left."

"Well, maybe that explains the soldiers." William shook his head. "Lockhart hates the Comanche only mildly more than he hates me. That letter explained our whereabouts and Lockhart probably called out the militia."

"If that's the case, we'd best leave with our steer tonight. No telling what he'll do if he sees what we're up to."

"I can't imagine that a strong Confederate supporter like Lockhart would interfere with such a patriotic task. He might hate me, but I doubt he would extend that hatred to the Confederacy. After all, he's in this war for what he can get out of it. I heard that he's been buying up properties all around."

Tyler nodded. "Yeah, he tried to approach my family about our ranch, but like Grandpa told him, the ranch is mine now— even if there's nothing but charred remains."

"Still, I wouldn't expect resistance from him when it comes to our efforts to help the starving Confederacy."

"There's no telling," Tyler said. "I do know I've worked too hard to see this fall apart now. If we can make this work, it can become a regular run, as far as I'm concerned. I'll see to it that you get paid, of course."

William ignored the comment. He wasn't at all certain he wanted to get into a routine of sneaking cattle to Louisiana. He sighed as he realized his plans for sleeping on the ranch that night were all but a dream. "Berto, can we have things ready in order to leave tonight?"

"I think so. You tell Juanita that you will need food and supplies. She will pack them. I will go help Mr. Tyler get the other things you will need."

"I guess we'll head out once it's dark."

He made his way to the house. Inside he found the children working on their studies in the front room. Andy jumped up at the sight of him.

"Hey, Will. I heard Hannah telling Juanita that you saved her life when the soldiers attacked the Indians. You're a hero like in a book."

William frowned. "Not exactly, Andy." He didn't want to dwell on the horrors of that battle. "I need to talk to Juanita, but I wanted to tell you it looks like you did a fine job of taking care of the house and family. The ranch looks to be in good order."

Andy seemed to grow a foot. "I did what you said. I was real good."

"I was, too," Marty declared. "I filled the water barrels every day."

"You did not," Andy countered. "You helped us once. You cried the whole time about how hard it was."

Marty's lower lip started to quiver and William could see a good cry was on its way. "Whoa there, Andy. I'd say Miss Marty did a good job to help even once. I don't like the womenfolk having to go down to the river so far from the house. It's not safe." He reached over and gave Marty a pat on the head. "You did real good, Miss Marty. When I get back, Andy, we're gonna have to see if we can't get a new well dug. It's a lot of bother to have to get our water from the river."

Marty seemed appeased and Andy had something new to think about. William found that he liked the brother and sister duo more than he wanted to admit. They were well brought up—Hannah had done a good job with them. She'd make a great mother to her own children one day.

The thought startled William. "You two get back to your studies now. I won't have your sister saying I kept you from learning." With that he left and headed down the hall to the kitchen, trying hard not to think of Hannah with a babe in arms. Reaching the kitchen, he could hear Hannah and Juanita discussing something quite intently and paused at the open archway to listen in.

"Mr. Lockhart, he was mad that you were gone with Mr. Will. He would not read the letter to us. Andy helped us to know some of the words, but Mr. Tyler had to read it to us later."

"I'm sorry about that, Juanita. I honestly didn't even think about the fact that you can't read English. I should have written it very simplistically so that Andy could read the entire thing. Anyway, Mr. Lockhart is only angry because he supposes that he will lose the chance to marry me if Mr. Barnett spends too much time with me. I've tried to explain that Mr. Barnett is not at all interested in me nor I in him. Still, Mr. Lockhart has proposed marriage."

"But you do not love him."

"I know that." Her voice sounded sad, almost resigned. Her next statement confirmed this to Will. "But if Father is dead, I may have no other choice. For the sake of Andy and Marty, I may have to forget about love and marry in order to keep them safe. Mrs. Terry said some things that make me more convinced that the ranch should go back to Mr. Barnett. If that happens, I don't know what I'll do. Mrs. Terry said the children and I could stay with them, but I hardly think that's the right thing to do."

"It not the right thing to marry a man you do not love."

With this William decided to interrupt. The idea of Hannah marrying anyone, much less Herbert Lockhart, was more than he wanted to contemplate. "Ladies, I'm sorry to cut in like this, but Tyler and I have decided we need to move the cattle tonight. We'll need supplies made ready."

"But you've only just returned from a wearying journey. You labored ceaselessly in the Numunuu camp, and I know your leg has been bothering you," Hannah replied.

"It can't be helped. Tyler and I feel that if we don't move out, we may get caught before we can get away."

"I already work to put together food for your trip," Juanita said, smiling. "I have it ready."

William smiled. "I kind of figured you might. We'll leave when it gets dark." He turned to Hannah. "With all of us gone, you'll no doubt feel like things are back to normal."

"I'm not sure what normal is anymore, Mr. Barnett. I'm not sure at all."

19

December 1863

"Gentlemen," Herbert Lockhart began, "we are visionaries, and as such we are often called upon to take great risks. The war will be over soon enough, but until that time we must take advantage of our circumstances."

He smiled at the six Dallas businessmen gathered in his office. "The area surrounding Dallas will no doubt see a huge boom after the war, and we will be a part of that. By securing the real estate surrounding the town proper, we will be in a good position to make a fortune."

"But every day we've seen more and more people pull up stakes and leave," one of the men spoke up. "The town is becoming deserted."

"True," Lockhart admitted, "but the end of the war will bring significant change. Now, we might not see that fortune for several years, but I have to believe it will come quickly enough.

However, with our currency continuing to be devalued by the rest of the world, we must act now to secure our position."

Walking to his desk, Lockhart picked up a stack of papers. "I have reviewed the reports that you brought. It looks like we're doing quite well. The most important pieces of property have been secured. I have had Mr. Wentworth draw up a map revisiting the possible routes for a main railroad line as well as the spur lines. Mr. Wentworth, if you would be so kind as to explain."

A middle-aged man got to his feet and tucked the watch he'd been checking into his pocket. "I believe after the war we will see a huge development in Southern railroads. The political talk definitely focuses on this one issue more than others. For us, the most important lines will be those that can connect Dallas to our capital and to the seaports, as well as to our sister states in the East."

"And where will the funding for such a project come from?" one of the other men asked. "Even if we manage to secure our position as the Confederate States of America, we will be steeped in war debt."

"That is true enough, but . . ."

Lockhart took his seat and ignored the ongoing debate. His mind was on more pressing matters, such as when and how he would tell Hannah Dandridge that her father was dead. So much time had already elapsed and here it was early December. The young woman had to already realize the likelihood that her father was deceased. However, he would make it easy on them all and let them know this fact for certain. It would be cruel to keep them guessing. Besides, Hannah might never consider his proposal seriously unless she knew there was no other hope of survival.

He had altered his plans several times, even creating another letter supposedly from her father. In this latest version the letter suggested that someone else had written it on behalf of her dying father. Thus, the handwriting needn't be an exact replica of John Dandridge. This had greatly relieved Herbert, who found his forging abilities better for small tasks such as signatures.

The Christmas season would only serve to enhance his position. He knew this would be a time of great family focus for the Dandridges. Hannah would be heartbroken over the loss of her father. She would need his comfort and strength. She would need a strong man to take charge of the situation.

An image of William Barnett came to mind. He had been a thorn in Lockhart's side since his return to the ranch. Lockhart had hoped to see him killed in the attack on the Comanche village, but that hadn't been the case. He frowned and realized all of his business associates were looking at him.

"Do you not agree, Mr. Lockhart?"

He shook his head. "I do apologize. I'm afraid other business momentarily distracted me. What was it you were asking?"

"I merely suggested," Mr. Wentworth explained, "that without railroads to move the cattle and other commodities that we can offer, the expenses would make the trips unmanageable. Cattle being driven for miles and miles to destinations far from their place of origin are always a risk. Not only do you stand to see the death of a small percent of cattle, but there are the Indians and weather to be factored in. Moving the herd too fast could also mean a loss of weight, and unless there is time to fatten them before sale, it would mean a greatly reduced price per head. If we control the railroads here, then we can also set the prices for such cattle deliveries. It will be extremely profitable for us, and less so for those who have no stake in our arrangement."

"I do agree," Lockhart said. "Railroads are imperative if this state is going to flourish and reach its fullest potential."

"But we have our ports, as well," another man declared. "Perhaps we should consider shipping via the water routes to be our main focus."

The meeting went on for another two hours before the men agreed to adjourn for the day. Lockhart had arranged a fine supper for them. "If you'll make your way to the hotel dining room, I believe Mrs. Englewood has prepared a sumptuous feast for us."

The men were only too happy to oblige. Lockhart hurried to secure some papers before joining them and was just about to lock up when a man appeared at the door. He recognized him immediately.

With his dark features and grizzled expression, Jesse Carter looked quite menacing. "Boss, I got somethin' you may want to hear."

Lockhart nodded and pushed the door open. "Let's go inside."

The man followed Lockhart into the dark office. He stunk of cigars, horse sweat, and body odor. Lockhart wanted to suggest the man use some of his pay to get a bath and a shave, but wisely held his tongue.

"So what is it you need to tell me?"

Carter leaned against the wall and grinned. "I heard tell that William Barnett and his bunch have been rounding up cattle. Heard they mean to drive them someplace, but nobody seems to know where or when."

Lockhart narrowed his gaze. "I see. Well, they certainly can't take them far—at least not legally." He tossed the man a coin. "I don't know what—if anything—this will lead to, but it may afford us an opportunity to put an end to Mr. Barnett's interference once and for all. Keep your eyes and ears open. If you find out where they plan to take the cattle, let me know."

⁓

Hannah looked at the letter Berto placed in her hands. He had gone to town and brought back a few meager pickings from the general store. This letter had been waiting. The return address was her grandparents' house in Vicksburg. Her heart began to beat at a quickened pace. Father! It had to be from him. She tore open the tattered envelope and pulled the single page free. She scanned the lines quickly and dropped to a nearby chair.

"She is dead. My grandmother is dead."

"Your father—he is all right?"

"No. I don't know. The letter was written by a local pastor. It's dated back in October." She looked up at Berto, tears streaming down her face. "The pastor regrets that Father could not be there, but assures him that Grandmother received a proper burial. She was laid to rest beside my grandfather."

Hannah felt as if someone had knocked the wind from her. For some reason, the arrival of this letter only served to convince her that her father most likely was dead. Surely if he were alive, he would have found a way to get word to her. If the Yankees were questioning him, they could easily have proven his story.

"I am so sorry, Miss Hannah. It is a sad day." Berto told her. "I get Juanita to be with you."

He hurried away, no doubt uncomfortable with her tears. Hannah wiped her cheeks with the edge of her apron. She felt so alone. Christmas was in three days, but she didn't feel at all like celebrating.

"Miss Hannah, Berto tell me about your *abuela*. I am so very sorry." Juanita knelt on the floor beside Hannah's chair, her orange-and-brown skirt swirling around her like the petals of a flower. Juanita gently touched Hannah's hand. "You are not alone."

Hannah startled at her words. How could Juanita know her thoughts so clearly? "I feel alone," she said, fighting to keep her voice even. "I feel abandoned. Why would God allow this to happen?"

"I do not know," the woman replied in a gentle voice. "But I know God see all. He see you here in sadness and He see your father, wherever he is."

"But God isn't helping us. It's like He has stopped listening. I prayed for my grandmother and for my father. I prayed that God would strengthen my grandmother and give her back her health so that she could come here and live with us. I've missed her so much, and now she's gone."

Folding the letter and stuffing it into her pocket, Hannah tried to figure out what she should or shouldn't say to the children. Thomas Early had taken Andy to get a Christmas tree, and Pepita and Marty were busy checking on the dairy cows. Nellie, usually their best milk producer, was due to calve any day. The girls were keeping close tabs on the cow's situation.

"We won't say anything to the children until after Christmas. They deserve to have a nice day even if I do not feel like celebrating." She dried her eyes again and drew a deep breath. "I want them to enjoy themselves."

"Sí, we say nothing," Juanita agreed.

Hannah nodded. "We will make cookies this afternoon, just as we planned. Thomas Early said he knew a draw where there was a scraggly pine. When he and Andy get back with it, we'll decorate it."

"I have popped some corn just as you ask. It will be ready for them to string," Juanita declared.

"Good." Hannah got to her feet. "We need to be as cheery as possible for the children."

Christmas morning dawned bright and cold. Hannah had been awakened early by the children. She didn't mind, however. They were eager for their gifts and for the joy of the day. She only hoped she could maintain a façade of happiness for their sake.

"It looks just like my dress," Marty announced after opening her last Christmas present. She held up the matching doll dress and laughed. "Now we can look alike."

"I'm glad you like it." Hannah felt her spirits perk up just a bit at the joy she saw in the children's expressions.

"I wish Pa would come home," Andy said, staring out the window.

"I do too, Andy," Hannah said, glancing at the clock. She'd arranged for Berto to bring Andy's Christmas present around to the back at exactly seven o'clock. The chimes began to ring and Hannah got to her feet.

"Andy, I believe there is one more Christmas present for you. I left it out back."

He looked at her with great expectation. "Another present—for me?"

"I want another present," Marty declared.

"You have plenty there," Hannah said, pointing to the girl's collection. Besides the clothes and outfits for her dolls, some candy, and some hair ribbons, Marty was now the owner of a small rocking chair. "Come on, let's go out back and see if you like it."

The trio made their way through the house, and when they reached the back door, Hannah made Andy close his eyes. She led him outside, putting a finger to her lips to remind Marty to be quiet. The little girl couldn't help herself, however. She let out a gasp of excitement, which in turn caused Andy to open his eyes.

When he did Hannah very nearly laughed out loud. His mouth dropped to his chest and his eyes widened.

"A horse! For me! And a saddle!" Andy ran to where Berto held the animal. The horse, a sixteen-year-old buckskin, very patiently endured Andy's petting and excited discussion. "He's really mine?"

"Yes," Hannah said, "but for now you mustn't try to ride him without someone helping you. You need to learn how to properly care for him, too. Berto has agreed to show you how in his spare time."

"Will said he'd show me how to ride," Andy declared. "But Berto can start me and then Will can show me the rest."

Hannah felt her chest tighten. She'd longed all of yesterday for Mr. Barnett's company, although she would never have admitted it to anyone. She found herself trying to imagine where he might be on the journey east and whether or not he'd encountered problems. What if he never came back? The thought caused a wave of emotion to envelop her body, but for the life of her Hannah couldn't figure out why. She knew she had developed feelings for him, but it seemed ridiculous that they should be so strong.

"Would you like to try him out?" Berto asked. "His name is Dusty."

Andy nodded. "Can I, Hannah?" he asked, looking over to her.

Smiling, Hannah knew there was no possible option of saying no. "Of course. But only with Berto's help."

Berto hoisted Andy into the saddle and motioned to the horn. "You hold on there and I keep the reins for now. I will lead him."

"Now I'm a real rancher," Andy said, his voice full of pride.

"I'm a rancher, too," Marty said. "I can rope and I have my own horse."

Hannah shook her finger. "Martha Dandridge, what have I told you about telling tall tales."

"It's not a tall tale. I saw a horse in the pen and I decided that one was mine."

"You can't simply decide a horse is yours, Marty. Most of the horses here belong to the ranch—to Mr. Barnett."

"They belong to Pa," Andy said, looking confused.

Hannah realized she'd opened a can of worms that weren't likely to get closed again. "We'll talk about it all later. Berto, why don't you take Andy down the road just a bit and then come on back."

"I wanna ride all day," Andy said.

"Today is Christmas, Andy. Berto needs to be with his children and Juanita," Hannah replied. "You will have plenty of time to learn to ride. For now, just enjoy what you have."

Her own advice echoed in her ears. *For now, just enjoy what you have.* Such a simple statement. Why was it so hard to heed?

"Miss Hannah," Juanita called to her.

Turning, Hannah saw that the woman was holding something out to her. "This is for you. *Feliz Navidad.*"

"Merry Christmas to you, Juanita." Hannah was surprised by the gift. She had given Juanita a small mirror and hairbrush for her present the night before. She certainly hadn't expected a gift in return.

"I make this for you. I sew it each night and pray for you. I finish it last night."

Hannah unfolded the present to find a beautifully embroidered Mexican blouse similar to the ones Juanita often wore on special occasions.

"Oh, it's beautiful. Juanita, I'm deeply touched." The workmanship was something to marvel at. Juanita's delicate stitches were crafted in a variety of roses and vining leaves. They edged the neckline, where a drawstring could be loosened and tightened. "I don't know when I've ever seen anything quite so lovely. And that you would spend your family time making this for me—praying for me . . ." Hannah felt the words stick in her throat. "Thank you," she managed before feeling completely incapable of speaking.

"I like the colors," Marty said, pointing to the flowers against the white cotton material.

"I make you one someday," Juanita promised.

Marty clapped her hands. "And make one for my dolly, too. That way we can look the same."

Berto led the horse and Andy back to where they started from. Hannah started to call out to the boy as he kicked out of the stirrups, but there wasn't time. Andy threw himself forward and slid down the side of the gelding, landing flat on his bottom. Luckily, the horse stood completely still.

He looked up in surprise. "Will doesn't fall down when he does that."

"You aren't Mr. Barnett," Hannah declared, helping him to his feet. "You mustn't show off around an animal this size."

"Your sister is right. A horse can be very dangerous, Andy. You must respect him."

The boy nodded. "I will. I promise."

Later that evening, Andy continued to chatter on and on about the horse. It seemed Dusty was like the brother he'd never had. Andy had all sorts of adventures planned for them, and Marty was extremely jealous. Hannah comforted her by reminding the little girl that one day she, too, would be old enough for a horse. Then Hannah qualified it.

"If you study hard and learn as well as Andy has, then you will prove you are ready for such endeavors."

"I'll learn my sums and my reading," Marty promised.

"Speaking of reading," Hannah said, "why don't you two go get ready for bed and I will read you the Christmas story. After all, this day is really about Jesus."

"Baby Jesus," Marty added. "He was a baby."

"Yes, He came to earth as a baby," Hannah agreed.

"Did He have a horse?" she asked.

"I don't think so. The wise men brought Jesus presents, but it doesn't say anything about a horse."

"I don't reckon they had a lot of horses," Andy said. "Mary and Joseph were poor. They had to sleep in the barn, remember?"

"I do remember they slept with the animals," Hannah replied. "And I don't remember any mention of horses. There were probably sheep and cows though."

"What about kittens? You said we could get two kittens after Christmas," Marty reminded her.

Hannah smiled. "The kittens are still too young to be away from their mother, but when they are ready we will have two of them." Miss Overbrook, the schoolmarm in town, had offered the gift when Hannah last saw her. Apparently Miss Overbrook's cat had given birth to a litter of eight kittens that she was determined to place in good homes.

"Did baby Jesus have kittens?" Marty asked.

"I don't believe so," Hannah replied.

Andy joined in. "They didn't have kittens, but they had a donkey. Mary rode on a donkey to Bethlehem."

"Did she now?" Hannah asked. "And how do you know that?"

"Well, didn't the preacher say that when we went to church last year?" Andy asked. "He said that Joseph had to pay a tax and he and Mary went to Bethlehem."

"Yes, that's true," Hannah said, impressed that Andy remembered so much. "But what if they had to walk the whole way? It really doesn't say. She might have had a donkey to ride, but she might have had to walk."

"How far away did they have to go?"

Hannah shook her head. "I don't know for sure, but it was far and probably took them a long time. It couldn't have been easy for either one, but especially not easy for Mary because she was going to have a baby."

"Like Nellie," Marty threw in. She was still most impatient for the cow to give birth. With great excitement, Marty appeared to get an idea. "Maybe they took a wagon."

Hannah shrugged, finding herself cheered by this new game. "Perhaps they did. Or maybe they got rides along the trail from other people."

"Yeah, like when Pa sees someone walkin' to town and he lets them climb in the back of the wagon."

"Exactly."

"It's hard to climb up there sometimes," Marty said, "but easier than walking."

"Do you think they had cowboys in Bethlehem?" Andy asked Hannah.

"I don't know. There were cows, so someone had to tend them. But I don't think they called them cowboys. Remember, most folks around here don't care for that title, so they might not have liked it then, either."

"David was a shepherd," Andy said, yawning. "He took care of sheep. Maybe there were cow shepherds, too."

Marty nodded and repeated the term. "Cow shepherds."

Hannah smiled. "There might have been. But it's getting late and I see two very sleepy children. Go on and get ready for bed and we'll read the Christmas story one more time."

Andy came and gave her a hug and Marty followed suit. "I sure wish Pa were here," Andy said.

"Me too," Marty added.

"That makes three of us, and I'm certain Papa wishes he were with us, as well," Hannah replied. "Now scoot."

She watched them climb the ladder to the loft and sighed. Her life was on a course she'd never imagined. So many unanswered questions haunted her.

"Please, God, help us. Help me. I don't know which way to turn." She whispered the prayer, but glanced to the loft just in case her words were overheard. The last thing she wanted was to spoil this otherwise wonderful day with her doubt.

20

Marty came running as if the barn were afire. "Nellie's havin' her . . . her baby, Hannah. Berto said . . . he said . . . to tell you the hooves are sticking out!" The breathless child didn't wait to see if Hannah had even heard, but turned to race back to the barn.

Hannah had been helping Juanita make tortillas and quickly wiped the corn flour concoction from her hands. She smiled at Juanita. "Hopefully I'll be back soon." She had known only one previous delivery, and it took more than an hour even at this stage of the labor.

Hannah looked up at the dull gray skies. The temperature had dropped again. She was grateful for her warm coat and pulled it close. Inside the barn was only marginally warmer, but the dim lighting made it harder to see.

"She's over here," Andy announced. "She's not lying down yet."

Hannah walked to the small birthing pen. Nellie, a black-and-white Holstein, had been purchased along with two other milk cows when the Dandridges had moved to the ranch. The cows had been bred to deliver at different times in order to ensure a good supply of milk, and Nellie was the second of the three to calve.

"See the hooves?" Andy questioned.

Hannah did indeed spy the little calf's hooves. Nellie seemed to hunch forward a bit and her tail stuck straight out behind her as another contraction seized her. Then the cow relaxed a bit and flicked her tail wildly as if to announce she'd had entirely enough of the whole procedure. Hannah couldn't imagine the pain the poor animal must be enduring. Nellie moved around the pen, rubbing her head against the barn wall and then the stall door. She paced and paced, then hunched again as her body tried to expel the calf.

This time the head appeared and Nellie determined it was time to go to the ground. For a large animal in the middle of laboring, Hannah thought the cow rather graceful in her descent. For a short while it seemed that everything had stopped. The calf was neither born nor unborn. Hannah watched in fascination as Nellie pushed once again.

"It will not be long now," Berto told her in a hushed voice.

A little bit more of the calf appeared, but not fast enough to suit Nellie. She jumped up to her feet and paced the pen with the calf dangling behind her. Then without warning she plopped back to the straw-covered floor and with two more pushes managed to finally expel the calf from her body. For a moment it seemed everyone held their breath. The calf just lay there without moving. Hannah wondered if it were dead.

As if in answer, Nellie bellowed and got up. She immediately set to licking the still calf. Within a matter of seconds, there was a flicker of life and then movement. The children cheered and Hannah felt like doing the same. What a wonder it was to watch new life begin.

"Is it a boy or a girl?" Marty asked.

"We can't tell just yet," Hannah said. "The baby hasn't gotten up on its feet. It will be a little while before that happens." But already the infant was straining to move. The insistent massage of Nellie's tongue did wonders to stimulate the baby.

Another ten minutes passed and then another. The calf struggled to get to its feet, but continued to fall down. Marty and Andy giggled at the hilarious display. The poor thing simply hadn't gotten used to having legs. About twenty minutes after its birth, however, the calf managed a wobbly stand. It was just long enough for Berto to announce it was a boy.

Andy gave a whoop. "Now we can raise a bull."

Hannah hadn't considered what would become of the calf. The other had been quickly passed off to another ranch, and Hannah had no idea what had become of it. She knew that on a ranch, however, an animal had to earn its keep or it couldn't stay.

"We'll have to see, Andy."

"Can we pet the baby?" Marty asked.

Berto shook his head. "This mama, she protect her calf. She get mean if you touch her baby."

"Come on back to the house," Hannah said, realizing just how cold her feet had become. The children had been out there a lot longer and were no doubt even colder. "Juanita made Mexican chocolate for you. It should be ready."

Andy and Marty liked the idea of this treat and hurried to follow Hannah into the house. They chattered all the way about what to call the new calf. By the time they were seated at the kitchen table with their drinks, Marty decided they should call the calf Cocoa.

"But that sounds like a girl's name," Andy protested. "Besides, he's not brown. He's black and white."

"Mostly black," Marty declared.

Andy's face lit up. "Then let's call him Blacky."

"I like that," Marty agreed and the matter was settled.

Hannah had already gone back to work making balls of the corn flour mixture so that they could press them into tortillas. Juanita had taken off the largest of the stove's iron burner plates and positioned a large round-bottomed pan over the open flame. She was busy frying the pressed tortillas and setting them aside to cool. The warmth of the stove made the work far more enjoyable, given the cold temperature outside.

"Hannah, do you think it might snow this year?" Andy asked.

"It's always possible, but not too likely. Frankly, it's more than cold enough for me. I'll be glad for the warmth of spring and summer."

A loud knock on the front door interrupted their conversation. Hannah once again wiped her hands. This time, however, she discarded her apron in order to be presentable to company. She made her way to the door and opened it to find Herbert Lockhart on the other side. Hannah tried not to show her immediate feelings. She was still certain he'd had something to do with the arrival of the army at the Numunuu camp, but wasn't yet ready to question him on it.

"Mr. Lockhart, this is a surprise. What brings you out here today?"

"I'm afraid it's bad news," he said. "Might I come in and explain?"

Hannah felt almost frozen in place. She nodded but didn't step back. "Have you . . . did you hear something . . . about Father?"

He nodded. "Please. Let's go sit down, and I'll explain."

She moved back just enough to allow him entrance into the house. Closing the door, Hannah felt an icy chill go up her spine. Her father was dead. She didn't know how she could be so certain without hearing it first, but something convinced her of its truth.

Following Mr. Lockhart into the front room, Hannah sat stiffly on a high-backed wooden chair and waited for him to speak.

"I had a letter. There was a note for you, as well. Apparently your father was ill and had someone write it for him."

"But now he's dead, isn't he?" She studied Lockhart's face, certain she would see the truth in his expression. She did. "How did he die?"

"The letter speaks of a long bout with a fever. He was apparently too weak to go on."

"Where did he die?"

"A small town in eastern Louisiana. He was buried there. I've forwarded funds to reimburse his expenses."

She nodded, feeling a terrible emptiness inside. "Thank you."

"If you'll take time to read his letter to you, you'll see it was his wish for us to marry right away. He wanted to see that you were cared for. I didn't say anything earlier, but your father and I were partners not only in the law business but in this ranch. I own half of it, and now it will come to me in its entirety."

Hannah tried to comprehend what he was saying. Her mind was already well down the road, however, trying to plan for her future and that of her brother and sister.

"I want you to pack whatever you need and come with me back to town. We can have your foreman drive you and the children. We will visit the minister and see how quickly he can perform the ceremony."

Shaking her head, Hannah got to her feet. "If you are now the owner of this ranch, surely you will not force us from it today."

"Of course not, but there is also news of additional Comanche and Kiowa attacks. I don't want to risk anything happening to you." He smiled and stepped forward. "My dear, I know that you have not yet grown to love me, but I have the deepest admiration and affection for you. Our marriage will be a good one. You needn't be afraid."

"I'm not afraid," she said, looking at him in disbelief. "I've just learned of my father's . . . death." She lowered her voice. "My brother and sister are in the kitchen, and I would not have them hear the news from you. I must speak with them privately."

"Of course," he replied. "Why don't you go speak with them and I'll wait here."

She shook her head. "I will need time with them. You should return to town."

"But I've only just arrived, and the temperature is quite

chilling." He smiled. "Please allow me to stay and help you with your grief."

"Help me? Help me explain to a five- and eight-year-old that they've lost their one remaining parent? I think not. This is a private matter, Mr. Lockhart. You may have been partnered with our father in business, but not in our family." Hannah hugged her arms close as if warding off Herbert Lockhart's very presence.

"Miss Dandridge . . . Hannah . . . please do not hold me malice for bringing such bad tidings," Lockhart said in a formal manner. "It was only my desire to bear this burden with you. As I stated, I have come to care quite deeply for you and your family. Your father was . . . well . . . a brother to me in many ways."

"Then as our . . . uncle," Hannah replied, "you will understand that we are now in a time of mourning. You will have to excuse me." She got to her feet. She could see the frustration, perhaps even anger, in Lockhart's expression as he stepped forward.

"I cannot allow you to risk your life or the lives of your brother and sister. I owe it to your father. You are not thinking clearly, therefore I will make the decision for you."

That was the wrong thing to say to Hannah. She felt defiance rear up in her. "I will not be dictated to by you or any other man, Mr. Lockhart. I will seek counsel and learn if you truly do possess this ranch or if it will in fact be returned to Mr. Barnett. Either way, I do not plan to marry you, and I find it cruel that you would even consider such a thing necessary at a time like this."

Lockhart took a step back, as if her words had struck him physically. "I am sorry, my dear. It was never my intention to be cruel."

"I am not your 'dear,' so please refrain from calling me such," Hannah said, narrowing her eyes. Her sorrow was pushed aside by her anger. "I am grateful that you brought us the news of our father. We have long suspected such an outcome, but it's better to know for sure. Now we face our true time of mourning. Please see to it that I receive all information regarding his burial. The day may come when we wish to visit his grave. I will take my leave from you at this time, and you must go."

She didn't wait for him to say another word. Instead, she gathered her skirts and made her way to the kitchen.

21

"Soldiers!" Tyler declared, hurrying into the small camp he and William shared. He jumped from his horse. "Cavalry—probably twenty or so are coming down the main road."

William extinguished the tiny campfire and prayed the scent of woodsmoke wouldn't be noticeable by the time the riders approached. Earlier they had driven the steers deep into the trees to a designated pen that Tyler had arranged to have built. It was a crude structure and they very nearly missed it all together, but after some searching Tyler had found it. Now it might all be for naught if the soldiers were out hunting for them.

William and Tyler pulled their mounts into the trees farther away from the road. They had been on the trail for just over a month and it had been far from easy. It had been a struggle just to get out of Texas. Then once they were in Louisiana, Tyler had found it impossible to secure additional men to help him so that William could return home. When they were in Shreveport they'd learned that the capital of the state had once again been moved, from Opelousas north and west to Shreveport to protect it from Federal control. Union soldiers had overrun Baton Rouge and then Opelousas. So far, the move seemed to have served them well.

Even so, the government was anticipating problems in the area and couldn't spare any manpower. William and Tyler had been promised help if they could make it to Monroe, some one hundred miles east of Shreveport, but the truth of the matter was that William didn't believe they would make it that far. The closer they drew to the heaviest areas of battle, the more hunger and need they found. People were starving, and a herd of cattle passing through the area—even a small herd—was almost taunting. Not only that, but things were progressively going wrong for the South. It seemed for every battle they won, the North held victory over even more.

A group of riders came on fast, and through the fading afternoon light, William could easily see that they were Union soldiers. They'd heard in Shreveport that there were pockets of Yankee scouts and forward observers, as well as renegades and mercenaries who favored Northern currency to Confederate dollars.

The routine, as they moved ever eastward, had been to hide as best they could during the day and move as far and as fast at night as they could manage. But even Tyler had to admit their chances of success were becoming slimmer and slimmer. There were marshes and swamps to contend with, as well as the soldiers.

William breathed with relief when the riders didn't so much

as slow. They were no doubt on their way to something more important. He looked at Tyler and shook his head.

"This isn't going to work. We might as well return to Shreveport and leave the cattle with the Confederacy there. Maybe they can find a way to get the cattle further east."

"I can't do that, Will. I can't turn my back on what I promised to do. I can only pray the others are having less difficulty, but I doubt it." Tyler tied off his horse and looked at William. "If you're gonna quit on me, at least have the decency to wait until we get close to the next town. I'll find someone to help."

"I'm not going anywhere," William said, knowing he couldn't desert his friend. "I just figure this isn't going to work."

"It was never going to be easy," Tyler countered. "In fact, I've known all along the odds were against us. And after all, what are twenty head of cattle compared to thousands of starving people? The whole idea was that if we could make this work, we could create a series of additional drives to smuggle more steer to the army and civilians."

"It was a good idea," William told him. "Your intent is good, anyway." He tied his horse off, as well, and took a seat on the ground opposite his friend. "The Mississippi was supposed to be your biggest challenge, though—not Louisiana."

Tyler shook his head and looked around. "Marshes, swamps, and forest. If it weren't for winter, we'd have to worry about malaria, too." He met William's gaze. "This isn't going to work short of a miracle."

"Whatever God's plan in the delivery of food to the Confederacy, we've given it our best."

Tyler heaved a sigh. "We're not gonna win this war. I think

Gettysburg proved that. The South keeps fighting, hanging on like a sick old man refusing to die. But sooner or later . . ." He left the thought unspoken.

William nodded. "Cooler heads should never have allowed things to get this far out of control. We have no business fighting each other—it's bound to scar this land and its people for generations to come. Even so, if the war would just come to an end, maybe we could get our lives back. You could rebuild the ranch—settle down and have a family."

"What of you and Miss Dandridge?" Tyler asked.

He looked at the ground. "I don't think there's a future there. Not that I wouldn't like one."

"So you finally admit you have feelings for her."

"There's little sense in it," William replied. "She could never have feelings for me. I represent everything that she hates. The war, the Battle of Vicksburg, where she lost loved ones . . . Not to mention the situation with the ranch. She knows I'm trying to reclaim it."

"Have the two of you talked about these obstacles?"

"No. I have to say that I've been a coward where matters of the heart are concerned."

Tyler picked up a stick and chewed on the end. "Seems to me you'd be a whole lot happier if you just sat down with her and explained what happened at Vicksburg like you did me. She can hardly hold it against you after that."

"Maybe not, but I hold it against myself," William said, getting to his feet.

❦

Hannah waited for the perfect moment to tell Andy and Marty about their father. She chose a time when they would have the house to themselves. Juanita was busy managing her own affairs, and Pepita had gone with her father to bring supplies from town.

"We're not going to have class today," Hannah told the children.

"Yippee!" Andy shouted with a jump. "Can I ride Dusty instead?"

Hannah shook her head. "No. Berto has gone to town, so no one can help you. Besides, right now I need to talk to the both of you. I'm afraid there's been bad news."

Andy sobered. "Is it about our pa?"

"Yes." Hannah could see the worry in his eyes. Marty, meanwhile, climbed into her lap. "I'm afraid," Hannah began, "Papa got sick on his trip to see our grandmother. His body was weak and tired from travel and he . . . he . . ."

"He died." Andy's voice was steady but his eyes filled with tears.

"Yes. He did."

Marty buried her head against Hannah's shoulder. "I want Papa to come home."

"I know, baby, but he can't. Mr. Lockhart arranged for him to be buried in Louisiana."

Andy stared at the floor. "What's going to happen to us now? How can I learn to be a man without a pa?"

Hannah reached out for him, but Andy resisted. She gave him a sad smile. "God will provide for us, Andy. God has never failed us. I don't know what tomorrow holds in store, but I do know that God will be there."

"He wasn't there for Pa," Andy said angrily. "I don't think God even cares." He ran from the room and from the sound of it, out the back door.

Hugging Marty close, Hannah fought to keep from crying. How could she possibly help Andy? She could barely contemplate the situation herself. How could she tell her little brother that the thought of him becoming a man was something that hadn't even entered her mind?

"Are you gonna die, too?" Marty asked.

Hannah stroked the little girl's head. "I don't plan to do so anytime soon. But, Marty, everyone dies. It's just a part of life. We live here for a little while and then we get to live forever with Jesus—so long as we've given Him our heart."

Marty nodded. "He's got my heart."

"Then you never need to be afraid of death," Hannah whispered.

"Did Jesus have Papa's heart?"

"Yes," Hannah answered. "Papa had a very sad heart because of losing your mama and mine. But he gave Jesus his heart a long time ago—when he was just a boy like Andy. Papa always said that we should put our trust in God, Marty. You must always remember that."

"I will. I promise."

⁓

The next day, Hannah was surprised when the Terrys stopped by the ranch. Ted and Marietta were driving a wagon and four mounted riders accompanied them.

"Won't you come in," Hannah said. "Your men are free to

water the horses in back and then join us. I'll have Juanita put together some refreshments."

"Don't worry about going to a lot of bother," Marietta declared as Ted helped her from the wagon. "We have to keep moving. We've mostly come because of this letter for Will, and problems with the Comanche. We were in town last night and heard this letter had arrived. Since we knew we'd be coming this way, we offered to bring it."

Hannah looked at the official-looking letter. It was addressed to William Barnett and the envelope showed that it was from a judge in Dallas. She felt her stomach clench. "Thank you. I'll see that he gets it."

They made their way into the house together while Ted went with the men to water the horses. Hannah was glad for the woman's presence. She had been struggling with Andy's sorrow and desperately needed advice.

"Won't you have a seat?" Hannah said. "I'll be right back." She placed the judge's letter on a small table between the chairs.

She quickly went to instruct Juanita and Pepita, then returned to join her guest. Hannah took the chair across from Marietta. "We had word that my father died."

"Oh, I'm so sorry."

"I've been afraid to spend the extra money to buy black dye for the clothes," she said. Laundry was the furthest thing from her mind, but for some reason Hannah didn't know what else to say. "The war is causing the price of everything to increase. It seems almost criminal to consider things like mourning clothes."

"Child, you needn't worry about traditions at a time like this. Tell me what happened."

Hannah shook her head. "Mr. Lockhart brought me a letter. It said that Father took ill and that he'd asked this person to write the letter for him. The letter said I should marry Mr. Lockhart right away. It said that this was Father's wish. At the end of the letter there was a postscript that mentioned Father had died. Mr. Lockhart said he arranged for Father to be buried in Louisiana and that he personally paid the expenses."

Marietta frowned. "Why was it that Mr. Lockhart had all of this information?"

"I suppose because of his partnership with Father. In fact, he tells me now that he and Father were co-owners in this ranch. The ranch now belongs to him."

"Hogwash," Marietta declared. "I do not believe that for a minute."

Hannah ignored her momentarily and glanced at the envelope on the table. "And now you've brought this letter from the judge in Dallas. I can only imagine it has to do with Mr. Barnett's desire to take back his land and ranch."

"Most likely that's the case. When is Will due to be back?"

"I don't know." Hannah met the woman's kind gaze. "They were sure to be up against all manner of trouble. The lieutenant told me that the situation would be quite dangerous."

"I'm sure they both know how to look out for themselves," Marietta said, reaching over to pat Hannah's arm. "I've seen Will get himself out of worse. Tyler too. You know those two have been friends for a long while."

Hannah nodded. "Mr. Barnett told me that Tyler was his first friend when they came to Texas."

"Well, I'll have to chide him for that. I was his first friend."

Marietta smiled. "But that will keep. Child, you know that you needn't worry about the future. As I told you, William would never put you out without somewhere to go. And our offer is still on the table. You are welcome to stay with us."

"I feel like such a hypocrite. I know God is watching over us, but I feel so alone. I feel like my entire world has collapsed around me. Andy is grief-stricken, and I don't know how to reach him. Marty is a little better, but the truth of it is, they don't understand the implications of their father's death. Unless I marry Mr. Lockhart, should his claim prove true, we would be forced to leave. And even if the ranch reverts to Mr. Barnett, I can hardly stay here and impose upon him."

"I don't think William would see it as much of an imposition. I don't think you would, either," she said, leaning forward. "I can see that you have feelings for him. You might as well admit it."

Hannah blushed. "Oh, Marietta . . . I can't deny that he's captured my thoughts and that my heart aches for his return. But there are things from the past . . ." Her words trailed into silence.

"Then you should tell him."

"I can't. I mean, especially now. The last thing I want him thinking is that I've taken on a sudden love for him now that Father is dead."

"But your love for him isn't a sudden thing, is it?" Marietta pressed. "I believe it's been developing for some time. I believe you were already quite smitten with him when you returned from the Comanche village."

Hannah knew she couldn't deny the truth. "I felt so confused then. I still am now. Mr. Barnett can make me so angry, and yet at the same time, set my heart aflutter. And then, as I said, there are obstacles . . . the war . . . and his participation. I don't honestly know if I can forgive him that."

"Forgiveness is the hardest act of love. Jesus died for just such a gift to us, so how dare we withhold forgiveness from any man—for any reason?"

"I know you're right," Hannah admitted. "But I learned that he was at Vicksburg. That is the battle that took the life of my brother and grandfather."

"Forgiveness is never easy, Hannah, but it is necessary for a life worth living. You can go on in bitterness and anguish over the past, but forgiveness will set you free. You have no way of knowing what responsibility William had in that battle. War is an ugly and painful thing to endure. Both sides have valid points and both sides are just plain wrong. Don't hold the war against William. He didn't want to go in the first place."

"I know that. At least that's what I've told myself over and over." Hannah's thoughts seemed to twist and churn. "I'm so confused."

Marietta chuckled. "Love is like that. No one vexes me as much as Mr. Terry, and no one blesses me more dearly. Love isn't about never knowing conflict—it's about making a commitment to endure through the bad times as well as the good. It's about choosing to forgive mistakes and intentional wrongs. It's never perfect and never without problems, but it is the most amazing gift God has given us."

Marietta took hold of her hand. "Hannah, I don't believe you could ever find a better husband. William Barnett is one of the best men I've had the privilege of knowing. And you are exactly what he needs in a wife. You are spirited and strong. You'll stand your ground with him, yet yield to his wisdom when needed." Marietta let go of Hannah and gave her time to consider what had been said.

Shrugging, Hannah shook her head. "I'm not very good at yielding, I'm afraid. I suppose that is another worry of mine. Of late, I've found myself rather rebellious. My father and I were once quite close. I was, as my mother once told me, the sparkle in his eye." Hannah smiled. "I could talk to Papa about anything. After Mama died, however, he changed. The sadness of losing Mama caused my father to close himself off. Later, he remarried without any consideration of Benjamin and me, but time proved that our new stepmother was a good woman. She wasn't all that much older than me, but she was quite wise. She became like a sister to me.

"I was to be married when my stepmother died giving birth to Marty. My father put an end to my engagement, saying I was needed to care for my sister and brother. We moved west and my young man was killed early in the war. Father said I should have been grateful to him for sparing me the sorrow of widowhood, but the loss was mine nevertheless. Even so, I loved my father and knew that he loved us. I wanted to please him, but it seemed nothing did."

"You poor thing. What a burden to bear."

"Then when we came here, Mr. Lockhart seemed to fall in step with Father's demanding nature. He was more subtle, but as the months passed he's been quite deliberate in pressing his desires."

"As I told you before, Mr. Terry and I feel that Mr. Lockhart is nothing but trouble. There are rumors about his dealings. In fact, when I was in Cedar Springs those rumors were told to me in great detail. I'm not a gossip so I will tell you only what pertains to me and Mr. Terry. Mr. Lockhart approached us and asked us about selling our ranch. He didn't say why, but suggested that if we wanted to sell out, he would be of a mind to buy and hoped we'd give him first chance. Mr. Terry told him we had absolutely no interest in selling. Later, when I was speaking with Mrs. Pritchard and mentioned the strange offer, she told me that Mr. Lockhart has been buying up land all around Cedar Springs."

"I can't imagine what he wants with all of that land. It's not like he intends to ranch or farm."

"Exactly my thoughts on the matter. Mr. Terry intends to investigate further."

Juanita entered the room with a tray of tea and cookies. "I will serve the men outside," she told Hannah. "Mr. Terry, he say that would be best." Hannah picked up Mr. Barnett's letter so that Juanita could place the tray on the table.

"Mercy yes," Marietta added. "We're all trail worn and covered with dust. I probably should have insisted on the same thing."

"Nonsense," Hannah said, straightening in her seat. She reached over to take up the teapot and placed the letter beside the tray. "You are perfectly welcome here. You took me in when I was in much worse condition. Put them in the dining room, Juanita." The woman nodded and hurried from the room. Pouring the tea, Hannah glanced up. "Do you take sugar? We were blessed to receive some of the sugar brought up from Corpus Christi."

"I like it without, thank you." Marietta took the cup and saucer.

Hannah then poured a cup for herself, Marietta's comments on love and forgiveness resonating in her mind. She had scarcely allowed herself to accept her feelings for Mr. Barnett, and the fact that she'd just spilled out her heart to Mrs. Terry surprised her. Perhaps, however, it was a blessing in disguise. By speaking to Marietta Terry, Hannah had had a chance to put her thoughts into words. Not only that, but Mrs. Terry had implied not once, but twice that William most likely had feelings for Hannah. Could that be true? Did she want it to be true?

Hannah thought for a long time about the things Marietta Terry had told her. She could see for herself that Mr. Lockhart was obviously planning something—but what? After a restless night, Hannah rose before anyone else. She dressed in an old worn skirt and blouse and then tied on an apron as she made her way down the stairs. She figured to get the stove fire built and start breakfast. Juanita was always so faithful to serve them, but Hannah liked the idea of giving the woman an occasional day or morning to herself.

When Hannah reached the kitchen, she lit a wall lamp and surveyed the immaculate room. Juanita liked to have a place for everything, and she wanted those places to be based on the article's usefulness. It took very little time for Hannah to find everything she needed.

With the fire built and heating up the stove, Hannah couldn't help but notice the letter for William. She'd left it on the kitchen table, thinking to later find a place where she could store it until William came home. Now, however, she was drawn to the letter. Her mind whirled with thoughts and fears. Did this letter hold the judge's decision regarding the ranch?

Though she knew it wasn't right, Hannah took a butter knife and slit the top of the envelope open. Her hands trembled slightly as she withdrew the letter and unfolded it.

Scanning the lines, Hannah didn't know whether to be relieved or worried. The judge said he'd made a decision regarding the Barnett property and wanted William to be in his chambers in Dallas on January the eleventh. That was just a few days away. Hannah frowned at the familiarities that passed from the judge to William. The two were obviously longtime friends. Would the judge find in favor of William?

"William," she whispered. When had she begun to think of him as William?

She folded the letter and put it back into the envelope. If asked about it, she would just admit to feeling the need to know if she should pack up the children and leave or remain there on the ranch.

But the letter hadn't resolved that question at all. Her father was dead, as were the only other members of her family, save Andy and Marty. She was responsible for them, but she had no idea of how she would care for them. The last thing she wanted was for things to become bad enough that she couldn't keep them with her.

"That won't happen," she insisted, moving back to the large bowl she'd placed on the counter. She considered a favorite meal of Andy and Marty's. She would make flapjacks and cover them with warm peach preserves and sweet cream. It was simple to make, yet a special treat for the children. God knew as well as she did that they deserved something good. Neither had been the same since the news came about Father.

Hannah grabbed her coat and pulled it on. She would need to collect eggs and get cream from the milk house. Stepping outside, she hugged her coat close and crossed the yard to the chicken coop. The chilly morning was rather bleak; the sun was barely peeking over the horizon and the skies were cloudy and gray. Perhaps Andy would see snow after all, she thought.

She saw the black horse that William had planned to have broken by now. The animal was far less skittish, but still quite green. He spied her and hurried to the side of the pen in case she had a treat for him.

"Sorry, boy. Nothing for you." She gave his velvety muzzle a brief touch, then moved on. Despite the cooler weather, the chickens were laying quite well. Hannah gathered three dozen eggs before heading back to the house. For some reason she paused at the back door and turned to look once again at the land and outbuildings. She loved it here. She would miss it when she was gone.

"When I'm gone?" she wondered aloud. Was this God's way of preparing her heart for the inevitable? Had He caused her to think of leaving in such a way that it wasn't *if* she went, but *when*?

The damp cold chilled her to the bone and Hannah hurried into the house and closed the door behind her. She didn't bother to take off her coat. It was colder in the house than she'd realized. Funny, but she hadn't even noticed the temperature earlier. Perhaps it was just the thought of losing her home that had stripped away her warmth.

Hurrying to wash off the eggs, Hannah quickly went to work mixing batter for the flapjacks. She pulled out a huge cast-iron skillet and then dipped into the drippings can for grease. Before long she had a nice bit of fat sizzling and was able to pour in her cakes. One by one she made a mound of them, and by the time Juanita appeared, Hannah had the peach preserves warming and was beating the sweet cream into a frothy whip.

"You are up very early," Juanita declared. She already had tied on an apron over a lovely green skirt.

"I couldn't sleep. I kept thinking about the letter from the judge and finally came down to open it."

"Mr. William's letter?" Juanita asked.

"Yes," Hannah replied. "I thought it might very well be something that would need attention before William returned. Turns out I was right. A judge has asked William to be in Dallas on the eleventh of January for his decision regarding the ownership of the ranch."

Hannah felt Juanita's gaze rest on her. "I believe that if William isn't here, I will go instead. I will also let Mr. Lockhart know and perhaps he can accompany me to Dallas."

"You should not go. You should wait for Mr. William," Juanita said, pulling plates from the cupboard. "He would not want you with Mr. Lockhart."

"Well, he doesn't have the right to tell me who I can or cannot be with," Hannah said. "The reality is that no matter what decision is made, this is no longer my home."

At that point everything suddenly seemed clear. This wasn't her home. Whether William now owned it or Mr. Lockhart, this ranch did not belong to her. It was really that simple. She put the whipped cream aside and realized that her only real choice was to take the children and go. If she stayed, William would feel obligated to provide for them.

The small amount of gold in her father's bedroom would see her through for a short time. Funds were still available in the bank, but they were being depleted quickly. "Can you manage here without me?" she asked Juanita.

"Sí, I finish up. The men, they will come to eat in a few minutes. Should I fry some ham for them?"

"Yes," Hannah said, nodding. "And feed them without us. I haven't yet gotten Andy and Marty up. Don't make the men wait."

Going to her father's room, Hannah couldn't help but worry about where to take the children. If the war were over, she could return to Vicksburg, where at least she had friends and acquaintances. But she knew the town had been ravaged by the battles, and its people were suffering greatly. If she were more skilled with a needle, she might apply to be a dressmaker or offer her help to a tailor. But her sewing was barely good enough for the family.

The room was dark and cold. Hannah lit a lamp and put it on the bedside table. Then she gently touched the Bible that lay atop the dresser. It was unopened, as it had been for many years. Had her father been able to make peace with God? Had he been able to overcome his grief and anger in order to die well?

"Oh, Father, our lives together could have been so different had you just learned to let go of the pain—to forgive and forget the past."

The words pricked Hannah's conscience. Would she make the same mistake?

Hannah pushed aside the iron bed. The loose floorboard where her father hid the gold was where the leg of the headboard had once rested. She reached down and used her fingernails to loosen the board and pull it free.

Inside, Hannah found a large black leather pouch. She sat on the floor and spilled out the contents of the bag onto her skirt. She gasped. There was over four hundred dollars in gold. In a time and place where Confederate paper money was losing its value, gold was a blessing and this was a fortune. They could live a long while on this. Hannah noted that among the gold pieces there were also two rings and a folded piece of paper.

She picked up the rings. One she recognized as having belonged to her mother. The other had been worn by Andy and Marty's mother. They were wedding rings. She hadn't realized that her father had removed them before burying the women he loved.

She touched the circular gold of her mother's ring. There were four garnet stones set atop the small band. Hannah slipped the ring onto her right hand and felt her eyes dampen with tears.

"Oh, Mama, how I wish you were here. You would know exactly what needs to be done."

She unfolded the piece of paper. It wasn't a letter, but rather a map of some sort. Her father had drawn it out by hand and put a dozen or so marks on the paper. There were also numbers and abbreviated words. She had no idea what it was supposed to represent. With a shrug she refolded the paper.

She replaced the gold, paper, and rings back in the pouch and forced the sadness aside. She had to think—she had to make a plan. There was still the question of where she should go. Hannah knew she didn't want to stay in Cedar Springs, and she definitely didn't want to go back to Dallas. A larger city would afford her more opportunities for work, but would also present more danger and problems.

She thought of William Barnett and felt an ache deep in her heart. She hadn't loved another since losing her beau in Vicksburg. Now, given the way she felt about William, she wasn't sure that she ever really understood what love really was. With her former beau she had been a child—barely a woman. As such her ideals and beliefs were simplistic and unchallenged. Taking on the responsibility for her siblings had changed that. So, too, the war. Now she was alone for the first time in her life, and she had to make a decision about her future. The ability to control her choices was hers for the taking. But, after all this time of longing for that power, Hannah felt it a hollow victory.

Gazing to the ceiling, Hannah prayed. "O Father, I don't know what to do or where to go. I know I must leave, but it is breaking my heart. However, I know if I don't go before William comes back, it will break my heart even more. I can't imagine facing him and still having the strength to leave."

❦

William's leg throbbed in pain. He'd tried to ease the misery by applying some warm compresses, but even that only helped for a moment. He rubbed at the site of his wound and remembered the feel of the bullet tearing through his flesh.

The shock of that impact had left him unable to move for a moment. He felt his leg muscle rip and the bone shatter. He could taste the blood in his mouth from where he'd bit his lip when the bullet had hit.

"You look awfully deep in thought there, Will."

Tyler motioned to the barn around them. "Pretty nice accommodations, given what we've been havin', eh?"

"Yeah," William admitted.

A family named Montague had taken them in and allowed them to hide the cattle and themselves in a large storage barn that had once been used for cotton. Tyler had met with Mr. Montague some time ago and arranged for him to quarter off the back portion of the barn so that they could corral the longhorns on their trip to the East.

Mr. Montague had informed them that very evening that Union troops had been sighted as near as twenty miles away. He didn't know if a battle was going to take place or if the soldiers had merely been forward scouts for a much larger group of men. Either way, they weren't going to be able to drive the cattle on without a great deal more difficulty.

"So, the way I see it, we need to make a decision about the cattle," Tyler continued.

"What's to decide? We can't press forward."

"Should we turn back then? Take the cattle with us? Leave them here?"

William had already thought it through. "The renegades make it too dangerous to go back. We're only three miles from Monroe. I say we drive the cattle on to town and leave them there."

Tyler considered that idea for a moment. "Or I could arrange to leave them here until things cool down a bit. That would give us time to know whether there's going to be a battle."

"I need to get back home. Judge Peevy promised me an answer by the first of the year and that's already come and gone. I want to get back to Dallas and talk to him, and then I need to talk to Hannah."

"It's about time," Tyler teased. "You gonna get up the gumption to propose?"

"First I need for her to know the truth about Vicksburg," William said. "Her reaction to that will let me know if we can even consider a proposal."

"She's a good woman," Tyler said, plucking a piece of hay from a nearby bale. "The truth will show her you're a good man."

"I'd like to believe that," William said, shaking his head, "but she's been through an awful lot. I couldn't blame her if she wanted no part of me."

Tyler grinned. "Well, if she wants no part of you, tell her to come see me."

William's brow rose. "You'd best watch how you talk. I could decide to get jealous." He smiled and lay back against his bedroll.

"Guess I'll take first watch." Tyler got to his feet. "You just stay there and dream those sweet dreams of Hannah Dandridge."

"I won't dream at all if you don't shut up," William said, pulling his hat down over his eyes.

It was sometime later when Tyler woke him up. "I hear something."

William jumped up and quickly reached for his rifle. "I'll go up," he said, pointing to the loft.

Tyler nodded and motioned to the stack of hay. "I'll be in there."

They went quickly to their places and waited. It wasn't long before the door to the barn creaked open. William aimed his rifle for the opening and waited.

"Lieutenant? You in here?" a voice called out. "It's me, Grubbs. Sidley is here, too."

William heard Tyler moving below. "I'm here," Tyler announced.

A lantern was lit and soon revealed the two men. William came down the ladder just as Corporal Grubbs explained their plight.

"Got into trouble north of Flower Point. Union soldiers caught wind of the cattle and that was the end of it. Sidley and me, we barely managed to get away. Figured to see if you'd made it this far yet. Talked to Montague at the house, and he said you was here."

"You very nearly made it to the Mississippi River," Tyler said, shaking his head. "We're not even going to get that far."

"No sir, you won't," Grubbs said. "That's why we was hopin' to find you. There's too many troops guarding the river. Ain't no chance to get them animals ferried across. There are a sight more patrols than when we went west, and I don't reckon they're gonna stop anytime soon."

"We've seen our share of renegade Yankees. Guess we're gonna have to get back to the captain and figure another way to smuggle in food." Tyler looked to William. "Since Grubbs and Sidley are here with me, you can feel free to head back anytime you like."

William nodded. That was the only encouragement he needed. Having had a few hours of sleep, he was more than happy to get back in the saddle. Tyler followed him to where William squatted down to gather his things.

"I want to thank you for what you've done."

"What I tried to do, anyway," William said, glancing up at his friend.

"I'll see to it that the captain knows about your help."

William shook his head. "Don't. There's no need. I wanted to help the hungry, not further the cause for either side. I'm sick of this war."

"I guess we all are."

Standing, William gave Tyler a smile. "Come see me after the war. You can stay on at my place while you rebuild yours."

Tyler nodded and the two men embraced. William gave Tyler a slap on the back as he pulled away. "Catch ya later, Johnny Reb."

"Not if I catch you first, Billy Yank," Tyler countered with a grin.

23

"But you must not go," Juanita insisted. Hannah put the last of their bags in the back of the wagon and Juanita continued to repeat her concerns. "It is too . . . how you . . . danger . . ."

"Dangerous," Hannah replied and turned to face her friend. "I know the dangers quite well. I have no choice. We will first let Mr. Lockhart know about the letter and then move on to hear what the judge has to say. I cannot suppose that it will be news in my favor, however."

She looked at the few things they had packed. "If we might impose upon you to keep the rest of our things until we can send for them, I'd be grateful."

"Of course, but you wait for Mr. Will. He not want you to risk this. He want you and Andy and Marty to stay here."

Juanita had taken hold of her arm, and Hannah put her hand over the woman's smooth brown skin. "I have to go, Juanita.

I think you know why I feel this way. My heart . . . well . . . if I don't go now, I might well make a fool of myself."

"To be a fool for love is not so bad," the older woman replied with a smile. "You and Mr. Will, you need each other."

"But don't you see? If I stay and declare my feelings for him, he will just think I'm doing it because of the ranch. I can't have him believe that of me."

Juanita shook her head vigorously. "No. No that is wrong. Mr. Will not think that. I know he care for you."

Hannah wanted to believe this, but it didn't really matter. There were so many obstacles to their love. An entire war stood between them.

Andy and Marty came dragging from the house. Their expressions were evidence of their unhappiness at Hannah's decision. Marty ran the last few feet and wrapped her arms around Hannah.

"I don't want to go," she told her sister.

"I know." Hannah let go of her hold on Juanita and lifted Marty in her arms. "But God has a plan for us, and we need to find out what it is."

"Maybe His plan is to just stay here," Marty suggested.

Hannah looked at the little girl and shrugged. "If God wants us to stay here then He'll make that clear."

"How?" Marty asked.

Andy said nothing as he climbed into the wagon seat. He was a different boy since the loss of their father. Hannah lifted Marty into the wagon and sighed.

"If God wants us to stay here," she told them, "then He will bring us back."

Juanita handed her a lap blanket, and Hannah passed it up to the children. "I hope we can send for the rest of our things and the milk cows once we're settled," she said, hoisting her skirts to climb into the wagon. She glanced to the back to recheck that Andy's horse was tied to the wagon.

"You wait until the men return. They come back today—maybe tomorrow," Juanita said, her tone pleading. "You wait."

Hannah shook her head. She had purposefully decided to leave while Berto and the others were out checking on the cattle. "In a few days the judge will wonder why William failed to show up. I want to make sure we are there on his account. He shouldn't lose his family's ranch just because he didn't know to be there. I owe him that much."

Pepita came to join her mother. She was every bit as downcast as the others. Juanita put her arm around the girl and hugged her close. Hannah would miss them more than she cared to admit.

"Juanita, you have been as dear as a sister to me. I pray God blesses you with His protection and peace."

"I pray for you," Juanita said, unable to hold back her tears. "I pray He bring you back to us."

Hannah nodded and wiped a stray tear of her own. "I would very much like that." She released the brake and snapped the reins. The same matched bays that had brought her and her family to Texas—to this ranch—were now taking her away. Only this time, Hannah had no idea where the road would take them. They'd come west "chasing the sun," as her grandmother and father had once said. She glanced up at the dull skies.

"We just didn't know the sun would elude us."

"What did you say?" Marty asked, huddling closer to Hannah. She smiled. "Nothing important." She looked over to her brother. "So are you two ready for a great adventure?"

"What kind of adventure?" Marty asked.

Andy remained uncommunicative and stared off toward the horizon. Hannah could only guess what he might be thinking. How she wished she could offer him comfort and reassurance. She had promised Andy that one day they would go and find their father's grave and have the body moved back to Vicksburg, where he could be laid to rest with their mothers. It seemed to offer him some degree of peace.

Hannah could only hope that Mr. Lockhart would have the answers she needed. She knew he wouldn't accept the fact that she intended to leave the area. For that reason she had told the children to say nothing to him about their plans. She would let him know about the meeting with the judge in Dallas, but that was all.

They rode in silence for a good long time. Hannah wanted to find a way to reach Andy, but she knew it wouldn't happen if she forced him to talk before he was ready. They were still a good three miles from town when he surprised her, however.

"Do you think Pa is in heaven?" he asked.

"I do," Hannah replied. "Or wherever Paradise might be. Jesus told the thief on the cross that he would be with Jesus that very day in Paradise."

"But Pa was mad at God. He told me so. Does God forgive you when you're mad at Him?"

Hannah considered his question for a moment. "I believe

God is a loving and just God. He knows when our hearts are burdened and we don't understand. He considers our hearts and the motives we have for every action. I think God forgives us for our confusion and misunderstandings. I think He knows," she told the children as much as herself, "that we are weak and human and we make so very many mistakes. But I know God loves us in spite of this."

"But how can you be sure, Hannah?" Andy questioned. "Isn't being mad at God like denying God? I remember my Sunday school teacher said that denying God was a sin that couldn't be forgiven."

The thought of this alarmed Hannah momentarily. She found herself praying for wisdom, and then it came to her as clear as any truth could be. "But that can't be true. Peter denied Jesus three times and Jesus forgave him. Jesus even knew Peter was going to do this well ahead of time. Do you remember?"

Andy shook his head, so Hannah continued. "When they were about to take Jesus prisoner, Peter wanted to fight. He said he would defend Jesus to the death, but Jesus knew that Peter was weak and human."

"Just like us?" Marty asked.

Hannah glanced at her sister. "Yes. Just like us. Jesus said Peter would deny him, but Peter said it would never happen. Then later, after they'd taken Jesus, some people recognized Peter and said, 'Hey, he's one of Jesus' friends.' Peter was terrified. He told the people he wasn't a friend to Jesus. He did it three times, and when he realized that he had done exactly what Jesus said he would do, Peter's heart was broken."

Andy shook his head. "But how do you know He forgave Peter?"

"Because later, after the wicked men put Jesus to death on the cross—after He was buried and rose from the dead—Jesus went to His disciples. He sat with them and talked to them. He talked to Peter about whether or not Peter loved Him and would serve Him. He loved Peter very much, even though Peter had denied Jesus. I believe God loves us so much that when we ask Him for forgiveness, He gives it. It's His gift to us."

"We're in for it now," Andy said, pointing to the north, where the land rose up in a series of small wavelike hills.

His change of subject surprised her almost as much as the problem he'd pointed to. Hannah saw the entirety of the hill fill with mounted Comanche and Kiowa warriors. They were wearing their war shirts, and while Hannah couldn't make out the details of their faces to any degree, they appeared to be painted for battle. Pulling back on the reins, Hannah halted the horses.

"Get in the back," she told the children. "Get under our bags and pull the feed sacks close. Stay down no matter what happens."

"Are we gonna die?" Marty asked, starting to cry. "Are they going to shoot us with arrows?"

"I hope not," Hannah said. "I would hope they have heard that we are their friends—that we want only to live in peace." She kept her sights fixed on the strengthening band and then back to the road. There was no hope of outrunning these mounted warriors. She could neither make it to town without them catching up to her, nor could she turn the wagon around and head back to the ranch without interception.

God, she prayed silently, *please send your angels to protect us. Help us now, Father, for we are all alone.*

Andy had already climbed over the seat into the back of the wagon, but Marty clung to Hannah. Prying the little girl's hands from her arm, Hannah smiled.

"God knows what we need, Marty. He's watching over us."

"He was watching over Pa, too," Andy added from behind her, "but that didn't do no good."

She looked over her shoulder at the boy. "God alone knows the truth, Andy. But He promised in the Bible that He would never leave us or forsake us. He didn't say we wouldn't have trouble." She looked back to the Indians, who had stopped advancing. They merely sat there, watching. Their silence and stillness were enough to make Hannah even more nervous.

"Marty, please do as I've asked," Hannah said. "I'm going to start for town very slowly and see what the Indians do."

The little girl began to sob. "Don't let them shoot you, Hannah."

"I won't."

Her sister reluctantly climbed into the back and took her place beside Andy. Hannah waited until both of them were lying flat before urging the horses forward once again. They had only gone about fifty yards, however, when two of the warriors broke from the gathering and started toward them. Hannah swallowed the dusty lump in her throat. No matter what happened in the next few minutes, she knew she had to be strong for Marty and Andy.

When the two warriors positioned their mounts in the middle of the road, Hannah felt her heart sink. One of the men raised his hand to indicate she should stop, and so she did. She reined in the bays and set the brake, all while praying that God would help them.

The riders moved forward and it was then that familiarity began to permeate Hannah's brain. "Night Bear? Red Dog?"

"It is as you say," Night Bear replied, moving his mount to the side of the wagon where Hannah sat.

"But how is it that you are here? I thought the soldiers made you go to the reservation."

"They did, but we escaped. We are now joined with our brothers to kill the soldiers."

Hannah frowned. "Must you always be at war?"

"They killed my people," Night Bear said, seeming years older than she remembered. With his red, black, and white face paint, he seemed every bit the formidable foe. "I must fight."

"But God loves you, Night Bear. He would not want you to go on killing. God is about peace and love."

He looked at her for a moment. "Your God, He does not make war?"

Hannah frowned. "Well, there were times when battle was necessary and God supported His people on those occasions."

"Your God would not fight for His people?"

She felt it was impossible to explain, but tried her best. "God does fight for His people. He's always with us—always providing for our needs. I wish I had the right words to make you understand. There is a time to fight, but also a time to refrain from fighting and lay down your weapons."

"This is not that time," Night Bear said

His dark-eyed gaze pierced Hannah's heart. "I do not wish to see you die," she said. "Nor do I want my family to be harmed. Will you kill us?"

He looked at her oddly. "I do not kill those who helped my people. You and William are my friends. Your people will not be harmed. I have told my brothers of your deeds. You are respected among the Numunuu." He reached behind him and drew around a leather war shield. It was fringed and there was beading across the top.

"This belonged to my father. It was used in great talks, but not in battle. You keep this with you and my people will know that you are a friend to us."

Hannah didn't know what to do. She knew after the soldiers' raid on the village that there couldn't be much the boy could claim as belonging to his family. She couldn't even imagine how he might have obtained this shield. "I can't take that," she said. "It should remain with you as a reminder of your father."

Night Bear shook his head. "I do not need this to remember my father. He was a great man—a great warrior. I will make him proud. I will fight his enemies and make war on those who made war on him."

Taking the shield in hand, Hannah held his gaze for a moment. "I will cherish it, but if one day you would like to have it back, I will return it to your care."

The young man reined his horse hard to the right, then looked back over his shoulder. "I will remember you."

He said something in his native tongue, but Hannah didn't understand. "What did you say?"

He smiled ever so slightly. "I said you make my spirit glad."

Hannah looked to Red Dog and back to Night Bear. "I will pray for you . . . for you both. I will pray you will find a way to be at peace with my people—that we will live in peace with the Numunuu."

With that, the two warriors gave a cry and raced back across the field to where the rest of the mounted Indians waited. Hannah watched Night Bear and Red Dog rejoin the men and head out in pursuit of their enemies. She looked at the leather shield for a moment, then hung it off the side of the wagon seat to be prominently displayed for all to see.

"They won't kill us now?" Andy asked.

Hannah turned in the seat to find both children had come out from cover and were sitting on their knees. She offered them a smile. "No. They won't kill us, because we're their friends."

Andy seemed to consider this for a moment, then climbed back over the seat to take his place. "That's good," he said, almost too quietly to be understood. His expression seemed torn between the sorrow he still carried and a look of pride. "You sure are brave, Hannah."

"I was brave, too," Marty said, climbing between them.

Hannah laughed, feeling the tension finally begin to slip away. "You were both very brave. I'm proud of you, and Pa would have been proud, too."

Andy glanced heavenward. "Do you think he saw us?"

Marty gazed upward, as did Hannah. "I wouldn't be surprised," Hannah replied.

In town, Hannah arranged for them to take a room at the hotel. Mr. Englewood was surprised by her arrival, but offered the best he had to see to their comfort.

"Room eight has the biggest bed," he told her. "You can all sleep there quite well." He nodded to her bags. "Why don't you just leave those right there and go on into the dining room for something to eat. The missus has been cooking most of the morning, and if the aroma is any indication, I'd say she's made a batch of chicken and dumplings. You go on and eat. I can take your bags up for you."

"Would you also be willing to have someone take the wagon and horse to the livery?" Hannah asked. She pushed a coin across to the man. "I'm happy to pay."

"No, ma'am. I'm glad to do it as a personal favor to you and your family. Your pa was a good man and a friend to me."

Hannah smiled and took the coin back. "Thank you. You are very good to say so. I won't forget your kindness."

She herded the children into the dining room and allowed Mrs. Englewood to fuss over them. The woman seemed almost starved for female company and began talking nonstop while helping them to take seats.

"We have some delicious chicken and dumplings, if I do say so myself. The recipe has been in my family for a long, long while." She reached down and rubbed Andy's head. "I swear you grow taller by the minute."

"I'm tall, too," Marty pointed out.

"Yes, you are and quite pretty. Why you're very nearly as pretty as your sister." Mrs. Englewood turned back to Hannah and frowned. "I was sure sorry to hear about your father. When

Mr. Englewood told me the news I was just about as sad as I could be. I said, 'Rusty, just imagine what it will be like for those poor children without him to provide. Why, they won't have a place to live or food to eat.' I knew you had no other living relatives to go to."

Hannah cringed at the look of worry that passed over Andy's face. She didn't want her siblings to worry and hurried to interrupt the woman's chatter. "Mrs. Englewood, the chicken and dumplings sounds wonderful. We're very hungry. Could we maybe have a bit of corn bread, too?"

The woman didn't seem to mind in the least that Hannah had interjected the request. "Why, of course. I'll fetch it right away. I'll bring milk for the children to drink. Would you like some coffee? I have some nice and strong."

"No, I will be fine without anything. The food will suit me perfectly."

The woman hurried away to the kitchen, leaving Hannah to figure out what to say to Andy. She didn't want to make too much of the woman's statement, but neither did she wish for her brother to feel he couldn't speak on the matter.

"You know," Hannah began, "Father left us some money and so we will be just fine. I'm trying to figure out what we should do next, but you needn't be afraid. Just remember, God directs our steps and He always will."

"I didn't believe it when I heard you were in town," Herbert Lockhart announced as he crossed the room to join them.

Hannah closed her eyes and uttered a silent prayer that the man might disappear, but when she opened her eyes again, there he stood.

"What's the meaning of this?"

She gave a patient smile. "I had some news that I thought you should hear."

"We're going to Dallas," Marty chimed in.

Lockhart looked at the child with a scowl and then back to Hannah. "What is she talking about?"

Hannah drew a deep breath and let it out. "There is a judge there who is handling the matter of the ranch ownership for Mr. Barnett. He sent a letter requesting Mr. Barnett appear on the eleventh of the month. We are journeying there to meet with him on Mr. Barnett's behalf."

"You will do no such thing," Lockhart declared. He pulled up a chair and plopped down between Hannah and Marty. "You are not going to drive all the way to Dallas alone."

"She's got us," Andy said, frowning.

"And she talked to the Indians," Marty threw in. "They like Hannah and so we don't have to be afraid."

Holding her breath, Hannah waited for Lockhart to question her on this, but instead he rolled his eyes.

"Does that child never tire of telling lies?" He didn't wait for an answer. "I won't allow for it, Miss Dandridge. Your father would never approve, and as his partner, you must heed me in this."

Hannah was barely containing her anger by this point. "First of all, Mr. Lockhart, you have no say over what I will or will not do. My father felt me fully capable of raising my brother and sister and of handling the affairs of our living in his absence. Second, Marty isn't telling lies." She looked at the pouting face of her sister and winked. "The Comanche have honored me for my kindness to them. I have been given a shield that will be a sign to other members that we are not to be harmed."

Lockhart's eyes widened at this. "And when did this happen?"

"On the way here. There was a war party heading off to search for the soldiers who destroyed the Comanche village." Hannah saw no reason to lie. "They are long gone."

"But you should have told me this immediately. We should get word to the authorities."

Hannah shrugged. "Do what you will, but I intend to head to Dallas in the morning. You are welcome to accompany us if you are that concerned for our safety. I figure since you believe the ranch to be in your possession now, it would serve you well to be there for the judge's decision. But whether you come or stay is of no concern to me. I will not be dictated to by you or any other man. This is my decision. I am an adult and fully capable of making such choices."

For a moment Lockhart seemed to battle with himself. Then without warning, he got to his feet. "I will ride along with you. As you say, this matter involves me." He looked as if he wanted to say something more, but refrained. "What time do you intend to head out?"

"Daybreak," she replied, satisfied that she had put him in his place. Perhaps he would leave her alone after this. "And Mr. Lockhart, I would like my father's things. I know he had a great many books and other items that he kept in the office. If you would be so kind as to gather those pieces and bring them tomorrow, I would appreciate it."

His eyes narrowed, but he said nothing. Instead, he gave her a curt nod and turned to walk away. Hannah had no way of telling if he understood the finality of the moment. As far as she was concerned, getting her father's possessions was the final act of severing all ties to Herbert Lockhart.

The next morning Herbert Lockhart stood waiting for Hannah at the livery. When she walked in with Marty and Andy, he tried once again to convince her to stay in Cedar Springs.

"I've thought about it all night," he said as she paid the liveryman. "I can go to Dallas on your behalf." He paused and reluctantly added, "And that of Mr. Barnett. I am, after all, a lawyer." He gave a nervous laugh. "I can surely see to this matter more effectively if not distracted, and by that I mean if my mind is not consumed with worrying for your welfare and that of your siblings."

Hannah all but ignored the man and helped Marty into the wagon before she climbed up beside her sister. Andy looked at Lockhart for a moment, then moved past him and scampered up to the wagon seat. Once her siblings were settled, Hannah adjusted her bonnet and picked up the reins.

"Mr. Lockhart, I thought I'd made myself clear yesterday.

I am driving to Dallas to meet with the judge. You are more than welcome to accompany us, but I have no intention of remaining here. Nor do I need for you to concern yourself with our welfare. Now, if you'll put my father's things in the back of the wagon, we can be on our way."

"About that . . . well . . . I'm afraid there wasn't time to gather everything," Lockhart said. "I figure you can get them when you come back to town. We'll have plenty of time then to discuss the future and what we must do."

She hadn't any intention of returning to Cedar Springs, but she wasn't about to tell Mr. Lockhart her plans. Why could the man not simply do as she had asked? Fighting her anger, Hannah shook her head. She didn't want to give away her hand and let him know that she was taking the children and leaving the area. "I suppose you leave me little choice."

Without waiting to see what Lockhart would do, Hannah maneuvered the horse and wagon out of town and onto the main road to Dallas. It wasn't long, however, before Lockhart had caught up to her. He was rather breathless and more than a little out of sorts. Nevertheless, Hannah noted that he had a small carpetbag hung over the saddle, so apparently he'd known better than to figure on her willingness to stay in Cedar Springs.

Good, Hannah thought. *It's better that he realize here and now that I'm a woman of determination. I won't be ordered about anymore. From now on, the children are my only concern.*

The day warmed only slightly and by the time they were drawing closer to Dallas, an hour and a half later, Hannah took pity on the children. She drew up on the reins and looked to Andy and Marty. "Why don't you two walk and run a bit. You can climb back up before we get into town and have to deal with the busy streets."

They didn't have to be told twice. Andy practically leaped from the wagon, while Marty was a little more cautious in her dismount. Together, they ran ahead of the wagon, challenging each other as to who could run faster.

"I didn't want to speak in front of the children," Lockhart said, drawing up alongside Hannah's wagon, "but I think it would serve us well to marry in Dallas."

Hannah looked at him in mute surprise. Lockhart quickly continued. "You have to be thoughtful of providing for the children. I believe the judge will see that Barnett was a traitor to the Confederacy and rule in my favor. Even so, as my wife, you will have a good home in Cedar Springs."

"Mr. Lockhart, I have not considered your proposal with any degree of seriousness. I'm afraid I have been much taken with grief over the loss of my father, and my concerns with the children's best interests." She flicked the reins and started the horses for town.

Lockhart was quick to catch up. "But that is just my point. You are not in a place to handle such decisions. Your sorrow will mar your good sense, and choices might be made that will be to your detriment."

"I believe God will keep me in His care," Hannah said, not bothering to look at the man. "I am trusting Him to guide my steps and show me the path He has chosen for me."

"Well, the Bible says that it isn't good for man to be alone," he said with a tone of amusement.

Hannah didn't wait even a heartbeat to reply. "Yes, but I am not a man, Mr. Lockhart. And with Andy and Marty in my care, I am certainly not alone."

After that, he said very little. Hannah drove in grateful silence, and when the time came for the children to reclaim their seats on the wagon, Hannah felt fairly confident that Mr. Lockhart would put aside his thoughts of matrimony.

She was wrong, however.

✑

After securing a decent hotel room, Hannah found herself once again forced to endure Mr. Lockhart's attentions and thoughts for their future. She wasn't at all happy that he'd chosen the supper table to continue speaking of such matters, and hoped that with the children present, he would refrain from making a complete idiot of himself.

"So you see, my dear, the house is nicely suited for you and the children. I have had the servants make ready the extra bedrooms."

"Hannah," Andy interrupted. "What's he talking about?"

Marty looked up and nodded. "I thought we were going on a trip."

She put her finger to her lips to hush the little girl, but made it seem as though it was the interruption that was a problem. "Mr. Lockhart is sharing his ideas."

Lockhart got a silly look on his face. Hannah thought perhaps he was suffering indigestion, since the pork they'd just dined on was quite fatty. Instead, Lockhart shocked her when he reached for her hand.

"I know we thought to keep this to ourselves, but I feel the children should know my intentions. I want to marry your sister. I want for us to be a family."

"You're too old," Andy blurted out. "Besides, I want her to marry William. He knows how to take care of the ranch and break horses, and he's not old."

"Or fat," Marty declared.

Lockhart turned beet red, while Hannah coughed nervously into her napkin. She had no idea why Andy would suggest marriage to William Barnett, but it had definitely irritated Mr. Lockhart. She wanted to say something, but Andy piped up again quickly.

"Hannah needs to marry somebody like William who can work hard." Her brother turned to look at her. "She works too hard and so she needs a man who can help her with the work."

"And who isn't fat," Marty added in a most solemn manner.

"Martha Dandridge, mind your manners," Hannah managed before turning to her brother. "And you . . . finish your dessert so that we might retire to our room."

Lockhart, however, was not to be put aside. "Miss Dandridge, am I to understand that Mr. Barnett has become a rival in winning your affections?"

Hannah shook her head. "There is no rivalry, Mr. Lockhart."

He smiled rather smugly and leaned back to tuck his thumbs in his vest pockets. "I could not imagine that there would be."

She didn't wait to continue. "There is no rivalry, because I have no affections for you." His expression fell. "Furthermore, I am not of a mind to consider matrimony at this time."

Marty leaned closer to her sister. "He's losin' all his hair, Hannah. You can't marry a man who doesn't have any hair."

Her sister's serious consideration of a beau very nearly sent Hannah into peals of laughter, but she held herself in check. "Marty, it doesn't matter as much what a fella looks like, but rather what's in their heart—if they love Jesus and if they are trustworthy."

She looked back to Lockhart and found him frowning. Apparently her words did not agree with him. Yet another reason to avoid marriage to this man, she figured. She pulled open the purse that hung at her waist and began to get coins to pay for the meal.

"My dear, I will not have you paying for this supper," Lockhart said, holding up his hand to halt her.

Hannah considered refusing his offer but thought better of it. She would need all the money they had just to get them somewhere to start anew. Nodding, she closed her purse and smiled. "That is very kind of you, Mr. Lockhart. However, before we conclude our meal, I would like to speak a little business." She turned to the children. "Please sit quietly while Mr. Lockhart and I speak. I promise it won't take long."

"Certainly you could send the children to their room," Lockhart suggested. "They needn't be bored with our affairs."

"Mr. Lockhart, this is a big city, and while it has been considerably depopulated because of the war and Indian conflicts, I would not begin to consider having the children fend for themselves—even in a hotel of this quality. Now, I wish to discuss my father's business. I know that you two were partners and that he invested a considerable sum to set up the offices in Cedar Springs. I wish to know how we might dissolve his interests and have you buy us out."

Lockhart had been in the middle of sipping his coffee. He all but spewed the liquid out across the table. "Please excuse my surprise," he said, dabbing the napkin to his lips. "I supposed you to know the truth of our arrangement."

Hannah eyed him seriously. "Which is what?"

The man put down the napkin and folded his hands. "The truth is, your father wasn't doing all that well financially. What with the war and the ranch not making money and having to provide for so many mouths to feed . . . Well . . . the truth is, I bought him out some time ago."

By the expression on his face, Hannah was certain he was lying. Lockhart watched her, as if to determine whether she'd accept his comments or protest them.

Hannah chose her words very carefully. "I think perhaps it would benefit us both if you and I discussed this matter with the judge in Dallas. It seems to me that Father did quite a bit of business without informing anyone else . . . but you." She smiled. "That must have been a tremendous burden. However, I believe the judge will be useful to us both."

"There's no need for that, I assure you. Your father and I were both capable lawyers. We drew up contracts and had witnesses. I have all of the papers back in Cedar Springs. You see, it was always your father's intention that you marry me." He looked rather uncomfortably at the children and then back to Hannah. "I even assured your father that I would adopt your brother and sister. You see, I care deeply about your welfare."

"Be that as it may," Hannah countered, "I have no intention of marrying you. If that was my father's wish, then he kept it well hidden from me. As for the children, I have raised them and they are as much my own as they were Father's."

"Still, a single woman cannot be responsible for herself, much less two vulnerable children. I would not feel comfortable allowing you to attempt such a feat on your own. Given your father's wishes for their well-being . . . if you are to indeed refuse my love, I cannot say that I could ignore my responsibility to them."

Hannah's eyes narrowed. "What are you saying?"

Lockhart's expression grew almost dour. "It would be a legal matter for the court to decide, of course, but I believe it would be my duty to your dear father to take on the guardianship of the children."

He couldn't have shocked her more had he punched her in the face. Hannah leaned back in her chair, feeling a sense of panic begin to creep over her. "You would force me into marriage in order that I might not be separated from Andy and Marty? Is that what you are saying?"

"My dear, I would never force anything upon you. I am simply saying that I have a responsibility to your father to oversee the welfare of his minor children. You are within your rights to ignore your father's wishes that we marry. I would never dream of imposing such a thing on an unwilling partner."

"I'm not going to live with you," Andy suddenly interrupted. "You aren't my pa, and I won't let you have Marty, either."

Lockhart pointed a finger at the boy. "You are out of line to speak in such a manner to your elders."

"Do not think to correct him, Mr. Lockhart," Hannah declared. "He is as shocked as I am at your harsh treatment. You cannot suppose that any of us would willingly participate in this scheme of yours to control our lives."

For a moment Hannah wasn't sure how Lockhart would take her comment. His face contorted, revealing emotions that suggested anger, fear, and finally deep sadness. "I am greatly wounded that you consider this harsh or a scheme. This is a hard land to live in, and your father was merely concerned for you. I don't suppose I should expect you, as a woman, to understand all of the dangers that could await you in the world. We do try to keep our women innocent of such matters." He gave a smile that suggested it was a heavy burden to bear. "This is the duty that falls upon the shoulders of all men, and I take that task quite seriously."

Hannah pushed back her chair and got to her feet. "I understand the dangers better than you might think, Mr. Lockhart. I believe now I will retire. We are weary from our long day." She helped Marty from her chair and was surprised when the little girl clung to her in a fearful manner. Lifting Marty to her hip, Hannah cradled the child close. "I'm certain you see the way you've upset my sister and brother. That could hardly have been our father's desire."

Lockhart was already getting to his feet, but Hannah could see that he didn't appear concerned with their feelings. He fixed his gaze on Hannah and delivered his next words with great care. "I am a man of my word, Miss Dandridge. Emotions are not what a man considers when following through on unpleasant concerns. I will do what must be done. In time, you will understand my position. I hope this will not lessen your opinion of me, but I must honor your father's wishes."

"Nothing at all could lessen my opinion of you, Mr. Lockhart. It's already at its lowest point. Good night."

She hurried Andy from the dining room and up the stairs to their room. Marty, for once, was surprisingly silent. Hannah wanted to rail at Herbert Lockhart. How dare he try to force her into marriage by using her siblings. She had never known such rage as she felt in that moment.

If only William were there. He would set the man straight.

The thought surprised her, though if she were honest with herself she'd admit that William was always the first one to cross her mind when times of trouble came.

"Hannah, will Mr. Lockhart really take us away from you unless you marry him?" Andy asked as soon as they were safely inside their room.

"You won't let him take us, will you?" Marty questioned, near tears.

"Of course I won't let him take you." Hannah smoothed back errant strands of hair from the girl's face. "Mr. Lockhart is mistaken about Father's wishes. That's all. He will soon realize that."

"He's a bad man, Hannah," Andy said matter-of-factly.

Hannah nodded. "I think I'm beginning to see that, Andy. We will have to pray for God's protection and trust Him. He won't let us be harmed."

"How can you be sure?" Andy asked. "He let Pa be harmed."

"He did," Marty said, supporting her brother's statement.

"We don't always know why things happen the way they

do," Hannah admitted. "I don't really know what happened to our father, but I do believe God was with him even in death. God is good, Andy. He loves us very much. We must trust Him to help us in this. I promise you, though, I will not leave you. Even if it means I have to marry Mr. Lockhart. I will never leave you."

"You can't marry him, Hannah." Andy's tone was almost pleading. "He's a bad man, and he don't love God."

"Doesn't," Hannah corrected. "He doesn't love God."

"No, he doesn't," Andy reiterated.

Hannah smiled at her brother. "I don't really know how Mr. Lockhart feels about God, but I do know how we feel. We aren't his judge, Andy. God is. We love God, and therefore, we will trust Him. He is our hope now—more than ever before."

Hannah was surprised to find the children dressed and ready to go to the courthouse when she awoke the next morning. She was even more surprised when Marty declared that she'd seen William on the street below.

"Marty," Hannah began in exasperation, "how many times have we talked about this? You simply have to stop lying."

The little girl bowed her head. "Well, I thought I saw him."

"Well, sometimes we see things and they aren't at all what we thought they were." Hannah lifted her sister's face to meet her gaze. "Do you understand?"

Marty nodded. "It sure looked like him."

"Maybe because you wanted it to," Hannah replied, caressing the youngster's cheek.

Hannah then smoothed out the lines of her chemise before reaching for her corset. She had long learned how to tighten her laces without help, but when Andy offered his assistance, she could only smile.

"You shouldn't have to help your sister with such a thing."

"Maybe someday I'll get married and my wife will need help," Andy told her.

At this Hannah could only nod and turn her back. "All right. Here's what you need to do."

After instructing him, Hannah quickly hooked the front of the garment, then waited patiently for Andy to adjust her to the proper tightness. After that she quickly donned her corset cover and petticoats. Her traveling outfit was well worn from the last few years of travel, but it would suffice.

After a hurried breakfast, Hannah and the children waited in the lobby for Mr. Lockhart. Hannah was about to give up on him when Lockhart walked in from the front doors rather than descending the stairs. Apparently he had already been conducting business.

"I see you're going to bring the children."

Hannah nodded. "As I mentioned last night, this is the city and I would not feel comfortable leaving them alone."

"I did consider that. The proprietor's wife agreed that they might stay with her, however." Lockhart looked at Andy and Marty with an authoritative expression. "I feel it would be best."

"They're staying with me," Hannah said, even as Marty hugged closer to her side.

Lockhart looked as if he might protest, then nodded. "As you wish."

The words clearly came hard for him, and Hannah knew he didn't mean them. She didn't care. It would be as she wished—despite his threats. She felt a sense of confidence and smiled. "I'm glad you understand."

❧

William had ridden hard and fast to get back to Texas. His desire to see Hannah had very nearly sent him to the ranch, but something inside urged him to stick with his plan and head to Dallas. Weary and worn, he'd made his way to the livery to see to his horse. It was while he was there that the liveryman, Horace Carter, invited him to spend the night and William eagerly agreed. The two had known each other for a long time and comfortably spent the evening with tales of war and politics.

Despite this and the comfort of a real bed, William awoke early, his leg throbbing from the abuse of riding for so many days without decent rest. He rubbed the old wound and wondered if he would ever know a day without pain.

Hunger soon became foremost on his mind, however, and William limped his way to a nearby hotel. He knew Horace would have happily fed him, but William desired to have a full hot breakfast of ham, grits, and biscuits with thick gravy. He'd been thinking about just such a meal since his days on the trail, and he wouldn't be deprived it now.

When he finished it was still too early to see the judge, so William walked along the main thoroughfares and marveled at how time had changed things. Dallas was still far busier than Cedar Springs, but many of the businesses were closed and the number of people and traffic seemed far lighter. Of course, the war had taken a good number of the men, and in their absence, many of the women had moved to be near relatives. He had heard that quite a few families had made their way to Austin and Houston in order to avoid the Comanche attacks, as well.

He stopped at a rather upscale mercantile and made his way to a display of dolls. He thought of Marty and the fact that she was soon to have a birthday. William picked up a doll dressed from head to toe in blue velvet. It was frilly and lacy and sported long blond sausage curls and a stylish bonnet. He grinned as a clerk made his way over to assist him.

"I reckon this ought to brighten the birthday of a six-year-old girl."

"Indeed it would," the man agreed. "And the price has recently been lowered." The man appeared eager for a sale as he continued. "Most folks don't have money for such frivolities these days, but those birthdays do keep coming."

William nodded. "I'll take it. Can you wrap it up in brown paper for me? I have a long, dusty ride home."

"Certainly, sir. Would there be anything else?" he asked in a hopeful voice.

"I think some peppermints would be a good idea—if you have some." He had the money given him by Tyler and knew such spending couldn't be the routine of his future. Still, he wanted to take some candy to the children. Andy and Marty would love it, but he knew Pepita and Pablo were just as fond of the sweet treat.

"I have some sticks in the back," the man assured him. "How many would you like?"

"Let me have six," he said, thinking he wouldn't mind a stick for himself.

"Yes, sir. I'll get those and I'll wrap up the doll while I'm at it."

William waited and noted the clock on a shelf behind the counter. It was nearly eight-thirty. No doubt Judge Peevy would be ready to open his doors to business. The clerk returned in a matter of minutes with the candy and the doll. William paid the man and hurried back to the livery, where he deposited his purchases. Horace was busy mucking out stalls and gave him a wave.

"I saw you were gone from the house mighty early. You should have hollered. I would have cooked you some grits."

William smiled. "I knew you would have—that's why I left early."

The man laughed. "Well, I've been thinkin' on gettin' me one of them mail-order brides who could cook me up a digestible meal, but there's a war on, you know. I'd probably have to send to the West or South for one."

"I wouldn't fret too much, Horace. Sadly enough I have a feeling we'll have plenty of widows after this dispute is resolved."

Horace nodded somberly. "I'm sure you're right. So you headin' home now?"

"Shortly. I have to see Judge Peevy first. I'm going to leave these things here and then I'll be back to settle up with you."

"You paid your keep just jawin' with me half the night. Ain't had a good conversation with anyone in a long time. That were worth the price of feed for sure."

"That's mighty kind of you, Horace. I'll remember it." William gave a little two-fingered touch to the brim of his hat in salute.

Judge Peevy was already hard at work when William got to his office. His secretary, an elderly man, greeted William and told him that the very subject of his ranch was now being discussed.

"With whom?" William asked.

The secretary didn't have time to reply, however. The door to the right opened and Andy and Marty came barreling out.

"I knew I heard your voice," Andy declared. "I'm so glad you're here. That Mr. Lockhart is trying to make Hannah marry him. He said if she doesn't marry him, he's gonna take us away from her."

William felt Marty wrap her arms around his legs. He looked down and she was nodding. "You can't let him marry Hannah. He's fat and mean."

"What's going on? Why are you here?" William asked Andy as he bent to lift Marty in his arms.

"Hannah said that we had to come here because the judge sent a letter. She said that the ranch belonged to you and it wasn't right for us to stay there no more since Pa was dead."

William frowned. "So you've had word about your father?"

"Uh-huh. Mr. Lockhart came and told Hannah. Then Mr. Lockhart told her that Pa wanted her to marry him."

"But we don't think she should," Marty added. "You won't let her, will you?"

"I'll do what I can." William had no intention of losing Hannah to Herbert Lockhart. She might not like the truth about what he'd done in the war, but he wouldn't stand by and allow her to make that kind of a mistake.

"I'm sure sorry about your pa. I know how much it hurts to lose a father. I hope you'll talk to me if you need to." He said this mostly for Andy's benefit, but smiled at Marty, too. "You two wait out here, and I'll go in and see what I can do." He put Marty down and gave Andy a nod. "I promise to do whatever I can to see that Hannah doesn't marry Mr. Lockhart."

"Good. I told her she needed to marry you," Andy declared in unabashed adoration. "I told her you were strong and a good worker and young enough to help her so she won't have to work so hard."

William was surprised by this. "And what did she say to that?"

Andy thought for a moment. "Well, she didn't say no."

William chuckled. "All right, then. I'll go do what I can."

He left the children to reclaim their seats in the inner chamber before knocking on the closed door to Judge Peevy's private office. Without waiting for a response, William opened the door and stuck his head inside.

"I hope I'm not late."

"William, I am glad to see that you've made it back," Judge Peevy said.

Hannah turned to look at him in surprise. There was a light in her expression that gave him hope for the first time. Dare he imagine that she cared?

"I figured since this meeting was about the ranch, I ought to be here."

"Indeed, indeed. Take a seat. I was just explaining to your lawyer—"

William held up his hand. "Hold on. I don't have a lawyer here. Mr. Lockhart certainly doesn't represent my interests."

Lockhart laughed rather nervously. "I felt given the situation and Miss Dandridge's insistence that we come here, that I would happily afford you my professional skills."

"Well, be that as it may, I don't want you for my lawyer.

Thanks anyway." He looked to Hannah and for a moment neither said a word. He found her eyes piercing, almost pleading. If Lockhart had threatened to take her siblings, she was no doubt beside herself with worry. It would be like someone ripping children from the arms of their mother.

William pulled up a chair and placed it between Lockhart and Hannah. "I suppose we should get right to the heart of the matter. What have you figured out regarding the ranch?"

"It is as I supposed," Peevy began. "I disagree with this war. I feel as Sam Houston did, that we shouldn't have seceded."

"That's ridiculous and traitorous," Lockhart declared. "We are one of the Confederate states. It truly doesn't matter what your personal desires are at this point."

"Nor does it matter what yours are, Mr. Lockhart. You not only do not represent either party in this affair, but you are treading dangerously close to being booted out of here all together. I'm only tolerating your presence because Miss Dandridge said you hold some claim on the ranch."

"You?" William said, turning to look Lockhart in the eye. "What possible claim could you have?"

"Miss Dandridge's father was my business associate and partner. In his will, he stipulated that I marry his daughter and care for his youngest children as my own. It was a little known fact, but due to certain financial problems, Mr. Dandridge included the ranch in our partnership."

"I don't believe you." William turned to Peevy. "This is the first time anyone has mentioned such a thing."

"I believe it is of no concern and a null and void point," Peevy declared. "It is my ruling that the ranch was removed from your family in an illegal manner. Therefore, the property still belongs to the Barnett family, which now, sadly, consists of no one but you."

"This is ridiculous. You would throw out a single woman and young children from the only home they've known this last year?" Lockhart questioned the judge. He looked to Hannah. "Do you see now? It is just as I warned you."

"Hardly," William countered. "No one is asking Hannah and the children to leave the ranch."

He turned to Hannah. "You have a home for as long as you want one." He wanted to say more, but not in front of Lockhart and the judge. He rubbed his aching leg and turned back to the judge. "Are we finished?"

"Not by a long ways," Lockhart interjected. "See here, Judge Peevy, I intend to appeal this decision. My deceased partner was awarded that property for his service to the Confederacy. Now, you may hold no respect for our Southern-formed government, but I do. My partner did, as well. He lost a son and father at Vicksburg. And I might add that Mr. Barnett himself was a Union soldier in that very battle."

Lockhart gave William a smug look before changing his expression to sympathy as he looked to Hannah. "As I told you long ago, my dearest, this man might very well have taken the life of your loved ones."

William felt gut-punched. He turned to Hannah, but to his surprise found no condemnation. She nodded and looked to the judge. "I have known for some time, Your Honor. However, God has given me a heart of forgiveness. I hold Mr. Barnett no malice. He was doing his duty not only to the country, but first and foremost to his father. That is an obligation that I well understand. I took on responsibility for my brother and sister from the time they were small for the same reason. I do not condone the fighting—on either side—but I do understand Mr. Barnett's position."

Lockhart refused to remain silent. "Your Honor, this only serves to further my point. The Barnetts left Texas to fight for the North. They clearly rejected the land and country that was founded here."

"Mr. Lockhart, as I see it, they did what their conscience demanded. Just as I am doing what my conscience demands of me. Appeal my decision, if you will. But I guarantee you that with the war, you won't see this case resolved for some time. Perhaps years."

Lockhart sputtered in protest even as William got to his feet and extended his hand to the judge. "Thank you. I appreciate all that you did to review this situation. Now, if you don't need me any longer, I plan to escort Miss Dandridge and her brother and sister . . . home."

"Good luck to you, William," the judge replied. "I'll see to it that the deed is recorded properly."

William nodded and turned to Hannah. "Are you ready?"

She hesitated. For a moment he thought she might refuse him, but then she reached out to take hold of his arm and stood. "Thank you, Judge Peevy. I believe you have made the right decision."

They didn't wait for Lockhart. Instead, William hurried her out the door to rejoin Andy and Marty. The children ran to her eagerly and Hannah hugged them close.

TRACIE PETERSON

"Did you win?" Andy asked William as he pulled away from Hannah.

"I did. The ranch is mine again."

"That's good." He seemed to sober a bit as he looked to Hannah. "Are we still going to leave?"

"I'm afraid we must," she replied. Hannah started for the outer office before William could stop her. It wasn't until they were outside that he caught up to her.

"Wait just a minute. What do you mean, you intend to leave?"

Hannah drew a deep breath, and William thought she looked very much like a woman preparing for battle. "Just what I said, Mr. Barnett. The ranch is yours. It's hardly appropriate for us to remain there. I intend to take the children and go."

"Where?"

She smiled. "I can't really answer that question. I don't know where we will end up. I can hardly go back to Vicksburg."

"Did you speak the truth in there?" he asked.

"Hold on just a minute!" Lockhart called out as he came barreling from the judge's quarters. "I do not intend to let you get away with this."

William looked at the man and shook his head. "You have no say in any of this. Your word and character have lost all credibility."

Lockhart's eyes narrowed. "Are you calling me a liar?"

"That, and a fraud and a bully. How dare you threaten this woman's well-being."

"You're the one who is doing that," Lockhart countered. "I won't stand here and allow you to deceive her with your

315

lies of valor and patriotic duty. Your only intention is to get her into your bed."

William didn't have time to think. He punched Lockhart squarely in the nose and watched as the man fell over backward. Blood spurted from Lockhart's face and the man was stunned into silence as he grappled for his handkerchief.

Turning to Hannah, William rubbed his thigh with the back of his knuckles. "My apologies that you had to see that."

"Apologies are not needed," she said with a smile. "I think I'm beginning to see a lot of things more clearly."

26

Hannah had barely stepped into the hotel when Herbert Lockhart caught up to her. He followed her up the stairs and when she still didn't stop to converse with him, he grabbed ahold of her arm. "I will have a word with you." She noted the blood splattered on his shirt. Then, looking up, she could see his nose was already discoloring and swelling.

"Andy, Marty, go inside the room and get your things packed up. Take these, please." She handed Andy two small packages. William had escorted her to the general store and was even now loading several other purchases into her wagon.

She unlocked the hotel door and waited until the children were inside and the door closed before turning to Lockhart. "What is it?"

He glared. "If you leave town with William Barnett, I'll have him arrested for assaulting me. Furthermore, I'll have the children removed from your care."

"On what grounds?"

He smiled, but it was cold and frightening to Hannah. "That you're a wanton woman. You're living in sin with Barnett and those children are in danger for their very souls."

"That's ridiculous and you know it. I might have feelings for the man, but I am not a wanton woman."

"So you admit it," Lockhart spat, his tone altered by his swollen nose. "You're in love with William Barnett."

"I am, but what of it? It's none of your concern, Mr. Lockhart. And I don't believe my father ever intended for you and I to marry. I think this is something you have assumed or created in your mind."

"I have proof. The letter and his will."

"Why should I believe you? Just as Mr. Barnett said, you are a bully. You have done nothing but impose yourself upon me since my father left. How strange it is that you should know so much about his comings and goings—his business and home affairs. I find it stranger still that my father never said anything to me about his intentions. My father was not one to keep such matters silent. Had he intended us to marry, Mr. Lockhart, my father would have made it quite clear."

Lockhart stepped closer, and Hannah could feel his breath upon her cheek. "It really doesn't matter anymore. I have the better hand, wouldn't you say?"

Hannah tried to step back, but he held her in place. "I didn't realize we were playing a game," she said, gritting her teeth.

"Sometimes that's the way life is," he said. "You do what you have to do in order to get what you want. I want you and I will have you. The choice is up to you as to how many people suffer in the meanwhile."

"What are you implying?"

He laughed. "Nothing. I'm promising retribution if you cause me any more trouble. Your father didn't take me seriously, but you would do well to learn from his mistakes."

"Mistakes? My father was your partner. He supported you and . . . made a business with you." Hannah feared her voice betrayed her uncertainty. "If he made mistakes, it was in that."

"You are truly dim-witted. Your father was, too, and that's why I had to put an end to our partnership."

Hannah felt her eyes widen and her breathing quicken. "You . . . you . . . hurt my father."

"Nonsense. I paid to have him killed." Lockhart seemed amused. "Not that you can ever prove it. No one would begin to believe you should you speak a word of it, but just in case you're tempted, remember that I've already arranged one murder—it's easy enough to arrange another . . . or two."

"You would kill innocent children . . . just to marry me?"

"My dear, while you are quite lovely, marriage to you is only a minor part in this. I don't expect you to understand the details, but I do expect you to obey. Otherwise, your brother will be the first to go."

Hannah quickly realized he meant business. He didn't care that such things would only make her hate him; a woman's hate or love were immaterial to his selfish needs and desires. What a fool she'd been not to recognize his true character sooner.

"I despise you. You are exactly the kind of man God warns against. Evil and vindictive, scheming and deceiving."

"Be that as it may," Lockhart said, tracing her cheek with his finger, "you will marry me. Now I suggest you gather your things and then allow me to escort you to get the wagon. We will find the nearest preacher and then we'll leave immediately. You will take your brother and sister and settle into my house."

She shuddered at his touch and didn't know what to say. If she protested, Lockhart would surely have William arrested and the children taken from her. She needed time to think.

"I'll need to let the children know," she said, stalling for time.

"Very well." He released her.

Hannah opened the door to the hotel room. The children rushed to her and clung to her as if she might disappear before their eyes. She wanted to ease their obvious worry, but she had no comfort to give. Instead, she put them from her. "Andy, Marty, Mr. Lockhart is taking me to get the wagon. Stay here with the door locked until I come back for you."

"But you said it wasn't safe," Marty protested.

"Why can't we wait for William to bring the wagon?" Andy asked, looking past Hannah to the hallway.

"Just do as I say, Andrew." She locked gazes with her brother, glad that he couldn't read the fear in her heart. "Just lock the door and don't let anyone in."

Once the children were secured, Hannah allowed Lockhart to guide her down the stairs and out of the hotel. She wondered if William would be at the livery. If so, the situation could get quite ugly. A fleeting thought crossed her mind. What if she could get the upper hand with Lockhart? What if she could pretend to agree to marriage and then work behind his back to prove he murdered her father? She gave a shudder at the thought of marrying her father's killer. Could she pretend agreement to such an arrangement?

"Pick up your pace, my love. I want to get out of here right away."

"I thought you intended us to marry here."

He stopped in midstep. "Does that mean you've come to realize the futility of fighting me in this?"

Hannah forced her expression to remain void of emotion. "I can hardly allow you to hurt my brother and sister."

"I'm glad you're seeing reason." He glanced down the street for a moment. "No, I believe we'll marry in Cedar Springs. You will convince the folks there how happy you are. They will attend our wedding. It will be quite the celebration, don't you think?"

"Why is this so important to you?" Hannah hadn't meant to ask the question aloud, but now that she had, there was no recourse but to await the answer.

"I have plans for my future. I am a man of business and I determine my fate. Your father didn't understand that, and look where it got him."

Hannah thought of all the people who might suffer at the hands of this man. "If I willingly marry you—give you the façade you desire—will you agree not to kill anyone else?"

He shrugged. "But of course."

"Including William Barnett?"

Lockhart scowled. "Barnett is not a part of this agreement. You have a brother and sister who need your consideration. Leave it at that." He pulled her along with him. "Now, my dear, we must hurry."

"I'm glad my father wasn't like you. Though he was a demanding man, there was still kindness in him. And love. My father loved us and he knew that a life without love wasn't worth living." She smiled suddenly, realizing why her father had insisted on bringing his family west with him. He had known that they would love him. She might have been angry and hurt when he broke off her engagement, but he knew she loved him enough to respect his wishes. The children would love him and be a reminder of the love he'd shared with their mother. It all made sense to her now . . . now that it was too late.

They reached the livery, and Hannah was relieved to see that William was nowhere in sight. She didn't want another fight, and she certainly didn't want a scene. The liveryman approached Lockhart while Hannah made her way to the readied wagon. She didn't know how she was going to make this work out, but she knew the solution would start with prayer.

Father, I need your help. She glanced over her shoulder, then cast her gaze heavenward. *And I need it now.*

⤞

William knocked on the door to Hannah's hotel room for a second time. Finally he heard Andy's voice call out.

"Who's there?"

"Andy, it's William. Open up."

The boy did as he was told and broke into tears. "You gotta help Hannah."

"What's wrong? What's happened?"

"Mr. Lockhart came and he told Hannah she had to marry him. Will, he said . . . he said . . . he killed our pa."

"He said he'd kill us, too," Marty declared.

Andy quickly nodded. "She's not lying. He said no one would believe her if she told them about pa. Then he said that he would kill us if she even tried to say somethin'."

Anger built to a roaring blaze in William's soul. "Where are they now?"

"Mr. Lockhart said we had to leave with him right now. He took Hannah to get the wagon."

Marty came alongside her brother. "He was holdin' her arm real tight, like he was trying to hurt her."

Andy nodded. "Hannah didn't want to go with him, but she did."

"And she told us to stay here and not unlock the door." Marty wrapped her arms tight around William's leg. "I'm scared."

"Don't worry," William told them. "You're with me now. I'll do what I can."

Marty took hold of William's hand. "Hannah loves you. She told Mr. Lockhart."

He wondered if this was just one more of Marty's exaggerations, but Andy chimed in. "It's true. She said she loved you."

"Come on," William said, motioning the children to the door. "We're going to need some help if we're going to keep Hannah safe."

"Who can help us?" Andy asked as they headed downstairs.

"We'll go talk to Judge Peevy again. I think he can tell us what to do next."

"Do you think . . . well, will God help us?" Andy asked. "He didn't help my pa."

William looked at the boy and shook his head. "Andy,

sometimes God's help doesn't look like we thought it would. I'm guilty of thinking God didn't help me when I was out there on the battlefield. I was wrong. God never left me. He's with me even now. I wish I'd seen it sooner, but that's the great thing about God. He's patient with us and He won't leave us to fight this battle alone."

⤴

Lockhart admired Hannah's shapely backside as she climbed into the wagon. She had refused his assistance, but that only freed him to watch her every move. Her beauty was something that had attracted him from the beginning, but it was her father's money he wanted. Hannah probably didn't realize how much money her father had brought with him to the West. Nor would she know about the shipment her grandfather had made shortly after the beginning of the war. Dandridge had confided in him about the collection of family heirlooms: gold, silver and jewelry that had belonged to his family for generations. Treasure that he had buried somewhere on the Barnett Ranch in order to keep it from enemy hands.

The stupid man had told Lockhart everything . . . except where the goods were actually hidden. That, he hoped to figure out after he married Hannah. He would have all the time in the world to search the ranch if he lived there. Unfortunately, the judge had put an obstacle in his way. But it was only a small obstacle.

His plans were coming together, and for once Herbert Lockhart felt that everything he wanted was within reach. He realized all at once that Hannah was watching him. If looks could kill, he knew he'd be hearing his eulogy spoken. But since they couldn't, he merely returned her glare with a grin.

"We're going to have quite a time, you and I. Marriage to you will be a challenge—rather like breaking a fine mare. I will look forward to the rewards and benefits."

"There will be neither for you, I promise you that."

"Oh, but that's where you're wrong, my dear." He tied his horse to the back of the wagon and came to climb up beside her. "You will make me a very happy man . . . or you will become a very sad sister."

"You are a poor excuse for a man."

"But not for long," he said. "As soon as we find your father's treasure, I will be quite wealthy."

Hannah looked at him in surprise. "What are you talking about?"

Lockhart looked at her in disbelief. "Didn't he tell you about it?" He frowned. This could complicate things a bit. He had always figured Hannah knew where her father had hidden their valuables.

"Your father told me he hid a great deal of wealth on the ranch." Lockhart tried to keep the frustration from his voice. She could be pretending not to know. "All those valuables he brought with him from Vicksburg."

Hannah folded her arms against her chest. "You're quite mad. My father had a small amount of gold, but I've been using that for the benefit of my family. There is nothing else."

"I pray for your sake that you're wrong in regard to that, my dear. Your father told me there was a map with instructions, and I intend to find it."

Hannah tried to move away as he joined her on the wagon seat, but he would have no part of that. "Stay where you are. I rather like the feel of you next to me." He picked up the reins and snapped them. He would soon have everything he'd worked so hard to gain.

They halted in front of the hotel, and to Lockhart's great frustration, William was standing in front of the establishment. The two men locked eyes immediately and Lockhart felt a sense of danger in his adversary's expression.

"What do you think you're doing, Lockhart? I thought I made it clear to you that I wasn't going to tolerate any nonsense."

"Miss Dandridge has changed her mind and is returning to Cedar Springs with me."

Barnett looked at Hannah and then back to Lockhart. "I don't think so."

"You have nothing to say about the matter." Lockhart narrowed his eyes. "We will retrieve the children and then we're leaving. If you interfere, there will be consequences."

"Such as putting an end to my life or the life of her brother and sister?"

Lockhart knew Hannah couldn't possibly have told Barnett about his threat. That left only the children. He threw a cautious look over his shoulder and then beyond William. Seeing no one in sight, he shrugged. "I'd just as soon see all of you dead. That would eliminate a great many complications in my life. However, at this point, if you don't leave us alone and do exactly what I tell you to, I'll be forced to make this young woman a very unhappy bride."

"I think you already did that when you had her father killed."

Lockhart fumed, determined that those mouthy children would suffer for giving him away. Now he had no choice but to kill Barnett. He jumped down from the wagon, but in his haste, twisted his knee in the process. Ignoring the pain, however, he stepped within a foot of Barnett. "I did have her father killed," he said, lowering his voice, "but I'll kill you myself. It will be self-defense, and Hannah herself will be my witness." He couldn't suppress a smile as he drew a gun from his pocket.

"Hold it there, Lockhart."

The sound of a pistol being cocked sounded from very near Lockhart's right ear. Herbert Lockhart felt all that he'd worked for slipping away as the sheriff stepped closer. The cold metal barrel of the sheriff's gun touched Lockhart's neck. For a moment, Lockhart thought only of pulling his trigger and ending Barnett's life.

"Give me the gun," the sheriff demanded, pressing his pistol painfully against Lockhart's neck. "Now."

Seeing the satisfaction in Barnett's eyes, Lockhart hesitated a moment longer. Then a thought came to him. He had friends. He had people who could help him out of this. People who owed him. He smiled and lowered his gun.

"Very well. But this is far from over."

Hannah continued to think of Herbert's comments as the sheriff led him away. He'd had her father murdered—probably for the treasure he believed existed.

"Treasure indeed," she muttered. There was no treasure. Was there?

"Are you all right?" William asked, coming alongside her.

"I don't know," Hannah said, slowly shaking her head from side to side. "It seems as if everything has suddenly gone crazy."

He chuckled. "The whole country is at war. The Comanche call you friend because you walked among them and offered them care, and you're just now thinkin' that everything is going crazy?"

She frowned. "Lockhart said my father had a treasure he'd hidden away. He seemed to think it was on the ranch and that he would lay hold of it by marrying me." She suddenly remembered the map that she'd found with the gold her father had left under the floor. "I think I know where the map is."

William shook his head and put a hand to her elbow. "Enough. We've got other business to settle. If there is a treasure to be found, it will keep. Right now, we need to discuss something far more important."

They were nearly halfway back to Cedar Springs when William halted the horses for a rest. Sunshine had warmed the day and the earlier clouds had drifted to the north, leaving a gloriously clear blue sky. The children were more than happy to get out of the wagon and play for a time near the full, wide creek. Thankfully, they seemed completely unharmed by the earlier trauma. Hannah was glad the children had been with the judge instead of on the street to see Lockhart pull a gun on William and hoped that they would forget all that they'd overheard through the hotel door. It was bad enough that they knew their father had been murdered.

Hannah felt awkward as William helped her from the wagon. They hadn't exchanged much conversation since the sheriff had taken Lockhart away, despite William declaring they needed to do just that. Now Hannah wasn't at all sure what to say or do. *Thank you* hardly seemed enough, and there was still the matter of the treasure.

William attended the horses, then approached Hannah as she contemplated Lockhart's actions. She wanted to believe the law would see justice done to Lockhart. But even so, it wouldn't take away the fact that he'd thoroughly wronged her family. No amount of punishment could bring her father back to life.

"Walk with me?" William asked.

She nodded and they set out a short distance to a rocky ledge that overlooked the creek. When William began to talk about the war, Hannah found herself engrossed in his recollection.

"We were positioned across a line of Confederate soldiers who were intent on keeping us from advancing into Vicksburg. We tried to spread out in order to cover more territory, and I had taken up a place near a stand of trees. I heard a noise in the brush and knew it was a Rebel soldier. I took aim from a standing position and was ready to fire for the first time in that battle." He fell silent as they reached the ledge.

Hannah didn't want to interrupt his thoughts, so she waited for him to continue. When he did, she could hear the pain in his voice.

"When the soldier came out of the brush I was just about to squeeze the trigger when I realized he was just a boy. He couldn't have been more than thirteen. I held the gun on him for a moment and when he saw me . . . well, there was a look on his face that I'd seen before. It was a sort of recognition that death had come to him. I lowered my gun. I couldn't kill a child—not for my country—not for my father."

William looked away for a moment. "I told him to go home. I told him he was too young to lose his life, and I was old enough to know it was wrong to take it. I turned and walked

away, and that was when someone fired and hit me in the leg."
He looked at her and shrugged. "I don't remember much after
that. I lost a lot of blood and very nearly lost my leg."

"He shot you after you showed him mercy?" Hannah asked
in disbelief.

"I don't know who shot me. It might have been the boy or
someone else. It really doesn't matter. I knew I didn't want to
be a part of this war anymore."

Seeing his eyes glisten with unshed tears, Hannah reached
out to take hold of his hand. She felt her breath catch as he
tightened his fingers over hers.

"I don't know why," he said softly, "but I wanted you to
know."

"I'm glad you told me," she said.

"Did you really mean it when you said you'd already forgiven me?"

Hannah nodded. "I know that this may sound strange to
you, but when I watched your compassion for the Numunuu . . .
well . . . I began to see you differently. The war seemed far
away then, and even though I knew you had been a part of
the attack on Vicksburg, my heart changed."

He turned and gazed into her eyes. Hannah didn't mind
his thorough study. She took the opportunity to return the
favor. She reached up to push back his thick brown hair
and smiled.

"I've wanted to do that for a very long time."

"I won't tell you what I've wanted to do," he said with a grin.

Her eyes widened. "Why, Mr. Barnett, I thought you to be
a gentleman."

His expression turned mischievous. "I am—that's why I'm not telling you."

She laughed and let go his hand, only to have William recapture it. "Don't go. I think we need to settle a couple of things."

"Such as?" she said, her curiosity more than a little stirred.

"Your brother and sister seem to think that you're in love with me." He drew her hand to his chest. "Andy says you said as much to Herbert Lockhart."

"I suppose . . . I did." She glanced away in embarrassment.

"Don't you figure that's tellin' the wrong man?" he teased.

"You weren't around to tell," she finally answered. "Not only that, but I wasn't sure you'd want to hear me say such a thing."

He put his finger under her chin and guided her eyes back to his. His voice was soft and low. "I've been waiting to hear that for all of my life."

"But you haven't known me all of your life," she countered.

William kissed her fingers. "I feel like I have."

Hannah shivered from the sudden rush of emotions crashing over her. She thought she might very well faint from the intensity of the moment, but just then Andy and Marty came running.

"Are you gonna kiss her?" Andy asked.

William looked at him and then to Marty. "Do you think I should?"

"Did you ask her to marry you?" Andy questioned, looking quite serious.

"No, I haven't yet done that."

Hannah wanted to giggle at the scene as Andy shook his head. "I don't reckon you should kiss until you get married."

Marty nodded. "Yeah, it's kind of better that way."

Hannah looked at her sister and shook her head. "Why in the world would you say that, Martha Dandridge?"

She answered nonchalantly, "'Cause if he doesn't like kissin' you, then you'll already be married and he won't be able to leave."

William roared with laughter. "She makes a very good point. I believe I'll wait until after we're married."

Putting her hands on her hips, Hannah turned back to him. "Well, I don't remember being asked."

Andy nudged William. "You'd better ask her."

William gave the boy a sober nod. "How do you suppose I should go about it?"

Hannah raised a brow, but otherwise forced her expression to be void of emotion.

"You gotta promise her that you'll work hard for her," Andy said. "And that you'll always do nice things for her."

"Like bring her flowers," Marty added.

"And sometimes you have to read to her. My pa said that our mama liked it when he read to her."

Hannah smiled at this. She hadn't known their father to be overly sentimental with his stories, but clearly he had shared this memory with his son.

"I think I can do all of that," William said, giving Hannah a wink.

"Then I suppose you should just ask her to marry you," Andy said. "Hannah doesn't like folks to talk around things. She's always sayin' that."

"He's right, you know," Hannah said. "I prefer people just be honest and forthright with me." She turned to gaze into William's eyes.

"I prefer that, too," he told her. Taking hold of her hand, he grinned. "Marry me?"

Hannah nodded. "I believe I will."

William looked to Andy and Marty. "Are you sure I have to wait to kiss her until after we're married?"

The children gave a quick nod and William let go his hold on Hannah. "Then I reckon we'd better get married tomorrow, 'cause I want to kiss her right away."

⁓

They reached Cedar Springs in the early afternoon. Hannah had hoped they could marry and head right out to the ranch, but talk ran high about recent trouble with the Comanche.

"It ain't safe out there," Nelson Pritchard declared. "Two fellas from over Denton way were scalped as they were makin' their way to Dallas. A third fella was able to get away and tell what happened. He said there must have been over seventy Injuns. Even the Terrys came in from the ranch. Your people, too."

"Where are they staying?" William questioned.

"Livery for the Mexicans and hotel for the Terrys."

William looked at Hannah and frowned. "If they came in there must have been a grave threat."

"But we saw Night Bear just before going in to Dallas. He told me we'd be safe."

"You conversed with the Comanche?" Nels asked in disbelief.

"Hannah's a friend to them," Andy said proudly.

"She's a fool then." Pritchard all but spat the words.

"You take that back. You can't call my sister a fool," Andy said, moving forward.

William put his hand out to stop the boy. "You would do well to watch what you say, Pritchard." He turned to Hannah. "Guess we need to go find the others and invite them to our wedding."

Hannah felt her face warm. "That's fine by me," she told him.

Mr. Pritchard looked surprised. "You two are getting married?"

Andy spoke up before anyone else could. "He asked Hannah just a little while ago."

"But they didn't kiss," Marty added. "They gotta get married first."

A sly grin spread across William's face as he turned back to Pritchard. "So you see, we need to talk to the preacher."

Nelson looked confused. "But I thought Miss Dandridge was marrying Mr. Lockhart. That's what he's told everybody."

"He told them wrong," Hannah interjected. "I have no romantic interest in Mr. Lockhart."

"He killed our pa," Marty declared.

Pritchard shook his head and waggled a finger at Hannah. "You'd do well to teach her about lying."

"She isn't lying," Hannah replied. "She's telling the truth, and Mr. Lockhart is in jail awaiting trial for the murder of our father."

"But . . . how could that be?" The storekeeper looked to William and then again to Hannah, his expression one of disbelief.

"The details are unimportant at the moment," William said. "What matters is that he can no longer harm this family."

"It's more important that Will and Hannah get married," Andy stated in an authoritative manner.

William smiled. "The boy is absolutely right. That's far more important."

"I knew your pa to be a good Southerner, Miss Dandridge. Mr. Barnett. . . ." Mr. Pritchard momentarily fell silent. He looked uncomfortable as he continued. "Mr. Barnett fought for the Yankees. Your pa wouldn't approve of this marriage."

"I believe my father would completely approve," Hannah said, turning her smile on William. "Especially given that William has just returned from risking his life to smuggle cattle to the Confederacy," Hannah declared. "He cares more about feeding the hungry than fighting, Mr. Pritchard. He's a hero for the betterment of mankind."

"You were a part of getting food to the troops?" Pritchard asked, looking to William.

Hannah could see that William wasn't exactly comfortable with the question. She gave him a reassuring smile and he nodded. Hannah turned back to Mr. Pritchard. "So you see, Mr. Barnett's heart is in helping people whether from the North or the South. He and some of his Confederate soldier friends drove cattle into Louisiana. He's just now returned."

Mr. Pritchard looked at William oddly. "But you and your family were Yankees."

"We were Texans first and foremost. I still am. I never wanted to go to war for either side," William answered honestly. "I think we could have better resolved things in a peaceful manner."

Pritchard considered this for a moment. "But your pa—"

"My pa is dead. My brother, too. This war has taken everything from me that I intend to give. Now, if you'll excuse me, I need to speak with the preacher."

They walked from the store in silence, the children trailing behind them. Hannah couldn't help but wonder what they were going to do about the ranch and the raiding Indians.

"You sure got quiet all of a sudden. You haven't changed your mind, have you?" William asked, escorting her toward the hotel.

"Changed my mind?" Hannah asked, shaking her head. "About what?"

He laughed. "About marrying me."

"Hardly. I've got plans for you, Mr. Barnett."

This made William pause in his steps and eye her seriously. He leaned close and whispered, "And I have plans for you, Miss Dandridge."

His low husky voice sent a delicious shiver through Hannah's body. Words caught in her throat and left her unable to speak. It didn't matter, however. She knew he understood.

Much to their frustration, Hannah and Will found their wedding delayed by three days. The preacher was sick and unable to perform the ceremony, and because of the threat of Indian attacks, no one wanted to travel back to Dallas. Marietta Terry thought it a very good thing, however. She immediately set to work with Juanita to create a wedding gown for Hannah.

"Every young woman deserves to get married in a lovely dress," Marietta declared as she helped Hannah into the new creation.

Hannah marveled at the beautiful white silk gown. The style was quite simple with its very full unembellished skirt and separate bodice. Juanita had worked with deft ease to fashion a bodice worthy of a wedding gown. Taking special care to fit it exactly to Hannah's slender frame, Juanita had given the bodice a V neckline and wide pagoda sleeves. Trimming both in delicate ruffles, she finished the piece off with lace up the back rather than buttons.

As Marietta pulled the lacings tight, Hannah could hardly believe the transformation in the mirror. She blinked back tears as she turned to face the two women who'd worked so diligently on her behalf.

"I've never seen a more beautiful dress."

Juanita smiled and adjusted a ruffle. "You are the beauty."

"She's right, you know," Marietta declared, taking a step back. "I've never seen a lovelier bride. But I think you could have married in broadcloth and been just as angelic."

Hannah dabbed at her eyes with a handkerchief. "I never thought to have a dress this beautiful. I don't know how to thank you." She looked to Marietta and then Juanita. "You don't think it too scandalous of me to marry so soon after Father's death?"

"Bah, who cares about that at a time like this?" Marietta countered. "There's a war going on. Not only that, but this is the frontier. Life out here often makes it impossible to align with the rules of polite society."

Marty came bounding in at that moment and froze in place. "Hannah! You look like a princess, 'cept you got no crown."

Hannah smiled at her little sister. "I don't need a crown to feel like a princess. This gown does that well enough by itself."

"It sure is pretty." Marty looked down at her own very simple calico dress. "I hope you let me wear it someday."

"I will save it for you," Hannah replied with a grin. "We will put it away, and when you grow up and find a beau, we will see if you are still of a mind to use it."

"It's time we made our way downstairs," Marietta declared as the clock on the mantel struck ten. "I have a feeling that Will is mighty impatient to see this through."

Hannah giggled like a schoolgirl. "He very nearly forced me to elope last night. If not for your and Juanita's hard work on this gown, I doubt I could have convinced him of our need to remain in Cedar Springs."

"I would have walloped that boy if he'd denied me the joy of a wedding," Marietta said, adjusting a panel of the gown to fall in a smoother fashion. "There's been enough sorrow around here. We needed a good old-fashioned reason to celebrate."

"I hope you know how much it means to me that you are both here," Hannah said, taking in as deep a breath as her tightly laced corset would allow. "Your friendship is so important to me."

"What about me?" Marty asked.

Hannah reached out to touch the girl's blond curls. Juanita had taken special care to ensure that Marty looked just as lovely. "You are my sister—which means you have a special place in my heart that no one else can ever have." She kissed the child on the forehead. "Now, if you're ready, I think we should go have a wedding."

Marty nodded in great enthusiasm. "I was ready when I got here. Will said if we didn't get downstairs, he was gonna come up here and get you. He said he'd carry you over his shoulder if he had to. I think he just wants to kiss you."

"Oh dear," Hannah said in mock horror. "Then we had better move quickly."

Juanita and Marietta laughed and hurried to the door. Hannah reached out to take hold of Marty's hand.

"Shall we?"

Marty nodded and started for the door. "I'm gonna close my eyes when you two kiss. I think kissin' is silly."

Hannah laughed, but it was Marietta who leaned in to speak. "You won't always think so, Miss Marty. Mark my words. One day you're going to find a boy who makes your stomach do flips, and then you'll be delighted to receive your first kiss."

Marty frowned as she appeared to consider the older woman's words. "I think I'd rather have a pony," she said rather thoughtfully. "Boys are just a lot of trouble. They get real dirty and eat all the time. I wouldn't want to kiss one."

The three women laughed heartily at this analysis, but offered no correction on the child's insight.

∽

"If she doesn't get down here in the next two minutes," William declared to Ted Terry, "then I'm going up after her."

Ted chuckled. "I remember being just as eager to wed Marietta. You need to practice a little patience, however. You two will have the rest of your lives together. A few more minutes won't hurt you."

William paced and glanced at the stairs. Andy came up alongside him. "You want me to go fetch her?"

"I've already sent Marty up." Will looked at the boy and shook his head. "Girls are a lot of trouble."

Andy nodded in a most solemn manner. "They always want to look pretty and smell good. I don't know why, but they even worry about cleaning their shoes all the time."

Ted put his arm around Andy's shoulders. "They worry about cleaning everything. You'll see someday when you have a wife."

"If she's too silly about cleaning, I won't help her with her corset."

"Andrew Dandridge, we don't speak of a lady's unmentionables in public. Besides, where'd you learn about corsets?"

Andy got a worried look on his face. "Don't you know about them? If you're gonna marry Hannah, you got to know how to help her with her laces." He looked to Ted Terry, who was barely able to keep a straight face. Andy seemed to consider the matter for another minute before turning to William. "I can show you sometime how to do it. Hannah taught me."

"Well, maybe she can teach me, too," William said with a sly smile.

Just then he heard the sound of footsteps on the stairs. Andy hurried to the railing.

"They're coming."

The small hotel wasn't as grand as a church, but Juanita and Marietta had worked to dress it up a bit with a few candles and bows. The lobby seemed a good place to draw everyone together, and the pastor had already taken his place behind the reception desk.

William felt Berto take his place beside him as the ladies finally came into view. Keeping his gaze fixed straight ahead, William felt his breath catch at the sight of Hannah in her wedding dress. Her hair had been curled and pinned into a stylish manner atop her head, and while she didn't have a veil, someone had thoughtfully laced her curls with blue ribbon. She was a vision . . . and she was his.

She smiled at him and William felt the pain of his war wounds pass away. There was an entire future in that smile—a world of hope and the promise of unspeakable joy. She stepped up to stand directly in front of him.

"You are beautiful," he whispered.

Her smile broadened. "And you are quite handsome."

Their gazes locked and for the moment they only had eyes for each other. The rest of the world disappeared, and William felt as though they were the only two people remaining. He reached out to take her face in his hands. Leaning closer, he was about to press his lips to hers when an insistent tug came on his coat. Looking down, he found Marty Dandridge's disapproving expression.

"You can't kiss her until the preacher says so."

Hannah laughed. "She's absolutely right. That way if you don't like it . . . well . . . you're just stuck with me."

William let go his hold. "Let's get on with it, then. I kind of like the idea of being stuck with you for the rest of my life."

⁓

By the middle of March the landscape had begun to green up nicely and Hannah and Juanita were well ahead of schedule with planting their garden. Married life suited Hannah quite nicely, and the valuables her father had carefully concealed kept the family fed and surviving the war's limited supplies. Thankfully, once she and William had taken the time to analyze the map, they had easily found the places where her father had stashed his treasure.

"We will have much work if all of this grows," Juanita declared.

Hannah looked at the planted rows and felt a great sense of accomplishment. There would be additional seed to plant in the weeks to come, but already she could see tiny shoots peeking through the ground from their earlier plantings.

"It feels good to have this done." She dusted off her hands, then wiped them on her apron. "I suppose we'd best get back to work in the kitchen, though. Roundup for branding will come in another week, and I promised Marietta we would furnish enough tortillas to feed a small army of workers."

Juanita nodded and picked up a hoe they'd been using. "We will be ready. Miss Marty promise to help and Pepita show her how to roll the dough into balls."

Hannah's attention was drawn by the shouts of some of the men. They sounded quite enthusiastic about something. She and Juanita picked up their pace and followed the ruckus. To Hannah's horror, William was atop the ebony horse he'd hoped to break. Unfortunately, it looked like the horse was about to break him.

"You got him!" JD yelled as he climbed to the top of the pen's gate.

"Don't let him throw you," Andy commanded.

Watching William bounce and twist from side to side, Hannah thought she might well be sick. After a few moments, however, the horse seemed to calm. With only occasional bucking, the gelding finally settled into a trot and yielded to William's commands.

Hannah let out her breath, not having realized she was holding it the whole time. William looked over and gave her a wave. "Mrs. Barnett, it's good of you to join us. What do you think of my new mount?"

She shook her head but offered him a smile. "I think he's probably just as stubborn and unruly as you are."

William laughed and let Berto take the reins. He threw his leg over and jumped to the ground, taking the full weight of his body on his left leg. Hannah marveled at his agility despite the injury.

"Hannah, William said he'd teach me how to break horses," Andy declared.

"I'm gonna break horses, too," Marty said, coming up from behind Hannah.

She threw her siblings a disapproving look. "I hope neither one of you will be breaking *anything* very soon. You have a great deal of schoolwork to finish up."

Andy muttered under his breath and kicked the dirt. "You're always spoilin' my fun."

"Why, Andrew Dandridge," Hannah said, looking her brother in the eye. "I thought you liked book learning more than anything else."

"That was before you married Will. Now I want to be a rancher and learn how to do everything Will does. He's gonna grow me up to be a man like him."

Hannah turned to her husband and gave him a look of adoration. "I certainly hope so," she whispered just before William wrapped her in his arms. He pressed his lips to hers and kissed her long and passionately. Hannah could scarcely draw a breath when he pulled away.

"I think she's startin' to get used to kissin' you, William," Marty said seriously.

"I think you just might be right, Miss Marty." He gave

Hannah a mischievous smile and winked. "I think with a little more practice we'll be just fine."

Hannah felt her cheeks grow hot, but she kept her gaze fixed on William Barnett and smiled. God willing, they would have a long, long life in which to perfect their skills.

TRACIE PETERSON is the author of more than ninety novels, both historical and contemporary. Her avid research resonates in her stories, as seen in her bestselling HEIRS OF MONTANA and ALASKAN QUEST series. Tracie and her family make their home in Montana.

Visit Tracie's Web site at www.traciepeterson.com.